A Clubbable Woman

A CLUBBABLE WOMAN

Reginald Hill

FELONY & MAYHEM PRESS • NEW YORK

All the characters and events portrayed in this work are fictitious.

A CLUBBABLE WOMAN

A Felony & Mayhem mystery

PRINTING HISTORY
First UK edition (Collins): 1970
First U.S. edition (Foul Play Press): 1984
Felony & Mayhem edition: 2007

ISBN: 978-1-933397-93-1

Manufactured in the United States of America

Printed on 100% recycled paper

Library of Congress Cataloging-in-Publication Data

Hill, Reginald.
A clubbable woman / Reginald Hill.
    p. cm. -- (A Felony & Mayhem mystery)
ISBN 9781933397931 (pbk.)
1. Dalziel, Andrew (Fictitious character)--Fiction. 2. Pascoe, Peter
(Fictitious character)--Fiction. 3. Police--England--Yorkshire--Fiction.
4. Yorkshire
(England)--Fiction. I. Title.
PR6058.I448 C58 2007
823/.914
                                2008052249

For Pat

The icon above says you're holding a book in the Felony & Mayhem "British" category. These books are set in or around the UK, and feature the highly literate, often witty prose that fans of British mystery demand. If you enjoy this book, you may well like other "British" titles from Felony & Mayhem Press.

For information about British titles or to learn more about Felony & Mayhem Press, please visit us online at:

www.FelonyAndMayhem.com

Other "British" titles from

FELONY&MAYHEM

MICHAEL DAVID ANTHONY
The Becket Factor
Midnight Come
Dark Provenance

ROBERT BARNARD
Corpse in a Gilded Cage
Death and the Chaste Apprentice
Death on the High C's
The Skeleton in the Grass
Out of the Blackout

SIMON BRETT
Blotto, Twinks and the Ex-King's
    Daughter

DUNCAN CAMPBELL
If It Bleeds

KATE CHARLES
A Drink of Deadly Wine

PETER DICKINSON
King and Joker
The Old English Peep Show
Skin Deep
Sleep and His Brother

CAROLINE GRAHAM
The Killings at Badger's Drift
Death of a Hollow Man
Death in Disguise
Written in Blood
Murder at Madingley Grange

REGINALD HILL
An Advancement of Learning
Ruling Passion
An April Shroud
A Killing Kindness
Deadheads
Exit Lines
Child's Play
Under World

ELIZABETH IRONSIDE
The Accomplice
The Art of Deception
Death in the Garden
A Very Private Enterprise

BARRY MAITLAND
The Marx Sisters
The Chalon Heads

SHEILA RADLEY
Death in the Morning
The Chief Inspector's Daughter
A Talent for Destruction
Fate Worse than Death

L.C. TYLER
The Herring Seller's Apprentice
Ten Little Herrings
The Herring in the Library

LOUISE WELSH
Naming the Bones

A Clubbable Woman

Confessions of a Crime Writer

I've been read my rights, I've talked to my legal team, and now I'm ready to make my confession.

I never set out to write a detective series.

I never even intended to be a crime writer.

Forty years ago, when I started writing, I just wanted to try my hand at all the kinds of fiction that I enjoyed—thrillers, detective novels, sf, historicals, war stories, comedy—and when I look back at the 20 or so books that I was lucky enough to get published between 1970 and 1980, I see that I touched most of my chosen bases.

The very first of those books was the inaugural Dalziel and Pascoe tale, *A Clubbable Woman*. Not the first written—that was a thriller called *Fell of Dark*—but the first published.

This was my try at a police procedural, not because I was particularly interested in police procedure, but because I thought it would be fun to explore how our notoriously reactionary and anti-intellectual UK police force might look to a young, liberally minded, reasonably idealistic graduate.

That was Peter Pascoe.

To show him to best advantage I needed a contrasting

background. That seemed easy. All I had to do was create a character the dead opposite of Pascoe—in other words an ageing, fat, vulgar, reactionary, hard drinking, flatulent, corner-cutting, seat-of-the pants, dark-age copper.

That was Andy Dalziel.

Like I said, easy. Except that, as all artists know, if you make your background too colourful, the viewer's gaze may be distracted from the significant figure in the foreground.

This is a problem I'm still wrestling with four decades on!

Not that I foresaw any of this back then. When I brought *A Clubbable Woman* to a close and wrote The End I meant it. Time for fresh woods and pastures new, and off I went, forgetting D&P until a couple of years and books later I settled down to have a bit of fun and write a *roman à clef*, a mystery set at a college not unlike the one where I was currently teaching. I needed a couple of cops. And why buy new when you've got what you want in the wardrobe? So out they came. I dusted them down and set them to work in that second Dalziel and Pascoe novel, *An Advancement of Learning*.

It wasn't a sequel, it certainly wasn't the second in a series. It was just another free-standing novel which happened to feature a couple of characters I'd used before.

But this time, by act of god or diabolical intervention, I'm still not sure which, I left a situation at the end that did cry out for a sequel. Pascoe discovers that one of the teachers at the college is an old student flame; they are still attracted to each other but now they are very much at odds. Everyone likes a good romance. I like to think my readers wanted to know where this one was likely to go. I certainly did. So, another couple of books later, I followed it up in *Ruling Passion*.

Now I had a series. And soon I had lift off. I've been translated into languages I can't even identify, let alone speak. I've won prizes, both for individual books and for the whole shooting match. I've even become a university set text! And back in the mid-nineties the TV series *Dalziel & Pascoe* was launched, eventually becoming one of the BBC's most successful and longest-running shows, currently just starting its eleventh season, with its forty-fourth episode.

Naturally I've been delighted with and grateful for all this success. Who wouldn't be? But us humans are contrary critters, else there'd be no point to fiction, and I must confess that from time to time I've looked back to that energetic young man starting out to try everything, and thought a tad wistfully of all those other books I might have written if I hadn't written more than 20 D&P novels.

On the other hand those twenty are still less than fifty per cent of my total output.

And as some of you may already have discovered, and those of you new to the series will, I hope, discover, creating an alternative universe for my detective duo and their associated characters has given me the chance to toss in elements of those thrillers, comedies, war stories, historicals, and even sf that I mentioned above.

I never had a cunning plan for the development of the series. It grew like life. My only conscious preconditions were that I would never repeat myself, that while doing my best to deceive my readers I would never cheat on them, and that I would make sure my characters aged and developed in a believable way—except of course not quite as quickly as their creator!

It's been a strange voyage in many ways. Like Columbus I set sail to find the Indies and ended up in America! Not a bad piece of navigation really.

I've had a great time making the journey and a large part of that pleasure is knowing that so many bright and intelligent readers have had and are still having a great time making it with me.

All journeys begin with a single step. *A Clubbable Woman* is that step. I hope you will enjoy taking it.

Reginald Hill
RAVENGLASS, UK
SUMMER 2007

Chapter One

"He's all right. You'll live for ever, won't you, Connie?" said Marcus Felstead.

His head was being pumped up and down by an unknown hand. As he surfaced, his gaze took in an extensive area of mud stretching away to the incredibly distant posts. Then his forehead was brought down almost to his knees. Up again. Fred Slater he saw was resting his sixteen stones, something he did at every opportunity. Down. His knees. The mud. One stocking was down. His tie-up hung loose round his ankle. It was always difficult preserving a balance between support and strangulation of the veins. But it was worth it. Once the mud hardened among the long black hairs, it was the devil's own job to get it off. Up again. He resisted the next downward stroke.

"Why do you do that, anyway?" asked Marcus interestedly.

"I don't know," said a Welsh voice. "It's what they always do, isn't it? It seems to bloody well work."

"You all right then, Connie?"

Connon slowly got up with assistance from the Welshman whom he now recognized as Arthur Evans, his captain.

"I think so," he said. "What happened?"

"It was that big bald bastard in their second row," said Arthur. "Never you mind. I'll fix him."

There was a deprecating little cough from the referee who was lurking behind Connon.

"I think we must restart."

Connon shook his head. There was a dull ache above his left ear. Marcus was rather blurred.

"I think I'd better have a few minutes off, Arthur."

"You do that, boyo. Here, Marcus, you give him a hand while I sort this lot out. Not that it matters much when you only get twelve of the sods turning up in the first place."

Marcus slipped Connon's arm over his shoulder.

"Come along, my boy. We'll deposit you in the bath before the rest of this filthy lot get in."

They slowly made their way to the wooden hut which served as a pavilion.

"Get yourself in that bath and mind you don't drown," said Marcus. "I'll get back and avenge you. It must be nearly time anyway."

Left to himself, Connon began to unlace his boots. The ache suddenly began to turn like a cogwheel meshing with his flesh. He bowed his head between his knees again and it faded away. He stood up, fumbled in his jacket pocket and took out a packet of cigarettes. The smoke seemed to help and he took off his other boot. But he couldn't face the bath, he decided. He wasn't very dirty and he hadn't moved fast enough to work up a sweat. He washed the mud off his hands and bathed his face. Then, after towelling himself down, he got dressed.

The others trooped in as he was fastening his tie.

"You all right, Connie?" asked Marcus again.

"Yes, thank you."

"Good-oh!" said Marcus. "Let's get into that water before Fred gets in."

He began to tear his rugby kit off. Within seconds the bath

was full of naked men and the water was sloshing over the side. There was a general outcry as Fred Slater settled in. Connon looked at the scene with slight distaste.

"Goodbye, Marcus," he said, but his voice was drowned in a burst of singing. He made his way to the door and out into the fresh air.

He picked his way slowly over the muddy grass towards the distant club-house. The hut the fourth team used had originally been all the accommodation the club possessed, but the present of an adjoining field and a large loan from the Rugby Union had enabled them at the same time to develop another two pitches and build the pavilion. But even here the showers could not really cope with more than two teams, so the Fourths soldiered on in the old hut.

Connon thought ruefully that he had rather missed out on the development. The season the club-house was opened had been the season he retired. All those years in the first team had been centred on the old hut. Now when he was stupid enough to let himself be talked into playing, it was back to the old hut again.

He pushed open the glass-panelled door and stepped into the social room. Tea and sandwiches were being served.

"Hello, Connie," called Hurst, the club captain. "Been over at the Fourths? How did they get on?"

Connon realized he did not know. He could not even recollect the score when he had left the field.

"I don't know how it ended," he said. "I got a knock and came off early."

Hurst looked at him in surprise.

"You haven't been playing, have you? Good lord. You'd better have a seat."

Connon helped himself to a cup of tea.

"I'm only thirty-nine," he said. "You're nearly thirty yourself, Peter."

Hurst smiled. He knew, and he knew that Connon knew this was his last season as captain.

"They won't get me out there, Connie. When I finish, I finish."

"Sandwich, Connie?" asked one of the girl helpers. Connon recognized her as the girl-friend of the second team full-back. He shook his head, remembering when Mary had used to come down on Saturday afternoon. The catering like everything else had been more primitive then. Once they became wives they stopped coming. Then they tried to stop you coming. Then they even stopped that.

"I won't do it again in a hurry," he said to Hurst. "How did you get on?"

But Hurst had turned away to talk to some members of the visiting team.

The ache was turning again in Connon's head and he put his cup down and went across the room to the door which led into the bar. This was empty except for the club treasurer behind the bar sorting out some bottles.

"Hello, Connie," he said. "You're early. You know we don't serve till tea's done and the girls have got cleared up."

"That's all right, Sid. I just feel like a quiet sit down. It's rather noisy in there."

He sank into a chair and massaged the side of his head. The treasurer carried on with his work a few moments, then said, "Are you feeling all right, Connie?"

"Fine."

He lit another cigarette.

"Make an exception and pass me a scotch, will you, Sid?"

"Well, all right. Medicinal purposes only. Don't let those drunkards smell it."

He poured a scotch and handed it over.

"Two shillings and sixpence."

"Isn't my credit good?'

"Your credit's bloody marvellous. It's my accounts which are bloody awful. Two and six."

Connon dug into his pocket and produced the money. He sat down again and sipped his whisky. It didn't help.

The door opened and Marcus stuck his head in.

"There you are, then. I saw your car outside so I knew you must be hiding somewhere. How are you feeling?"

"Not so bad."

"Good-oh. I see you've got a drink. Hey, Sid!"

"No."

"Right, I'll have to share yours, Connie."

He sat down beside Connon. Connon pushed the drink towards him.

"Have it."

"Here. Watch it or I'll take offence."

Connon smiled.

Marcus Felstead was short, bald, and fat. His face was not really the face of a fat man, Connie thought, but of a tired saint. He could not recall the name of the tired saint he had in mind but he remembered very clearly the picture in his illustrated Bible which was the source of the idea. The saint, his sanctity advertised by a dome of light which sat round his head like a space helmet, had been leaning on a staff and looking despondently into the distance which seemed to offer nothing but desert. Perhaps the thing about Marcus's face was that the fleshiness of it formed a framework round rather than belonged to the thin nose and lips and narrow intelligent eyes which peered at him now curiously.

"Are you sure you're OK, Connie? You're not usually knocking the booze back so early."

"Well, I did feel a bit groggy. But it's gone now. How did we get on by the way?"

"What do you think? Two men short with one of their reserves playing at full-back? Can you imagine? A reserve for a fourth team. Jesus, he made me feel young. They scored another couple after you'd gone. Thirty-two—three it was at the end."

Connon was surprised. He could not recall any scoring at all, certainly not the kind of regular scores needed to build up a total like that.

"Who scored for us?"

Marcus looked at him strangely.

"What are you after? Flattery? You did, you silly bugger. A moment of glory, like the old times."

Connon drank his whisky absently. He had distinct memories of the game, but they bore no relation to Marcus's account.

The door burst open and a group of youngsters came in, their faces glowing with exercise and hard towelling.

"Come along, barman, this isn't good enough, this bar should be open now!" one cried.

"It'll be open at the proper time," said the treasurer, "and then I'm not sure you're old enough to be served."

"Me? The best fly-half the club's ever had. I'd be playing for England now if I hadn't got an Irish mother, and for Ireland if I hadn't got an English father."

"And for Wales, if you didn't fancy Arthur Evans's old woman."

Marcus frowned disapprovingly and spoke sharply into their laughter, affecting a Welsh lilt.

"Somebody talking about me, is there?"

There was an edge of silence for a moment, but only a moment.

"It's only Marcus!"

"It might not have been," said Marcus sharply.

Unconcerned, a couple of the boys strolled over and sat down at the table. They were only eighteen or nineteen. Still at the stage where they were fit rather than kept fit, thought Connon.

"Did you play today, Marcus?"

"Yes."

"Great! How did you get on?"

"Lost."

"Pity. We won and the Firsts won."

"Not playing for the Firsts yet, a young and fit man like you?"

The youth smiled at this attack on his own condescension. "Not yet. But I'm ready. I'm just waiting for the selection committee to spot me." He grinned, a little (but not very) shyly, at Connon. "Didn't you like my line-out work today, Connie?"

The boy had never called him Connie before. In fact, he couldn't recollect the boy's ever having called him anything. This was the way with these youngsters—noncommittal or familiar, there was no earlier formal stage. Not that I mind, he admonished himself. This is a Rugby Club, not an office party.

"I didn't see it, I'm afraid," he replied.

Hurst stuck his head through the hatch which led into the social room.

"Right, Sid," he said. "All clear."

"Your order, gentlemen. Marcus, you're on tonight as well, aren't you?"

"Christ, so I am. I could have been legitimately behind the bar all this time. Are you staying, Connie?"

Connon shook his head.

"I'm late already. Mary's expecting me for tea."

"She doesn't know you were playing, then?"

"How could she? I didn't know myself till Arthur grabbed me when I got here and wept Welsh tears all over me."

"Best of luck, then. See you tomorrow."

"Perhaps."

"Come on, Marcus!" came a cry from the bar. The room was now full and the social room hatch was also crowded with faces. Marcus barged his way through the crowd and was soon serving drinks from the other side of the counter.

Connon held the last of his whisky in his mouth. He felt reluctant to move though he knew he was already late. In fact he tried to catch Arthur Evans's eye but the little Welshman either missed him or ignored him. Connon smiled at himself, recognizing his own desire to be pressed to stay. A group of young men with their girls crowded round his table and he stood up.

"Thank you, Mr Connon," said one of the girls as she

slipped into his chair. Connon nodded vaguely at her, suspecting he recognized one of his daughter's school-friends under the mysterious net of hair which swayed over her face. She brushed it back and smiled up at him. He was right. Seventeen years old, glowing with unself-conscious beauty. She had a piece of tomato skin stuck in the crack between her two front teeth.

"You're a friend of Jenny's, aren't you?" he asked.

"That's right," she said. "How's she enjoying college?"

"Fine," he answered, "I think she's very happy there. She'll soon be home for the holidays. Perhaps we'll see you at the house. It's Sheila, isn't it?"

"That's right. It depends where I fit into Jenny's new scale of friends, I suppose. I'd quite like to see her."

Connon reluctantly digested another piece of the revolting honesty of the young and turned to go. He heard a burst of laughter as he moved to the door. Arthur noticed him this time.

"Hey, Connie, how are you there, boyo? How's the head?"

"It's all right now."

"Good. I settled that fellow's nonsense anyhow. Time for a drink?"

"No thanks, Arthur. Gwen coming down tonight?"

"Why yes, she is. Always does, doesn't she? Why do you ask?"

"No reason. I haven't seen her for a while, that's all."

"That's because you're always bloody well rushing off home, isn't it? Why doesn't Mary come down nowadays?"

Connon shrugged. For a second he contemplated offering Arthur a long analysis of the complex of reasons governing his wife's absence.

"Too busy, I expect," he said. "I'd better be off. Cheers, Arthur."

"Cheer-oh."

The car park was quite full now and his car was almost boxed in. He had once proposed at a committee meeting that the club-house facilities be restricted to those who at least watched the game but this voluntary restriction of revenue had not won much support. Finally he got clear without trouble and drove away into the early darkness of a winter evening.

He glanced at his watch and realized just how late he was. He increased his speed slightly. Ahead a traffic light glowed green. It turned to amber when he was about twenty yards away. He pressed hard down on the accelerator and crossed as the amber flicked over to red.

There was no danger. There was only one car waiting to cross and it was coming from the right.

But it was a police-car.

Connon swore to himself as the car pulled ahead of him and flashed "Stop." He drew carefully in to the side and switched off his engine. Its throbbing continued in his head somehow and he rubbed his temple, in an effort to dispel the pain. Out of the car ahead climbed two uniformed figures who made their way towards him slowly, weightily. He lowered his window and sucked in the fresh air.

"Good evening, sir. May I see your licence?"

Silently he drew it out and handed it over with his insurance cover-note and test certificate.

"Thank you, sir."

The gears in his head were now grinding viciously together and he could not stop himself from rubbing his brow again.

"Are you all right, sir?"

"Yes, thank you."

"Have you been drinking?"

"No. Well, no. I had one whisky, but that's all."

"I see. Would you mind taking a breathalyser test, sir?"

Connon shrugged. The policeman accepted the negative result impassively and returned his documents.

"Thank you, sir. You will hear from us if any further action is proposed concerning your failure to halt at the traffic lights. Good evening."

"Good evening," said Connon. The whole business had taken something over fifteen minutes, making him still later. But he drove the remaining five miles home with exaggerated care, partly because of the police, partly because of his headache. As he turned into his own street, his mind cleared and the pain vanished in a matter of seconds.

He drove carefully down the avenue of glowing lamp-posts. It was a mixed kind of street, its origins contained in its name, Boundary Drive. The solid detached houses on the left had been built for comfort in the 'thirties when they had faced over open countryside stretching away to the Dales. Now they faced a post-war council estate whose name, Woodfield Estate, was the sole reminder of what once had been. This itself merged into a newer development so that the boundary was a good four miles removed from the Drive. Mary and her cronies among the neighbours often bemoaned the proximity of the estate, complaining of noise, litter, overcrowded schools, and the comparative lowness of their own house values.

This last was certainly true, but Connon suspected that most of his neighbours were like himself in that only the price-depressing nearness of the estate had enabled him to buy such a house. Even then, it had really been beyond his means. But Mary had wanted a handsome detached house with a decent garden and Boundary Drive had offered an acceptable compromise between the demands of social prestige and economy.

His gates were closed. He halted on the opposite side of the road and went across to open them. While he was at it, he walked up the drive and opened the garage doors. It was quite dark now. The only light in the house was the cold pallor from the television set which glinted through the steamed-up lounge windows.

When he went back to his car a man was standing by it with the driver's door open. Connon recognized him as the occupier of the house directly opposite his own, a man named Dave Fernie whom he also knew as a chronic grumbler at work.

"Evening, Mr Connon. You left your engine running. I was just switching it off."

"Thank you," said Connon. He never knew how to address this man. He worked in the factory of the firm for which

Connon was assistant personnel manager. But he was also a neighbour. And in addition, possibly with malice aforethought, Mary had made of Mrs Fernie the only friend she had from the council houses.

"I was just opening my gates," he added, climbing into the car.

"That's all right," said Fernie graciously. "I've just been down the match. Were you there?"

"Yes," said Connon. "I mean, no. I was at the rugger match."

"Oh, that. I meant the football. We won, 3–1. How did your lot come on?"

"Oh, we did all right."

"Good. Rugby, eh? Here, you used to do a bit of that, didn't you? My wife saw the pictures."

"Yes, I did once."

He turned the key in the ignition and felt the turn in his skull so that the pain in his head shook with the roar of the engine, then settled down as quickly.

"You OK?" asked Fernie.

"Yes, thank you.

"Well, good night then."

"Good night."

He swung the car over the road and into the drive, slamming his foot hard on the brake as the branches of an overgrown laburnum slapped against his wing. He was used to this noise, but tonight it took him completely by surprise. He had stalled the engine and this time it took two or three turns of the starter to get it going again.

At last he rolled gently into the garage. He shut the main doors from the inside and went through the side door which led into the kitchen.

In the sink, dirty, were a cup and saucer, plate and cutlery. From the lounge came music and voices. He listened carefully and satisfied himself that the television was the source of everything. Then he took off his coat and hung it in the cloakroom.

He looked at himself in the mirror above the hand basin for a moment and automatically adjusted his tie and ran his comb through the thinning hair. Then, recognizing a desire to delay, he grinned at his reflection and shrugged his shoulders, grimaced self-consciously at the theatricality of the gesture and moved back into the entrance hall.

The lounge door was ajar. The only light within was the flickering brightness of the television picture. A man was singing, while in the background a lot of short-skirted dancers sprang about in carefully choreographed abandon. His wife was sprawled out in the high-backed wing chair he thought of as his own. All he could see of her were her legs and an arm trailed casually down to the floor where an ashtray stood with a half-smoked cigarette burning on its edge. The metal dish was piled full of butt ends, he noticed. The burning cigarette had started another couple of stumps smoking, and Connon wrinkled his nose at the smell.

"Hello," he said. "Sorry I'm late," still hesitating at the door.

The music and dancing seemed to be approaching a climax. The trailing hand moved slightly; a gesture of acknowledgment; a request for silence, a dismissal.

Connon let his attention be held for a moment by a close-up of a contorted face, male, mixing to a close-up of a shuddering bosom, female. The cigarette smell seemed to catch his throat.

"I'll just get a cup of tea, then," he said and turned, closing the door behind him.

Back in the kitchen he found a slice of cooked ham, evidently his share of the meal whose debris he had noticed in the sink. He slapped it on a plate and lit the gas under the kettle. Even as he did so, he felt his head begin to turn again and this time his stomach turned with it. He pressed his handkerchief to his mouth and moved shakily upstairs. Distantly the thought passed through his mind that he was well conditioned. Being sick in the downstairs toilet might disturb Mary. Now he was on the landing and his knees buckled and he gagged almost drily. Wiping his mouth, he pulled himself up, one hand on the handle of his bedroom door.

The next time he fell, he fell on to the bed and the wheels in his head went spinning on into darkness.

❄ ❄ ❄

"Do we have to have that tripe on?" asked Dave Fernie.

"Please yourself," said his wife. "You usually like it. All those girls. You must be getting old."

"Too old for that."

Alice Fernie glanced across at her husband with a smile, half ironical, half something else.

"Old enough for what, then?"

"Aren't you going to switch it off?"

"I didn't switch it on."

"No. I did. So you could see your precious football results after you rushed back from your precious match. And when you didn't come, I even marked them down for you. Don't you want to see?"

Fernie reached across and took the paper from the arm of his wife's chair.

"Thanks," he said.

The singer was off again, alone this time; a ballad; his voice vibrant with sincerity.

"For God's sake, switch that bloody thing off, will you!"

Angrily she rose and pulled the plug out of its socket.

"I don't know what's wrong with you these days. I'm getting pretty near the end of my tether with you. Other women wouldn't put up with what I do."

Fernie ignored her and peered down at the newspaper, but she sensed he wasn't really seeing it. She stood in the middle of the room and glowered down at him. He was in his early thirties, the same age as herself, but there was a puffiness about his face and a sagging at the belly which made him look older. Normally the contrast to her own advantage pleased her. Now she screwed up her face in distaste. Then, quickly as it came, her anger drained from her and she sat down again.

"Are you ready for your tea yet?"

"No, love. I told you I wasn't hungry."

"Is there anything bothering you, Dave? Are you feeling all right?"

She steeled herself for the irritability her concern for his health always seemed to cause, but unnecessarily.

"No, I'm fine."

"You were late tonight."

"Yes, I'm sorry. I got held up. It was a good gate. I met his lordship on my way up the road."

He jerked his head towards the window which faced the street. Alice affected not to understand.

"Who's that you mean?"

"You know who. Connon. Bloody twat."

"Why? What's he ever done to you?"

"Nothing," he grunted. "I just don't take to him, that's all. Too bloody stand-offish for me."

"That's what he was. A stand-off."

"A what?"

"Stand-off. His position at rugby. Mary told me."

Fernie laughed. "Stand-off, eh? That's bloody good. Wait till I tell them on the bench. That fits him."

"Anyway I think you're wrong. When I met him he was very nice. Charming. A bit quiet perhaps but he's just a bit shy, I think."

"If he's shy he shouldn't be a bloody personnel manager, should he? Anyway he's more than that. He's a snob."

Alice laughed with a slight edge of malice. "I'd have thought you could say that about Mary Connon. But not him."

Fernie shook his head dismissively. "Her. That's different. She'd like to be better, but knows she isn't. He believes he is. Bloody rugby club."

"Oh, Dave, don't be daft. It's not like that these days.

Anybody plays rugby. Maisie Curtis's boy next door, Stanley, he's in the Club."

"So what? Things don't change all that quick. What a game. Organized thuggery, then they all sing dirty songs like little lads. Yet they all tut-tut like mad if one of our lads runs on the field and someone shouts 'shit' from the terraces."

"There's no need to get excited, Dave."

"No? No, I suppose not. Here, I think I'm ready for my tea now."

Alice rose and went into the kitchen.

"I'll tell you something about your precious stand-offish Mr Connon, though." His voice came drifting after her.

"What's that, then?"

"He'd had a couple tonight. He was swaying around a bit. And I thought he was going to drive across his lawn and in through the front door."

Alice came back to the sitting-room door.

"That doesn't sound like him."

"Doesn't it? Don't tell me that you've only heard good of him from Madam Mary?"

"She doesn't talk much about him at all."

"I don't know why you bother with her. You've only got your age in common."

Alice took an indignant step forward.

"What do you mean? I can give her ten years, and more."

Fernie caught her hand and pulled her down beside him on the settee.

"As much as that? Mind you, she's well preserved. And game too, I should think."

"I don't know what you mean," said Alice, struggling to get up.

"She must have caught him young then, very young. He's only thirty-nine, you know."

"How do you know?"

He didn't answer but went on, "And they've got that girl of theirs..."

"Jenny."

"Yes, Jenny, at college. He must have been caught young. Very young. She's a pretty little thing, now."

"Don't you want any tea, Dave?"

Fernie's brawny arm held his wife in a clamp-like grip round the waist. He looked thoughtfully into her face, then pressed gently with his free hand where it rested on her leg just above the knee.

"No," he said, "I think I've changed my mind again."

❖ ❖ ❖

Jenny Connon hadn't quite made up her mind what to do about the hand on her knee. Adaptability was an important quality in a teacher, her education tutor had told the class that morning. How to cope with the unexpected.

Though, as she herself had arranged that her roommate should go out and she herself had turned the key in the door to prevent interruption, the situation was not all that unexpected.

"Do you really want to be a teacher?" she asked brightly.

Antony (he insisted on the full name) pushed the hair back from his brow with a gesture almost girlish (but he used the hand not on her knee) and smiled.

"If you mean, have I got a sense of vocation, no. If you mean, are my natural inclinations to be something else being repressed, the answer is equally no. Being at college is less distasteful than most of the alternatives, and it pleases my parents. Anyway, think of the holidays. I have a sense of vacation very strongly developed."

Antony Wilkes was without doubt the smoothest man in the South Warwickshire College of Education at the moment. As he was in his third year and Jenny was in her first, the opportunities for the relationship to develop were limited. As it was, Jenny had decided to feel flattered that she was the second girl he had chosen from the year's new supply. Her college "mother" in the second year had assured her (rather sadly) that Antony was most discriminating in his selection. Her room-mate had been even more positive. She had been the first of the year. This gave Jenny the advantage of being well briefed in the Wilkesian technique, but being forewarned she was discovering did not prevent her from being disarmed. Antony was one of the few people she had met who really did talk in long well-organized speeches like people in plays. Most of her acquaintance, she realized, hardly ever strung together more than a couple of dozen words at a time except when telling an anecdote, and in fact the few who did talk at length were down in the catalogue as bores and therefore to be avoided.

But Antony talked eloquently, interestingly, without strain; with none of those changes of direction, grammatical substitutions, syntactical complexities, whose existence her linguistic lecturer assured her was the real framework of the spoken language.

His speech, Jenny decided, was the smooth, reassuring surface of his amatory technique. Even the slight sense of staginess it conveyed worked for him, creating a faintly non-real, therefore non-dangerous, context. But beneath the surface...

The obvious survival tactic was to stay afloat. She seized at a bit of driftwood in his last speech.

"Is it important to please your parents?"

"But of course. It's important to please everyone who deserves it, even a little beyond desert if possible. Financially it's not important. My father has a strict scale of values. He gave me the precise amount necessary to bring my grant up to the level he has worked out to be sufficient for my well-being. Less would be neglect; more would be luxury. So I never get more or less for any reason. And to use money as punishment or reward is quite out of the question."

"He sounds like a Puritan banker."

"Not at all. If you wish to combine his religion with his profession, you'd have to call him an Aston Villa butcher. Mind you, my mother slips me the odd note now and then. But, as I say, this has nothing to do with the question. The only real answer is that, despite the fact that in many ways they find me utterly incomprehensible, they have always felt inclined by nature to please me; similarly I them."

"You mean you love them?" asked Jenny, half-consciously trying to embarrass him.

"Yes, of course. Had I not made that clear? I'm sorry. And you, do you love your parents?"

"Yes, I think so. My father, I like him a lot and we mean a lot to each other. It's a matter of talking and understanding, but my mother's different. Irritating in so many things. I want to scream at her sometimes."

"But you never do?"

Jenny grinned. She had tried to stop grinning. She thought it made her face fall apart in the middle, and she still had to count her teeth to assure herself she had not got twice as many as other people. But she kept on forgetting.

Antony Wilkes was glad she forgot.

"Oh, sometimes. I give a quick forty-second psychoanalysis. Rather nasty stuff it can be. She's a bit of a snob; uses me to get at Dad, whom she resents in some odd way. She's a few years older than he is, though I only use that as a last resort. I don't know why, I suppose I just know that for her, age is the ultimate insult, stuck a long way after vanity and dishonesty! But sometimes I feel I'm a lot more like her than Dad, than I'm like Dad I mean, though I like him more."

Ruefully she compared her own performance as a speech-maker with Antony's. Still, it wasn't all that bad. And her hesitancies arose from uncertainties of emotion. Perhaps it would have flowed more smoothly if she hadn't been so aware of the tensions, the fight for survival at home.

Antony's hand patted her knee sympathetically. She realized that her attempt to stop on the surface had somehow gone wrong. She had entered into a conversational intimacy with him without even noticing it. She would have to keep very much on the alert now. His other hand was pressing her shoulders round. She turned to him and he kissed her. She'd have to do something about his other hand. But not yet. Miniskirts and tights, she thought dreamily. Action and reaction. The invitation to attack might be more compelling than ever before, but the defences were stronger. She grinned again, which produced a very invigorating kind of kiss.

She could postpone her decision for a while yet.

❀ ❀ ❀

"Christ, Marcus, where the hell have you been? You just said half-an-hour. It's been more like an hour and a half."

Marcus Felstead manoeuvred his bulk under the flap into the bar.

"Sorry, Ted, old son. Got held up a bit. Look, have a pint on me and push off now. I'll spell you when you've got a Saturday."

"OK. And I'll have that pint. I've been so bloody busy that not a drop's passed my lips since you left."

"It'll do you good. Give you an edge when they start fighting for the spare."

"Some hope. There won't be much of that around now. See you, Marcus, Sid."

Sid Hope, the club treasurer, looked askance at Marcus.

"Nice of you to come back and give us a hand."

"Come off it, Sid. I did get Ted to stand in."

"Ted! Have you seen him at the till? He's got some peculiar decimal system of his own. Where have you been to anyway? On the prowl?"

"Nowhere important. Just out."

A peal of uninhibited female laughter cut through the noise and fume of the bar. Marcus turned. Sitting in the furthermost corner surrounded by half a dozen men was the woman he expected to see after hearing that laugh. Dressed in a low-cut cocktail dress whose demure whiteness set off the gleaming black of her hair and the shining silver of her tights, she was looking up and smiling at the young man who bent over her, obviously telling a story.

The treasurer followed Marcus's gaze and shook his head.

"Trouble," he said laconically.

"What do you mean?"

"You know what Arthur is. He's been hopping around like a cat on hot bricks all evening waiting for his precious wife to turn up. Finally off he goes about half an hour ago to fetch her. Decides she must have forgotten. Forgotten! Well, he's hardly out of the place before she comes sailing in like the figurehead on the good ship Venus. And of course within two minutes of coming into the most crowded room in the county with a queue six deep at the bar, she's sitting in the corner surrounded by drinks. Just wait till Arthur gets back."

Sid drew a couple of pints for a complaining customer, then looked over at Gwen Evans again.

"Mind you," he said, "what a pair of bristols, Jesus! There hasn't been anything like that in here since Nancy Jennings went off with that traveller. And Mary James—Connon, I mean—was the only thing I've ever known who could have beaten it."

"Connie's wife?"

"Yes. She doesn't get in here much now, does she? Nor does Connie for that matter. But I can remember the days. Jesus! Connie was married when you came to live here, wasn't he, Marcus?"

"Yes. Just."

"It must have been a full-time business with that one. No wonder he lost his edge after that. God, he once looked a cert for a cap. First we'd have ever had. Never been a sniff since. All for love."

Marcus poured himself a scotch.

"He did crack his ankle."

"Of course he did. I'm not really suggesting, mind you, that kid of theirs came out pretty smartly. Like Connie's pass, they said. And the responsibility can't have helped. But they seemed to make out all right. Didn't see all that much of Mary after that. But it was before. Like her over there. And Nancy Jennings. Trouble."

Marcus, his eyes still fixed on the noisy corner, ran his glass along his lower lip.

"Are you putting forward as a general proposition, Sid, that women with big breasts cause trouble?"

"Not absolutely. Though there's a bit of truth in it, isn't there?"

"Mary Connon never caused any trouble down here that I saw."

"Like I said, after they married, she didn't get in here so much. Tailed off. That's an apt phrase if you like. She was six years older than him, you know."

"Still is, isn't she?"

"You know what I mean. She'd had her fling down here. Not here exactly. That was in the days before this bloody road-house came into being. Remember? We had the tea-hut. None of your polished floors. You could get splinters through your shoes if you weren't careful. Then over to the Bird-in-Hand. No, Mary did the right thing—for her, anyway. Married someone half a dozen years younger. And stopped coming so much. Nancy Jennings, she buggered off. It's when they marry someone ten years older than themselves *and* keep their wares in the shop window that the trouble starts. Here, my lad, if you're going to have another whisky, pay for the last one first."

"Sorry, Sid. There it goes; and for this one too. Witnessed?"

But Sid wasn't paying attention.

"Here we go," he said in a low voice. "Here we go."

Marcus had never seen anyone whose face was really black with rage, but Arthur Evans was pretty close to it as he pushed through the door. A path opened up before him. It led to the corner where his wife sat. She looked up, flashed him a quick smile, then returned her attention to the youngster who had been talking to her. But he had seen Arthur too and seemed disinclined to talk further.

With a tremendous effort, obvious to all who watched, which was about three-quarters of those in the room, Arthur turned to the bar. Marcus could almost feel the man's will forcing his broad shoulders to turn. Then his trunk followed. And finally his legs.

Quickly Marcus thrust a glass up against the whisky optic. And again.

"Arthur, old son, I'm in the chair. Wrap yourself round this and tell us about your childhood in the green valleys of old Wales."

Evans took the drink in one.

"Thanks," he said.

Over his shoulder, Marcus saw Gwen casually disengaging herself from the group in the corner. Exchanging a word here and there as she came, she passed easily across the room till she arrived at her husband's shoulder.

"Hello, dear. Going to buy me a drink? I've got no money and I can't sponge off your friends all night."

"Where've you been, Gwen?"

She smiled ironically.

God, you're a beauty, thought Marcus. Sid, in an excess of desire to share his admiration of the sight before them, kicked him painfully on the ankle.

"Oh, I got tired of waiting, so I came on by myself."

"But you were supposed to be coming with Dick and Joy."

"Was I? Oh, I forgot."

"They called for you."

"Then I must have left."

"To come here? You took your time, didn't you, girl?"

"Do you want to quarrel, Arthur?"

She raised her voice just sufficiently to cut into the attention of those immediately adjacent to them.

Marcus looked at Arthur. Surprisingly, he seemed to be considering the question on its merits.

Finally, calmly, "No," he said.

"Then let's have that drink. Marcus, love, see if you can add a bit of gin to that slice of dried-up lemon which seems to be all that's left of a once-proud fruit."

"A pleasure, ma'am," said Marcus. "A real pleasure." He meant it.

❀ ❀ ❀

Two hours or so later, just after eleven, he put the lights out in the bar. Outside he could hear the din of departure. Car doors. Impatient horns. Voices. Song.

As he passed the Gents, the door opened and a large figure fell out.

"Marcus," it said.

"Ted. Christ, you certainly caught up, didn't you? Come on, old son. We'd better get you home."

Arm in arm they walked out into the car park.

❀ ❀ ❀

Jenny Connon opened the door to let her roommate in.

"Hello," said the newcomer brightly. "Not too early, am I? It's after eleven."

"What you really mean is, not too late, you hope. How are you, Helen?" said Antony. "Well, must be off. See you both. 'Bye."

Jenny watched him go down the corridor.

"Had a nice time?" asked Helen.

"Oh yes," said Jenny noncommittally as she closed the door. She hoped she had done the right thing.

❀ ❀ ❀

"The time is ten minutes past eleven," said the announcer with evident relief. "You are watching…"

Alice Fernie switched him off in mid-sentence and yawned.

"Well, I'm off to bed. Coming?"

Behind her, her husband stood in the small bay of the window looking out into the front garden.

"No, dear. You go on. I'll be up in a minute."

"What are you looking at?"

"Nothing. I thought I saw that bloody black and white cat from next door digging up my lawn. Off you go."

"All right, then. Good night."

"Good night."

And over the road, Sam Connon stood pale-faced and trembling in the darkened hall of his house, the telephone in his hand.

Behind him in the lounge, stretched out in the high-backed chair he would never want to call his own again, was his wife.

She was quite, quite dead.

Chapter Two

Superintendent Andrew Dalziel was a big man. When he took his jacket off and dropped it over the back of a chair it was like a Bedouin pitching camp. He had a big head, greying now; big eyes, shortsighted, but losing nothing of their penetrating force behind a pair of solid-framed spectacles; and he blew his big nose into a khaki handkerchief a foot-and-a-half square. He had been a vicious lock forward in his time, which had been a time before speed and dexterity were placed higher in the list of a pack's qualities than sheer indestructibility. The same order of priorities had brought him to his present office.

He was a man not difficult to mock. But it was dangerous sport. And perhaps therefore all the more tempting to a Detective-Sergeant who was twenty years younger, had a degree in social sciences and read works of criminology.

Dalziel sank over his chair and scratched himself vigorously between the legs. Not absent-mindedly—nothing he did was mannerism—but with conscious sensuousness. Like scratching a dog to keep it happy, a constable had once said within range of Dalziel's very sharp hearing. He had liked the simile and therefore ignored it.

"You should have seen him, Pascoe. He went round their cover like a downhill skier round a line of snowmen. And he was a big lad, mark you. Still is, of course. But even then. Not one of your bloody Welsh dwarfs, but a good solid-built English fly-half. How we roared! He'd have captained the Lions if we'd been selectors."

"Yes, sir," said Sergeant Pascoe with the resigned condescension of one certain of the intellectual superiority of Association Football.

"Graceful, too. Ran upright. Always looking for the quickest way to the line. God, he found it that day. He was picked for the final trial, of course. Nearest thing to a certainty since Lily Jones left Crown Street. Then bang! his ankle went. The week before. No one's fault. He was overtaken by a loose scrum. Never afraid to mix it, was Connie. Solid defender, sharp attacker. But he never came again after that. Played for another eight years. No difficulty in holding his place in the club. Stood up for the County a dozen times. But never sniffed at a cap again. But he was a great runner with the ball, a great player."

He nodded two or three times and smiled faintly as though at some pleasant memory.

"A great player."

"Then he could hardly commit a murder, could he?" said Pascoe, hoping by this irony to recall his superior to the realities of their work.

"No. Probably not. Or not one like this. He'd use his head, that one. Which," added Dalziel, standing up and walking to the window, "is what you should do, Pascoe, before wrapping up another of your little ironies for me."

Pascoe refused to be squashed.

"Perhaps he is using his head, sir. Perhaps he is, in the sporting idiom, selling us a dummy."

Dalziel flung up the window with a ripping sound from the parts where the paint had fused, and let in a solid cube of icy air which immediately expanded to fit the room.

"No one ever sold me a dummy. Point yourself at the man and bugger the ball, you can't go wrong."

"But which man?" said Pascoe.

"No," said Dalziel, slapping his thigh with a crack which made Pascoe wince, "at this stage the question is, which bloody ball? Is that enigmatic enough for your scholarship, eh?"

Pascoe had grown used to jokes about his degree when a constable, but Dalziel was the only one who hung his wit on it now.

The trouble is, he thought, looking at the broad slope of the back whose bulk stopped the light but not the draught, the trouble is, deep down he believes that everyone loves him. He thinks he's bloody irresistible.

"What did you make of him last night anyway?"

"Not much. That doctor of his had pumped him full of dope and was hovering around like a guardian angel when I got there."

Dalziel snorted.

"At least you saw him. He was tucked up in bed by the time I arrived. I'd have liked a go at him while the iron was hot."

"Yes, sir. The early bird…"

"Only if it knows what it's all about, Pascoe."

Pascoe did not let even the ghost of a smile appear on his lips. He went on speaking.

"In any case, the iron wasn't all that hot at eleven. She'd been dead at least three hours, possibly five. The room temperature seems to be a rather uncertain factor. Signs of a big fire, but the place was like an ice-box by the time we got there. That was a sharp frost that set in last night."

"Bloody science. All it does is give us reasons for being imprecise. I can manage that without logarithms."

"The cause of death's a bit more exact, isn't it, sir?"

"Oh, yes."

Dalziel rippled through the papers scattered on the desk before him. Pascoe tried to show none of the offence this lack of organisation caused him.

"Here we are. Skull fracture...bone splinters into frontal lobes...blow from a metal implement, probably cylindrical... administered with great force to the centre of forehead... perhaps long enough to permit a two-handed grip. That's a great help. Found anything yet, have they?"

"No, sir."

"I should bloody well think not, eh? Not if you knew and I didn't. Where is this man, anyway?"

Pascoe pushed back his stiffly laundered white cuffs to glance at his watch.

"The car went for him half an hour ago."

"Waiting for him to finish breakfast, I expect. Hearty, I hope. He'll need his strength."

Pascoe raised his eyebrows.

"I thought you said..."

"I didn't think he'd done it? But I might be wrong. It's been known. Twice. But whether he did it or not, if it wasn't done casually by an intruder, he'll probably know why it was done. He might not know he knows. But know he will."

"Have we dismissed the possibility of an intruder, sir?"

"We? We? You're not my bloody doctor. No, I haven't. But if you look at your bloody scientifically based reports, you'll see that she seems to have been sitting very much at her ease."

"Couldn't it have been from behind? With, say, a narrow-headed hammer. That way you'd get the force..."

"Pish and cobbles, Pascoe! Didn't you see the height of that chair-back? And she was sprawling in it at her ease. You'd need arms like an orang-outang. No, I think it was someone she knew pretty well."

"And how narrow does that make the field?"

Dalziel grinned lecherously.

"Not as narrow as you'd think. Twenty years ago there were a hell of a lot of people down at the Rugby Club who knew Mary James pretty well. I've had a bit of a nuzzle there myself. And that kind of acquaintance doesn't get forgot all that quickly."

"You make her sound like a professional."

"Don't get me wrong son. She wasn't that. Not even an enthusiastic amateur. She just liked the gay life. There's one in every club. Where the booze is strongest, the dancing wildest. The girl who doesn't flinch when the songs get dirty. Who can even join in. It's the gay crowd she likes, not the slap and tickle in the dark corners. But her image demands she has a large following. And she's bound to be overtaken from time to time."

"Was Connon an overtaker?"

"Oh no. He was taken over. Your old stager begins to smell danger when the gaiety girl passes the quarter-century with no strong ties. Your young lad's easy meat, though. Easily frightened too."

"Frightened?"

"They got married at a dead run. Their girl appeared eight months later. Premature, they called it."

Pascoe listened with distaste to the rasp of laughter which followed.

"But you'll find out all about that, my lad. Have a walk down there this lunchtime. They always get a good crowd in. Have a chat with one or two of them. See if anything's known. They'll all be eager to natter. Here, I've scribbled out a list of who's who down there. It's not definitive by any means, but it'll tell you whether you're talking to a mate of his—or hers—or not."

He passed over a scruffy sheet of foolscap, one corner of which looked as if it had been used for lighting a cigarette.

"You're best at this stage. If we haven't sorted this lot out in a couple of days, I'll drop in for a social drink myself. The tension'll have gone by then and they'll all imagine they're pumping me for information."

Whereas you pump stuff into barrels, not out of them, thought Pascoe.

Dalziel turned to the window again and took a couple of deep breaths. His fingers drummed impatiently on the sill.

"Anything in from house-to-house yet?"

"Not yet, sir."

"They'll all be in bed. Christ. Bloody Sundays!"

There was a long pause. Then...

"Here he comes," said Dalziel, slamming the window shut with even more violence than he had used to open it. "Anything you want here, laddie?"

"Well, no; I mean yes," said Pascoe in puzzlement.

"Grab it and go, then. What's the matter? Did you hope to see the master at work?"

"No. But I thought that as you know him—I mean, you are a vice-president of the Rugby Club and something of a friend..."

"A friend?" said the superintendent, twisting his fingers in one pouchy cheek so that his big mouth was dragged sinisterly out of shape. "You've jumped to conclusions, Sergeant. Perhaps I better had let you watch the master some time. He's a great player, but I never said I liked him. Nor he me. Oh no, I never said I liked him. Push off now. We'll save you for later if need be."

Quickly Pascoe gathered a couple of files and some papers together and made for the door. There was a knock and it opened just as he reached it.

"Mr Connon, sir," said the uniformed sergeant standing there.

"How are you, Mr Connon?" said Pascoe looking at the pale-faced man who stood a pace or two behind the sergeant.

Solid. Yes, he looked solid all right. Still firm. No flabbiness in the face. Just the paleness of fatigue. But what is it that has drained your blood, Mr Connon? Grief? Or...

"Please come in, Mr Connon." The loud voice broke his thoughts. He glanced round. Dalziel, his face a mask of sympathy so obviously spurious that Pascoe shuddered, was advancing with his hands outstretched. He stood aside to let Connon enter, then stepped out into the corridor leaving them together.

"He's like Henry Irving," he said to the sergeant, shaking his head.

"Which one?"

"Which one? I don't know. Perhaps both. I'll be in here if I'm wanted."

And for all his resentment at his dismissal, he found he wished that he had been wanted.

"It might be nice to see the master at work."

The sergeant turned round, but Pascoe had closed the door of his temporary office behind him with a bang.

The sergeant went back to his desk whistling, "Dear Lord and Father of mankind."

It was, after all, Sunday.

❀ ❀ ❀

"Sorry to get you out of bed, Mrs Fernie," said Detective-Constable Edwards.

"Don't apologize," interjected Fernie. "I told her this might happen last night."

"Last night? Why was that, Mr Fernie?"

"Well, I happened to notice your cars pull up outside Connon's house…"

"Happened to notice!" sneered Alice Fernie, pulling her nylon housecoat closer round her. "You must have been standing at that window for half an hour or more."

Fernie started to reply but the constable interrupted them.

"The important point to ask both of you is, did you notice anything earlier on?"

"Anything? What kind of thing? How much earlier?" asked Alice.

"Anything at all concerned with the Connons or their house. Any time yesterday."

"Well, no. I was over there in the afternoon…"

"Over there?" The constable leaned forward.

"Did you know the Connons well, then?"

"Mary Connon, I know—knew her very well. We were friends," said Alice; then, "We were friends," she repeated softly to herself, as though the import of the comment was just beginning to sink in.

"And how did Mrs Connon seem to you then?"

"Oh fine, fine. Just the same as ever. Nothing out of the ordinary."

"Did she say anything that struck you as unusual?"

"No."

"Were there any phone calls? Any callers?"

"No, nothing."

"What time did you leave?"

"Shortly after four. I don't know exactly. I came back to get Dave's tea ready."

"What were Mrs Connon's last words?"

"Last words?"

"I'm sorry. I didn't mean it to sound...what did Mrs Connon say as you left?"

"Well, nothing really. Cheerio. And something about getting Mr Connon's tea ready, if he got home in time for it."

"What did she mean by that?"

"Well," said Alice, "I'm not sure..."

"Come off it, Alice," said Fernie. "She meant that if he didn't get home on time he'd get his own tea. She was a stickler for that, you've often told me. And he didn't get home on time either."

"How do you know that?"

"I saw him. About half past six. And I'll tell you something else."

"Dave!" said Alice with real annoyance in her voice.

"What's that?"

"He was drunk. Could hardly stand."

The constable scribbled assiduously in his notebook.

"You're certain of that?"

"Dave!" said his wife again.

"Oh yes," said Fernie, looking at his wife. She ignored his glance.

"If you're finished with me, I think I'll go back to bed,"

said Alice, standing up so that her housecoat fell open revealing her thin nightdress.

"Thank you very much, Mrs Fernie," said Edwards. "You've been most helpful. We might want to see you again."

"I'll be ready."

She went out, leaving the constable smiling and her husband scowling.

"Now, Mr Fernie. What exactly happened when you met Mr Connon last night?"

❀ ❀ ❀

"So that's all you can tell me, Mr Connon?"

"That's right, Superintendent."

"You got home about half past six. How positive is that time?"

"I don't know. Pretty approximate."

"That's a help. You say the television was on when you stuck your head into the lounge?"

"That's right. I see what you mean. There was some variety show. Dancers, girls, not much on. Dancing behind a singer. Big youth, rather Italianate, singing something about flowers."

Dalziel smiled sardonically.

"So you were out for four hours?"

"That's right."

"Nasty, that. What'd your doctor say?"

"I don't know what his diagnosis was. He just seemed concerned with getting me to bed."

"You'll be seeing him again?"

"Of course."

"I wonder if you'd mind if our man cast his eye over you while you're down here? It might save your McManus a crisis of conscience."

Connon smiled wanly.

"Again I see what you mean. I have no objection."

"Good. Good. But first, there's one thing that puzzles

me. You felt sick in the kitchen. You end up by passing out on your bed. Why not be sick downstairs? The kitchen-sink. Or if your notions of hygiene are so strong, why not use the downstairs toilet? I noticed you had one."

Connon spoke the words of his reply very slowly and distinctly as if learned by rote from a linguaphone record.

"I did not wish to disturb my wife."

Dalziel crossed his legs cumbersomely and started prying into his nostrils with thumb and forefinger.

"Tell me, Mr Connon, Connie, I always think of you as Connie, do you mind?"

"I always think of you as Bruiser, Superintendent."

Dalziel was amused and gave a few snorts of laughter.

"If the name fits, wear it, eh? Give a dog, eh? But yours doesn't tell us much. Doesn't fit, does it? Connie. A bit girlish. Which reminds me. You did not wish to disturb your wife. Now me, I'm a blunt Scottish lad by birth, a blunter Northcountryman by domicile. So perhaps the finer points of marital diplomacy have passed me by. (I wish my lad Pascoe could hear me!) But I don't quite follow the workings of your mind here. You come home, you're a bit under the weather, your wife ignores you, you've got to make your own tea. And you don't want to disturb her. There are some men would've disturbed her. Men you've played rugby with who'd have put their boots through the telly screen."

"Men who have no respect for their wives do not deserve to keep them, superintendent."

That was a mistake, thought Connon. He's taking it personally.

Dalziel's wife, now divorced, had gone off with a milkman fifteen years before. At least, she had gone off. The milkman might have been malicious invention.

"Yes, Mr Connon. You're right. We should respect those who are weaker than us. Or older. Of course we should. Like forgiving our enemies."

The phone rang.

"Excuse me," said Dalziel. He listened for a moment.

"The doctor's ready for you now, if that's OK."

Connon stood up.

"He won't keep you long, I expect. Like the Army. Just a cough and a piddle."

"Will you want to see me again, superintendent?"

Dalziel opened the door for him.

"Just for a moment perhaps. Sergeant!"

The uniformed sergeant who had brought Connon to the room appeared. The expression of unctuous sympathy with which Connon had been greeted reappeared on Dalziel's face for the first time since the interview began.

"This is very good of you. It's a trying time. Sergeant, show Mr Connon to the doctor. And get him a cup of tea, or coffee if you prefer it."

"No, thank you," said Connon and set off after the sergeant.

"No," said Dalziel to himself as he watched them go. "I expect you'll manage a piddle without it. Or I'm losing my touch. Sergeant Pascoe!"

❀ ❀ ❀

"You're not intending to go down to the Club in that rig, are you, girl?"

Gwen Evans turned before the mirror and peered back over her shoulder.

"What's the matter? My bum's not too big, is it?"

She was wearing a tight-fitting dress of flowered silk, whose style was distantly Chinese in origin.

"No, but if that slit went any further up the side, you'd be able to see your belly-button."

"Don't be vulgar, Arthur. What's the matter? Don't you want me to go to the Club?"

"No, it's not that at all..."

"No? I think you'd much rather have me here slaving over

roast beef and two veg, waiting for you to come back full of love and beer."

"Be fair, Gwen. Most of the time you complain that I'm too keen to get you down there."

"Oh ay. Where you can keep an eye on me at night. But it doesn't seem to worry you at lunchtime. Do you think I've got a time switch on it, then, and can't get it to work in hours of daylight? You should know better."

Evans crossed to her in three swift strides. Instinctively she cowered back, holding her hands before her face, but he made no move to strike her. Instead he reached down, seized the hem of her dress and tugged violently upwards.

There was a tearing noise as stitching came apart and the oriental split up the side extended to the waist.

"There," he said. "Now you can really see your belly."

She relaxed, leaned against the wall and began to laugh. At first there was a very faint note of hysteria in it, but this rapidly faded and the laugh deepened to genuine amusement.

"Give us a fag, will you, Arthur?" she said finally, regarding her husband with something like real affection. "You're not such a bad old faggot when you're roused."

Evans sat on the bed and lit two cigarettes, one of which he passed over to his wife.

"Thanks," she said, drew on it deeply and placed it carefully on the edge of the dressing-table while she began to remove her ruined dress.

Evans watched her impassively.

She went to the wardrobe in her slip and opened its door.

"Well," she said, "what's it to be? Clubwear, or kitchenwear?"

"Where were you last night, Gwen?"

"At the Club with you, dear. Remember?"

She smiled sweetly.

"Gwen," he said, "you're right. It's a daft question, isn't it, girl? I know where you were. Or at least who you were with."

She stiffened and reached down a dress from the hanging rail.

"Oh, do you?"

"Yes, of course I do, Gwen. And I suppose if I know, every other sod in the Club has known for months. But I don't understand you, Gwen. I can see why you encourage all those young lads who come sniffing around you. That'd be flattering to any woman. But a man of my own age. And a friend. What made you pick him, Gwen? What made you pick Connie?"

❧ ❧ ❧

"A-1, I hope," said Dalziel when Connon reappeared.

"I hope not, Superintendent. That would mean I couldn't get better. And I don't think I've recovered from that knock yet. I hope we won't be much longer."

"This is a murder enquiry, Mr Connon. We need your help. Your wife is dead."

"I think that I am at least as aware of that as you, Superintendent. My daughter will be arriving home some time this morning. I'd like to be there to meet her."

Dalziel looked sympathetic.

"Of course. A father's feelings. But have no worries on that score. My sergeant was just telling me. Your daughter's got here safe and sound. We were able to assist a little there."

Connon stood up.

"Jenny? Here? You mean, here?"

"Oh no. Never worry yourself. I mean at home, of course. We wouldn't bring her *here*."

"At home. Then I must go."

Dalziel let him reach the door.

"Just one question, Mr Connon."

"If you must."

"You left the Club at twenty to six, and got home about six-thirty. Rather a long time isn't it? It's only seven or eight miles at the most. And there's not much traffic about at that time."

"There was enough."

Dalziel, expert at detecting ironies, thought he heard one here.

"You didn't stop for any reason? A drink perhaps? Or had you had enough at the Club?"

"Why do you ask?" said Connon quietly.

"Well, it's just that we've had a statement. Not guaranteed reliable, mark you. But admissible, and voluntary, and therefore carrying some weight. This man..."

"Which man?"

"A man called Fernie, says he met you last night. Is that true?"

"Yes."

"About six-thirty?"

"Yes."

"Outside your house?"

"Yes again."

"He says that you were acting oddly. In various ways. He says, in fact he was willing to swear, but we introduced a degree of moderation, as is our wont. He says he got the distinct impression that you were drunk. Very drunk."

"Thank you for telling me, Superintendent. Now I must go. Goodbye."

"Wait!" bellowed Dalziel.

Connon turned once more, half out of the door.

"If you want a fairly precise statement of the amount of alcohol I had taken up to about ten past six, I suggest you contact the constables who administered a breathalyser test to me at that time in Longtrees Road. I thought that this was what you were going on about, not malicious gossip. Good day. I must get to my daughter."

Dalziel sat for a minute looking at the open door. Then he stood up and walked slowly over to it, scratching the back of his neck with an intensity that made his skin glow redly through the grey stubble.

"Sergeant," he called, pitching his voice low, but with an intensity which easily carried it along the corridor to the desk.

"Would you step along here for a moment, if you'd be so kind? To discuss an organizational point."

At the desk, the sergeant stopped whistling.

❀ ❀ ❀

"Sorry, we don't start selling till twelve."

"I'm a police officer," said Pascoe. "I don't start buying till I'm off duty."

Sid Hope slowly rose from his crouching position behind the bar.

"Oh yes? I'm Hope, the club treasurer. What can I do for you? Is there some trouble? About the licence, I mean?"

"Should there be?" said Pascoe. "You don't allow non-members to buy drinks, do you? Normally?"

"Of course not. When we know, that is. But I didn't know who you were. On my knees, trying to set up a new keg. It's like a bloody heart-transplant operation getting one of these things operational."

Pascoe merely looked thoughtful at this attempt to bring in a lighter note.

"Anyway, I don't know them all. You could be a member. There's one or two from the police who are. Superintendent Dalziel for one."

"Is that so? How do you run the bar, Mr Hope? A duty roster?"

Sid looked happy to get on to more general ground. "That's right. We have a committee, me in charge, plus half a dozen others. We take it in turn to look after things for a week."

"Just one of you? By himself?"

Sid laughed.

"Not bloody likely. No, we get some of the boys to help us when it's very busy, like weekends. Or even take over for a couple of nights. Some of us are married, you know. But, like I say, weekends the committee man in charge has really got to be here all the time. It's not just the serving, but the stock, and the till."

"Sounds like hard work."

"It is. Like now. Getting things set up for the great rush."

"Popular, is it?"

"Christ, yes. It's our main source of income. Apart from the odd dance or raffle. We've just about paid back our loan now and…"

Pascoe turned on his heel. The man was beginning to be at his ease. He stopped talking at the sight of Pascoe's back.

"How many do you get in here on a Saturday night?"

"I don't know. Sixty, seventy, and there's the other …"

"You'd be on last night?"

"That's right."

"Busy?"

"Very."

"Was Mr Connon in at all, Mr Sam Connon?"

"Connie? No. Well, yes. I mean he was in at the beginning of the evening right after the match. Look, what's all this about? Have you got any proof you really are a policeman?"

"I thought you'd never ask."

Pascoe produced his warrant card. Sid examined it closely.

"What time did Connon leave?"

"I'm not sure. About five-thirty. Quarter to six, I think. I can't say for certain. He stopped to have a word with Arthur on his way out, but he might just have gone through into the other room."

"Arthur?"

"Evans. Captain of the Fourths. That's right. Connie had been playing. Got a knock. Wanted a medicinal scotch. Hello, Marcus."

Pascoe looked to the doorway. Standing there was a short fleshy man dressed in slacks and a polo-neck sweater. Pascoe felt that he had been standing there for some time.

Now he came into the room.

"Hello, Sid. Sorry I'm late again."

"That's all right. I've been managing. As long as you didn't send Ted."

Marcus didn't look at Pascoe but went behind the bar as though he wasn't there and began to busy himself with bottles.

"Marcus," said Sid, "this is—who is it?"

"Sergeant Pascoe."

"Sergeant Pascoe. He's asking about Connie."

Marcus looked at Pascoe now.

"What about Connie?"

"You know his wife?"

"Mary? Yes. What about her?"

"Was she a friend?"

Sid and Marcus looked at each other.

"Not exactly. But I know her pretty well. Connie's a close friend," said Marcus.

"Why do you say 'was'?" asked Sid.

"She's dead I'm afraid."

You learn nothing from their faces, thought Pascoe. A split second of surprise, incredulity, shock; perhaps not even that. Then they're all busy arranging their features to the right expression.

"She was killed last night. I'd like to ask a few more questions, please."

Marcus sank down on a bar stool. His left foot hooked repeatedly at a non-existing cross-rail.

"Where is Connie?" he said.

"I don't know. Home by now, I expect. His daughter's arriving."

"Jenny. That's good. That's good."

But the look on his face didn't seem to go with the words somehow.

❀ ❀ ❀

"Daddy?"

"Yes."

"Is that you?"

"Yes."

She was sitting on the edge of a dining-room chair like a nervous candidate for interview.

For a moment they looked at each other as though this indeed was why she was there.

Then she ran to his arms and sobbed once into the wool of his overcoat, then rested there quietly for a long minute.

"Come and sit down, Jenny," he said.

"Yes."

They sat side by side at the table.

"Why don't you take your coat off?" he said.

"Why don't you?"

"Yes. I will."

He stood up and undid the buttons. Jenny glanced down at the white and brown mock-fur coat she wore.

"It's all I had. I had to wear something, it was so cold coming. There was nothing else. And I was so worried about people seeing me in this. It's a bit gay, isn't it? That's all I thought as I walked up the path. But I don't have anything darker. Jesus! I never thought I'd give a damn about the neighbours."

"You never used to. Some of the things you'd lie around the garden in when it was hot."

"Oh yes. Do you remember old Mr Hawkins? He'd go in to get behind the curtain. But Mr Hall would come rushing out with his lawn-mower. All to look at my bumps."

She laughed, then stopped in mid-note.

"We're talking about them as if they're all dead."

He laid his coat on the table and put his arm round her shoulders.

"No, my dear. Not them. Just those days."

She stood up away from his arm and took off her coat. He looked at her, long-legged, short-skirted, well-rounded.

"They were wise to look," he said with a smile.

She trailed her coat along the floor as she walked to the window and ran her finger along the sill.

"Tell me about it, Daddy."

"Are you sure?"

"Yes. Please."

"There's not much to tell."

"Not much. My mother's dead! And that's not much?"

"No, I mean."

She sat down on the sill.

"I'm sorry. I know what you mean."

"I came home. I was late. I'd let myself be talked into playing and I got a bit of a knock. Your mother had had her tea and was sitting watching the television. I just stuck my head into the room and said hello. She didn't say anything. I could feel the atmosphere. You know how she hated anything to spoil her timetable, no matter how unimportant. So I went into the kitchen to get myself some tea."

He stopped and after a moment Jenny turned from the window which she had been staring out of since he started talking. Connon was resting his head in his hands, his elbows on the table.

"Are you all right?"

"Yes, yes. It's just this pain again. That's what happened on Saturday. It came on then, in the kitchen. I couldn't eat. I felt sick, so I went upstairs. And I passed out on the bed."

"What is this pain? Have you seen about it?"

"Not really. McManus has had a look. And a police doctor, but he didn't give me a diagnosis. I told you I got a knock during the game. Anyway, when I awoke it was nearly eleven. I still felt a bit groggy, but I remember thinking it was rather odd your mother hadn't been up to look for me. I came downstairs. The telly was still going in the lounge. I went in."

He stopped and made a gesture which might have been a shudder, or a shrug, or an incipient reaching out to his daughter. Jenny didn't move and Connon became still again.

"Go on."

"She was sitting in the big chair. Sprawled out. She was dead."

He was silent again, studying his daughter from between half-closed lashes. As if making a decision, he stood up and walked over to her so that he was standing close to her, not touching, not offering to touch, but there if required.

"Her eyes were open. Her forehead was smashed in just above her nose. She was obviously dead. I stood there for a minute. It was odd. I was quite calm. I thought, I mustn't touch anything. And I walked out into the hall and picked up the telephone. Then this thing in my head started again. I could hardly dial. But I managed."

"Who did you ring?"

"Old Dr McManus first. Then the police. McManus was more interested in me than your mother. Just took one look at her. But gave me a shot of something and put me to bed. There were police all over the place, but they didn't get far with asking me questions. I was out like a light."

"And this morning?"

"They were round first thing. That's where I've been. They told you that?"

"Yes."

"It's that fellow Dalziel. I know him vaguely from down at the Club. He's a brute of a fellow. I don't know what they expected him to find out."

"Have they any ideas?"

"Yes, I think so. A couple."

"What are they?"

"Firstly, that I am lying about this pain in my head and passing out. I came in last night, smashed your mother's head in and waited a few hours before calling the police."

"Secondly?"

"That I'm telling the truth about passing out. But, unknown to me or forgotten by me, I nevertheless killed your mother."

Now there was the longest silence of all. Finally Jenny opened her mouth to speak but her father gently laid his index finger across her lips.

"You needn't ask, Jenny. The answer is no, I did not consciously kill her."

"And unconsciously?"

"I don't think so. What else can I say?"

Now she took his hand and pressed it to her cheek. Connon looked fondly down at her flowing golden-brown hair.

He ran his fingers through its softness; it was a happy mixture of her mother's once vivid red and his own light brown.

"Don't worry, darling. It'll soon pass over, all this. Perhaps we can go away. It's almost your Christmas holidays. Would you like that, to go away, I mean?"

She looked up at him.

"Is that what you want? To go away?"

He rolled the question round in his mind for a moment, trying to read her thoughts. But nothing of them appeared in her face.

Finally he settled for the truth.

"No, I don't think so. No. It isn't."

She nodded her head in serious accord.

"No. Neither do I. We'll stay. There'll be lots to do here. We'll stay and do whatever we have to. Together."

She kept on nodding her head till her hair fell in a golden curtain over her white face.

Chapter Three

It was a glorious day. The sun laid a deep shadow obliquely across the polished oak of the coffin as it was lowered into the grave. The sky was cloudless, its blue more thinly painted than the blue of summer but the sun was too bright to stare in the eye. The air was just cold enough to make activity pleasant and the mourners shifted gently, almost imperceptibly, under their coats from time to time.

Only Connon and Jenny stood in absolute stillness.

Dalziel was scratching his left breast, his hand inside his coat moving rhythmically.

"Ironical," he whispered loudly. "Suit you, my boy. Subtle."

"What?" said Pascoe.

"This," he said. "Nature."

"Human nature? Or red in tooth and claw?"

"Don't get bloody metaphysical with me. The day, I mean. Fine day for a funeral. Sun. No wind blowing dead leaves or any of that. Fine day for golf."

"What are you doing here then, sir?"

Dalziel sniffed loudly. A few heads turned and turned away. He obviously wasn't about to break down.

"Me? Friend of the family. Last respects must be paid. Heartfelt sympathy."

He fluttered his hand inside his coat so that the cloth pulsated ludicrously.

"What's more to the point, what are you doing here? I come within smelling distance of having a reason. You're a non-starter. Bloody policeman, that's all. You'll get the force a bad name. Intrusion of grief, it could be grounds for complaint."

"In his master's steps he trod," murmured Pascoe softly.

"Which of us does that make the very sod? And what are you looking for, Pascoe? You're not nursing any nice little theories, are you? And not telling me?"

"No," said Pascoe, "of course not."

Not bloody much, thought Dalziel. You keep working at it, lad. Nothing like the competitive spirit for sharpening the wits.

❀ ❀ ❀

"Not a bad gate," whispered Arthur Evans to Marcus.

"Arthur!"

Evans looked sideways at his wife. She had put hardly any make-up on in deference to the occasion and wore a plain black coat, loose-fitting. But the bite in the air had brought the red blood to her lips and cheeks and the looseness of the coat just made it more obvious where it did touch.

Dressed like that, thought Evans with bitter admiration, she wouldn't stay a widow long.

Marcus, on his other side, looked pale beyond the remedy of frost. He swayed slightly.

"You all right, boyo?"

Jesus, on and off the field, I spend half my life nursing them.

"Yes, I'm fine. Just a bit cold. Poor Connie."

Poor Connie. Poor bastard. Evans remembered the shock last Sunday when they had finally got to the Club, arguments buried for an hour. That detective had been there, he was somewhere around now, bloody ghouls, one of Dalziel's lackeys, there's a right thug for you, like all these Scotsmen, no finesse, first up first down, feet feet feet. Sid had got in first. Snipped his indirect line, gave the news right out, loud and clear. Mary Connon's dead. And all I could do was look at Gwen, watch Gwen, see her age beneath the words, then gradually come back to life with awareness of her own life.

Poor Connie. He deserves sympathy. He deserves... perhaps he will get what he deserves. There he stands with that little girl of his. Not so little. She's a pretty little thing.

She's a pretty little thing.

❀ ❀ ❀

The service was over. Out of the corner of his eyes Pascoe had noticed two men with spades move tentatively forward from the cover of a clump of trees, then retreat. Their movement startled half-a-dozen crows whose caws had been a harsh burden to the words of the prayer-book and they went winging from the tree tops in ragged grace, as the black-coated mourners moved in twos and threes away from the grave-side, silent at first, but speaking more and more freely as the distance grew between themselves and the motionless couple who remained.

At the car park they formed little groups before dispersing. Dalziel convened with three or four elder statesmen of the Club, his face and manner serious. He produced a cigarette-case and passed it round.

Black Russian perhaps, thought Pascoe. That would amuse Dalziel if I could tell him. Do I want to amuse Dalziel? And if I do, is it to keep him sweet so I can manipulate him, like I pretend? Or is it because he puts the fear of God into me? Just how good is he anyway? Or is he just a ruthless sucker of other men's blood? "Don't get bloody metaphysical with me!" But said quite nicely really. Like a jocular uncle. Uncle Andrew.

You had to laugh. But not here. It's colder now. Christ, I'm holding conversations with myself about the weather, the mental Englishman, that's me. Now there's something to warm us all up, that woman getting into the back seat, back seat's the place for you, dear, are you sitting comfortably, now get them off. Don't be shocked, love, that's what all the detectives are thinking this year, you'll be giving yourself a scratch in a minute Andrew, you randy old devil. Randy Andy. Now if she'd been killed, her, Gwen, wasn't it? Evans, that would have been easy. Jealous husband, spurned lover, or one of those tumescent young men who'd been hanging around her from the moment she set foot in the bar, yes, one of those provoked just that bit too far, just over the edge where playing starts to be for real. But not Mary Connon, not that parcel of middle-aged lumber they'd just stored away. Though why not? She'd been built on the same lines, streamlines, take a hundred lines, so they said. Forty-five. Inches. Years. Was forty-five too old? No kind of age at all these days.

And she wasn't looking her best when I saw her, was she? There's something about a hole in the head...

So who knows? But I don't quite see the young men...more like one of these old fogies Randy Andy's chatting up, best prop-forward the Old Sodomites ever had, don't you know; or perhaps the best fly-half who never played for England, himself perhaps, selling us all a dummy as he stands there remembering how he smashed her head in so he could look for it inside, for the years lost, the place out in the glow of the crowd at Twickenham, could a man love a game that much? And smashed her with what, for God's sake? Where was it? I'd like a look round that house. Whatever it is could be lying at the bottom of his wardrobe. He'd get used to it after a while, like an egg-stain on a waistcoat, you get used to anything after a while. Lying there for someone to find, a friend, Felstead, Marcus, what's he got to look so sick about? And what'd he be doing in Connon's wardrobe anyway? Homosexual jealousy, that's the answer, I'll try it on Dalziel for a giggle. More likely his daughter, she'll find anything there is. Christ, what a thing to find out about your father, she'd do all right in the back seat too, I wouldn't mind carrying her away at a student riot. Here they come. And there goes fat Marcus, I come to bury Mary not to, he's taken his time about extending heartfelt sympathy though there's always the phone. Still, for a nearest and dearest friend...

❀ ❀ ❀

"Hello, Connie, Jenny."

"Marcus."

"Hello, Uncle Marcus."

Marcus had invited her to stop calling him "Uncle" about three years earlier when she had flourished into young woman-hood. "It makes me feel old and you sound young." So he had become plain Marcus.

Till now.

I have reverted to my old role, thought Marcus.

"I would have called round," he said apologetically, addressing himself to Jenny rather than Connon. "But you know how things...how are you both?"

"Well," said Connon. He did not look as if he was really listening, but glanced back to the grave.

"What will you do now, Jenny? Is your term over?"

"No, there's another couple of weeks yet, but I've got leave of absence. I needn't go back till after Christmas."

"How is it? Are you liking the life?"

"It's not bad. A bit crowded. There's more students than space. I can sympathize a bit more with these people who write indignantly to the Express about 'smelly students'."

Thank God for the resilience of youth, thought Marcus. No damage there, or not that's going to show. But you, Connie, out of the cage at last, you look as if another sniff of free air will shrivel your lungs. No bloody wonder, the shock, the strain of investigation. There's a new life waiting, if only you'll believe that, I must make him believe it before it's too late...

Jenny made a move down the path towards the car park. Marcus touched her arm.

"I'll stay here and chat to your father a bit till the others have thinned out. We'll catch you up. You'd better go and sit in the car out of the cold."

Jenny was surprised to find herself resenting Marcus slightly as she moved away.

She was my mother after all, and he's my father. Why should he be treated like the sensitive plant and me chucked down to face this lot?

Because you can think like this at a moment like this, she admonished herself humorously and the shadow of a smile must have run over her face for she caught "Bruiser" Dalziel eyeing her sharply as she stepped on to the car park.

Standing a little behind Dalziel she saw a tall young man, elegantly dressed, with a thin intelligent face—the kind of actor-type who played ambitious young Foreign Office men on the telly. She thought momentarily of Antony. She hadn't had time to see him before she left, everything had happened in such a hurry. But no doubt Helen would have passed on the news to him. Perhaps even made a come-back in her original starring role.

Definitely her last appearance, thought Jenny, but didn't find it particularly funny. She intended to make straight for the car and shut the door firmly on all condolences, sympathetic noises, keen-edged questionings probing for vicarious pain. But her arm was taken firmly and she was brought to a halt.

"I just wanted to say that I shall miss your mother, Jenny," said Alice Fernie.

The annoyance that had tightened her lips for a moment eased away. She could not remember anyone else saying this. They were all "dreadfully sorry," it had come as a terrible shock to them, but no one had really suggested that Mary Connon would be missed.

"Yes. I shall too," she replied, then feeling this was a bit too cold she squeezed the gloved hand which still rested on her arm and went on, "I know how much she relied on you."

This was nothing more than the simple truth, she realized, as the words came out. Mary Connon had rarely mentioned Alice Fernie to her except in faintly disparaging or patronizing terms. Her lack of taste; the unfairly large wage her husband earned on the factory floor; the excessive subsidization by the rate-payers of council-house rents. She was capable of blaming the Fernies ("and all those like them," she would say inclusively) for the very existence of the Woodfield estate. It had only been a very few years previously that Jenny had realized that the council estate had been there already when her parents bought the house. She had come to accept a picture of rolling country-side being savaged before her mother's eyes as the bulldozers rolled in, prompted by the Fernies and "all those like them." But Alice Fernie had been, perhaps by the mere accident of proximity, the nearest thing to a real friend she had. And now Jenny felt real gratitude that this large handsome woman who could only be in her early thirties had thought enough of her mother to accept the condescension of manner and get closer to her.

Closer than me perhaps, she thought.

"How did you get here, Mrs Fernie?" she asked. "Can we give you a lift back?"

There were no funeral cars other than the hearse. "I will judge what is fitting," she had heard her father say to the oblique remonstrances of the man from the undertakers.

"No, thank you, dear. You'll want to be with your dad. And I'm not going straight back anyway. 'Bye now."

"Goodbye. Please call round, won't you? I shan't be going back to college till next month."

I'll have to watch myself there, she thought as she watched Alice move away with long confident strides, I could become as patronizing as Mum.

As she got into the car, she glanced back and caught the eye of the young man who could have been from the Foreign

Office. He took a step forward. She thought he was going to come across and talk to her. But a rumbling, phlegmy cough from Fat Dalziel caught both their attentions and the young man turned away.

Policeman, she thought, angry at her disappointment, and slammed the car door.

❀ ❀ ❀

Connon watched Marcus walk away from him down the path through the rank and file of headstones.

The car park was nearly empty now. The Evanses' car was just pulling away. He looked after it thoughtfully. Gwendoline. He formed the syllables deliberately in his mind and smiled. All those youngsters competing to provoke the loudest laugh, craning forward to get the deepest view of bosom, pressing close to feel the warmth of calf or thigh, and imagining a returned pressure. Tales to be blown up into triumphs over a couple of pints. But the real triumphs were never boasted of, but remembered in secret; first with reminiscent delight, but soon with fear and cold panic.

Dalziel was gone, he observed, and his puppy-dog, Pascoe. Mentally he corrected himself. He had no reason for thinking Pascoe was merely that, though he was sure Dalziel would make him that if he got the chance.

And me, what would he make of me if he got the chance? he thought.

A parcel for the lawyers. Strongly wrapped, neatly labelled.

Samuel Connon. Wife-killer. There must be some long Latin word for a man who killed his wife. Dalziel might know it, though he probably wouldn't admit to it if he did. Pascoe would know. He seemed a highly educated kind of cop. The new image. Get your degree, join the force, the Yard's the limit. Or...leave school at sixteen, start as office boy. You can be assistant personnel manager by the time you're forty. If you're lucky. And if the general manager is a big rugby fan.

I'd better be getting down to Jenny. Poor Jenny. I wish I knew how hard this has hit her. Perhaps I was wrong. Perhaps we should get away for a bit. Where? What on? There's not all that much spare in the account. All this costs a bit. Even if you haggled over headstones. Now if I'd gone first, Mary'd have been sitting pretty. But what kind of man insures against his wife's death?

At least they can't say I killed her for profit. But it'd be nice to get away. Soon. When things had quietened down. It'd be nice to get far, far away. To somewhere as unlike this as possible.

Back to the desert.

Over twenty years earlier, Connon had been sent to join his unit in Egypt at the start of his National Service. He had only been out there a couple of months when the regiment returned home, and at the time the few weeks he spent there seemed to consist of nothing but endless liquid motions of the bowels. He had been as delighted as the rest to return to England and it was this period that saw the blossoming of his rugby career. He had played only a couple of times since leaving school but now he became quickly aware of the advantages traditionally enjoyed by the athlete in His Majesty's forces. His natural talent exploded into consummate artistry in these conditions and only the simultaneous service, as officer, of the current Welsh stand-off kept him out of the Army XV.

But something of his brief acquaintance with the desert did not easily die. It remained with him as dreams of luxury hotels in the remote Bermudas haunt some men. He read anything he could get hold of on the desert. Any desert. He collected colour brochures and handouts from the travel agents. Fifteen days in Morocco. Three weeks in Tunisia. Amazing value. But always too much for him.

In any case the desert Connon really wanted to visit was not in any of the brochures, not even the most expensive. He recognized it by its absence, that is, he knew what he wanted was something out of the reach of a camera; something untranslatable into colour photography and glossy paper. He wanted rock that had absorbed terrible, endless heat for a million years, that had writhed in infinitely slow violence till its raw bowels lay on the surface, yet without a single movement noticed by man. He wanted sand which rose and fell like the sea, but so slowly that it was only when it drowned his own civilization that a man recognized its tides.

It was a vision he confided to no one. Least of all Mary, who had found his collection of travel brochures nuisance enough.

Perhaps Jenny...

He saw that she had got out of the car again and was standing against the bonnet looking up towards him. Otherwise the car park was now completely empty.

He began to walk towards her.

❀ ❀ ❀

"I wasn't going to ask her anything," repeated Pascoe. "Not then. Not there. I felt sorry for her. Just standing there. She looked, I don't know, helpless somehow."

This, he thought, is a turn up for the book. Bruiser Dalziel lecturing me on tact and diplomacy. It was like Henry the Eighth preaching about marital constancy.

"Well, watch it. We don't harry people at funerals. At least not unless we think they did it. And we don't think young Jenny Connon did it, do we?"

"No, sir."

"You checked, of course?"

"Of course. She was nearly a hundred miles away. We know that."

"It's about all we bloody well do know. The only thing we make any progress with is the list of things we don't know. Item: who had a strong motive to kill her? No one we know, not even the great Connie as far as we know."

"Strength of motive is in the mind of the murderer, sir."

"Confucius, he bloody well say. To continue. Item: what did he kill her with? A metal object or at least an object with a metal end, cylindrical in shape, long enough to be grasped probably with both hands and smashed right between the eyes of a victim who sits there smiling and doesn't even try to duck."

"The pathologist's report did say that Mrs Connon had unusually fragile bones, sir. Perhaps we're overestimating the strength needed."

"So what? Thanks for nothing. And Mary Connon fragile? I don't believe it. It couldn't be true. With tits like those she'd have broken her collar-bone every time she stood up. To continue again. Item: who saw anything suspicious or even anyone anywhere near the house that night? Not a soul. Not even the eyes and ears of the Woodfield Estate, your friend Fernie. All he can swear is that Connon was rolling drunk. Which Connon can disprove with con-bloody-siderable ease."

"It does fit with Connon's account, though. About his giddiness, I mean. Makes his story that bit stronger, don't you think? And our doctor did find signs of a slight concussion. He's still seeing his own man, too. I checked."

Dalziel slammed his fist so hard on the desk that Pascoe broke his rule of stony non-reaction to his superior and started in his chair.

"I'm not interested in the bloody man's health. If he's innocent, he can drop dead tomorrow for all I care."

"A sentiment that does you credit, sir. But there is one thing about this injury to Connon that's a little bit odd."

"What's that, and why isn't it in your report?" asked Dalziel suspiciously.

"Apparently irrelevant. But I felt you might like it, sir."

Dalziel licked his lips and looked as if the task of strangling Pascoe personally and instantly might not be unattractive.

"It's just that when I was down at the Club, I talked among others to a chap called Slater."

"Fat Fred. I know him."

"Slater remembered Connon being laid out. But, he added casually and as far as I could see without malice, that he reckoned the boot that did the damage belonged to Evans, his own captain. He seemed to think it was just a case of mistaken identity."

"Fred would. He's thick as pigshit, that one. But Arthur Evans isn't made that way. He plays hard, but he'd never put the boot in."

"So?"

"So Fred Slater should start wearing his glasses on the field. Or better still, give up. It's indecent a man that size exposing himself in public. I don't know how his wife manages him."

He chuckled to himself at the thought and murmured, "Levers, I should think."

"Pardon?"

"Sergeant," he said quietly, "is there anything we've left undone which we ought to have done?"

"I don't think so, sir."

"Right. Then somewhere, in some area we are covering, or have covered, lies the clue."

"The clue?"

"There's always a clue, boy. Don't you read the Sunday papers? All this started somewhere and it wasn't Boundary Drive. Or if it was, we're not going to get much help there. Now where's our best bet?"

Pascoe spoke like a bored actor who was thinking of things other than his lines.

"At the Club."

"That's right. I think I'll just drop in there tonight. No, tomorrow. That's a training night. They'll all be there. Socially, I mean, for a pot of ale. If there's anything known, they'll tell me by chucking-out time. They'll tell me."

He spoke with some satisfaction.

Like a…but the phone interrupted Pascoe's search for the right simile. Dalziel nodded at it.

"Well, get it, then."

Pascoe lifted up the receiver.

"Sergeant Pascoe here. Yes?"

He listened for a few moments then replaced the receiver and stood silent.

"Not a private call, I hope, Sergeant," said Dalziel. "Or are you just playing hard to get."

"I'm sorry, sir," said Pascoe. "No. It's the Connons. They got home and there was a letter. For the girl, it seems. Something unpleasant. Connon wants us to go out there straight away."

❊ ❊ ❊

Alice Fernie had gone straight home from the funeral, not doing some shopping first as she had told Jenny. She possessed a great deal of natural tact as well as independence of spirit, a quality which had made possible her friendship with Mary Connon. But the journey had involved two buses and a great deal of waiting. So she had plenty of time to think.

Buses and trains both set you thinking, she thought. But not in the same way. Trains gave you a rhythm, sent you into dreams, cut you off from reality. Buses were always stopping and starting; traffic, road-junctions, lights; and of course, bus-stops. The world you passed through was observable. And real.

So was the world inside your head.

Buses were good places to worry on.

Alice Fernie was worried. She was wondering what the law might do to her husband if it caught up with him.

"Hello there, Alice. What a grand drying day it is, eh?"

Maisie Curtis from next door had got on the bus and was easing herself into the seat beside her. They were both broad-hipped women and the woeful inadequacy of the Corporation's transport service was very apparent. Alice didn't mind. The Corporation didn't provide much heating either and the warmth generated by the collision of two such large areas was very welcome.

"Hello, Maisie."

"You're looking smart. You've been to her funeral, then?"

"That's right."

There was a short pause while Maisie paid her fare.

"Many there?"

"A few."

"Oh."

She'll want names, thought Alice resignedly. She'll want a guest-list. And she'll get it.

"There's no funeral meats, then?"

"No. Everyone's just going home. Quietly. Like me."

"Was there anyone from the police there?"

Alice sighed.

"As a guest, I mean, a mourner. They wouldn't be there official, would they? Not unless…"

"What?"

"Unless they wanted to watch him, keep an eye on him."

"Who?"

"Mr Connon, of course."

Alice shifted herself in the seat so that Maisie had to give a couple of inches. The conductor looked in awe at the overhang.

"Why should they want to watch him?"

"I don't know. In case he decided to skip, that's why. Well, he might, mightn't he? If he felt like it."

"Like what?"

"Like getting away."

"In his shoes, who wouldn't feel like getting away?"

Maisie was used to deliberate obtuseness on the part of her neighbour and was neither distracted nor offended by it.

"I mean escaping. If he did it."

"If he did it? What makes you say that? You should watch what you say, Maisie. That kind of talk could get you into trouble."

Alice found herself speaking with greater vehemence than she'd intended, but once more Maisie greeted the affront with a smile.

"Well, if I'm in trouble, I won't be the only one. There'll be lots of company," she said smugly.

Alice's heart sank.

"Who do you mean?"

"Why, your Dave for one."

Oh God, she thought. Was he still at it? In spite of the row last night? He'd say it to someone who mattered sooner or later. And then, then the law would have its course with David Fernie. Alice knew nothing of the law of slander. But she knew how much compensation she herself would demand for being falsely accused of murder.

She tried to speak casually.

"Dave? What's he been saying to you?"

To you. Maisie Curtis. Queen gossip of the Woodfield Estate. Which meant of the town.

"To me? Nothing. Your Dave doesn't pass the time of day with me. No, it was our Stanley he was talking to."

This was worse. Maisie Curtis's Stanley was a direct channel to the Rugby Club. The only one Dave had, probably. And, equally probably, he'd know it. There'd be gossip enough at the Club. Bound to be. Suppose Stanley, young, bumptious, keen to impress...lived nearly opposite the murder-house...next to a key witness.

Witness! To what?

Like that time in Bolton. That was a few years ago, but her memory was longer than her husband's. The law had been brought in then, but only to ask why anyone should have wanted to break Fernie's jaw and kick three of his ribs in.

But Mr Connon was a different kettle of fish. It wouldn't be the law of the jungle this time. Gossip was one thing. Innuendo, knowing winks, impudent questionings. But someone saying he knew was quite different; someone saying he was certain.

Dave Fernie, big Dave Fernie. He knew. He always bloody well knew. Not even God Almighty was as certain about things as Dave Fernie.

"What's Dave been saying, then?" she asked as calmly as she could, shredding her ticket with meticulous care.

"Well, according to my Stanley, your Dave says he knows how he, Mr Connon that is, killed his wife. And he knows why."

Maisie nodded as affirmatively at this point as if she had been Fernie himself.

Soul-mates, thought Alice. They're soul-mates. Born under the same star.

"Was that all?"

"All? Wasn't it enough? It quite upset our Stanley, it did. That's how I got to hear of it. I could see something was bothering him. And he's not been in the best of health lately, had a few days off work with one of his tummy upsets. So I asked him and he told. He's always looked up to Mr Connon, you see. Well, I mean, they all do, down at that Club. He's on the selection committee as well, you see."

Alice didn't see, because she'd stopped listening. To think they said that it was women who had the vicious tongues. There'd been one or two near things since Bolton. One or two unpleasant moments. One or two lost friends.

But this could mean the law.

"Alice! Are you not getting off, then?"

The pressure had gone from her flank. Maisie was standing in the aisle, looking down at her.

"Yes, of course."

They set off down the main road together, Maisie chattering away about other matters now. She was unoffendable herself and never considered for one moment that anyone could be hurt or angered by anything she might say.

After fifty yards they turned left into Boundary Drive.

It was quieter here, away from the main course of traffic. The private side of the road was lined with trees which, even though stripped for winter, added something to the peacefulness of the scene. The trees which should have been on the other side of the road had been swept away at one fell swoop, without warning, when the Corporation bulldozers had moved in at the end of the war. An act of civic vandalism, the residents had called it, complaining even more when they realized they would have to pay road charges now the council was making up the road-surface. But the trees had gone beyond recall, and their absence accentuated as much as the architecture the differences between the old and the new.

Still, the trees and the pleasant outlook over to the more solid and architecturally varied private houses had made Alice glad that they had been offered a house here rather than in the middle of the estate.

Up till now.

Maisie's voice suddenly rose so sharply that it penetrated the confused web of her own thoughts.

"That's them, isn't it, Alice? In that car. I thought I recognized them."

Her eyes focused ahead. A black saloon had just driven by them. She remembered seeing it in the cemetery car park. She watched with trepidation as it slowed down further along the street. For a moment of heart-sinking shock, she thought it had pulled over to stop in front of her own house. But the driver was merely giving himself enough room to swing round to the left, over the pavement and into the Connons' drive.

"I wonder what they're after?" asked Maisie, increasing her pace.

Alice didn't wonder. She didn't care. As long as they weren't after Dave. She'd have to talk to him again. She'd have to make it quite clear that he was worrying her silly with his slanderous gossip. She'd have to get him to realize that he could get himself into very serious trouble with these terrible accusations against Mr Connon. Very serious trouble.

Unless…

It was curious that the thought had never entered her mind before.

Unless they were true.

She began to lengthen her stride to keep up with Maisie Curtis.

❁ ❁ ❁

"'Dear Miss Connon,

It must be terrible for you to find that your mother is dead and to realize your father is a murderer. Nothing can bring your mother back. But it may be some comfort to you to know that the man you think is your father is not. Your mother married him only so that her baby (you) would have a name. What a name! It is a murderer's name. Think yourself lucky he is nothing to do with you.'"

"No signature."

"Let me see," said Dalziel.

Pascoe handed over the letter. The superintendent took it carefully by the same corner that Pascoe had used and glanced down at the writing.

"At least it's clean," he said.

"That's little consolation," said Connon, who was standing with his arm protectively over Jenny's shoulders. To Pascoe the girl did not look particularly in need of protection. In fact she had the same rather dangerously angry look he'd seen wrinkle her brow after the funeral.

"Let's get this clear..." Dalziel began.

Connon interrupted him.

"I presume that means you want me to repeat myself."

Clever sod, thought Dalziel. Clever-clever. I'm beginning to hope you did it, clever Connie.

"No, I'll repeat you," he said. "You just confirm. It's a question of making sure we're talking the same language. Now, you came straight back after the funeral arriving... when?"

Connon looked at his daughter.

"Quarter to twelve," she said. "I put the radio on. There was a time-check."

Then she added, almost apologetically, "I wanted a noise in the house. Something lively."

Pascoe looked at her sympathetically. She didn't avoid his gaze but stared back till he looked away.

"You picked up the letter as you came in, but didn't open it immediately?"

"No," said Jenny. "I thought it'd be just another condolence note or card."

"Anyway, you made a pot of tea, brought it through to your father who was sitting in here, then you opened your letter?"

"That's right."

"And?"

"And what? I showed it to Daddy."

"And I," cut in Connon, "decided we ought to get in touch with you instantly."

"Quite right too, sir."

"Well, Superintendent, what next?"

Dalziel looked around with the kind of heavily underlined hesitance that could be clearly marked in the back row of the gods. Pascoe watched in awe.

He invites them to join in his games, he thought. That's the secret of his success. He reduces it all to the level of a pantomime.

"I wonder," said Dalziel, "I wonder if I could perhaps have a word with you alone, sir?"

Connon looked doubtful.

If he's not careful, he'll be playing. If he's not playing already.

"My sergeant can be taking a statement from Miss Connon while we're talking," added Dalziel.

That'll be nice, thought Pascoe, trying to keep any trace of the thought off his face.

Jenny Connon did not seem to think it would be particularly nice at all and made little effort to keep her thoughts off her face. But she turned readily enough and went to the door.

"We'll go into the lounge, then," she said. Connon nodded. Dalziel wondered if he detected a hint of relief.

Perhaps he doesn't like to go into the lounge any more.

The chair had been moved, Pascoe noticed. He didn't suppose anyone else had sat in it since Mary Connon had relaxed to watch television on Saturday night. Then he laughed inwardly and changed his mind. The chair probably hadn't come back from County Forensic where Dalziel, despite the scorn he poured on Science and all its works, had sent it. The boys down there, their work once finished, would have no compunction at all about sitting in it.

"Well," said Jenny, "are you just going to stand there, all hawk-eyed, or are we going to get on with this statement? What would you like me to state?"

"Yes, the statement." Pascoe fumbled in his pocket for his notebook. "Won't you sit down?"

"In my own home, I prefer to issue the invitations. Please sit down, Sergeant."

Only the remembrance that her mother had died in this room not a week earlier stopped Pascoe from grinning.

He sat down.

"The words in that letter were printed, of course, but even printing is sometimes recognizable. Did the writing remind you of anyone's you had seen before?"

Jenny shook her head.

"No."

"Sure?"

"Yes, I'm sure."

"Can you think of anyone who would send such a letter to you?"

"Yes."

Startled, he ceased his pretence of making notes.

"Who?"

"The man who killed my mother."

He shook his head slowly.

"Now why should he do that?"

"To divert suspicion from himself."

"How can he hope to do that when we don't know who wrote the letter?"

"But you do know who you're suspicious of."

Of whom you are suspicious, Antony might have said. But it sounded a little clumsy for Antony. He never let his passion for correctness trap him into clumsiness. In any field.

She noticed that this time Pascoe had let his grin show through. She felt like grinning back, whether at Pascoe or at the thought of Antony she wasn't sure. But she didn't, for at the same time she felt guilty, as she did whenever she found herself acting normally, as if her mother hadn't been done to death, here, in this very room, last week, on an ordinary Saturday evening with the television set babbling uncaringly on in the background.

The thought had stopped the grin even if her willpower had failed. But even now she recognized how diluted the emotional shock of remembering had already become.

I could go out tonight, she thought. Have a drink and a laugh, no bother. I know I could. I feel I shouldn't be able to, but I could. They've got to catch him soon, they've got to, I'll make sure they do, he deserves it, he must be caught. Must.

That'll be an end of it then, some more distant part of her mind whispered.

Dear God! the most conscious level replied, aghast. Is that it, then? Is that what the pursuit of vengeance is—not the instinctive reaction of deep and lasting grief, but an attempt to compensate for shallowly felt grief, to give it body, to make testimony to it?

Confused, she became angry. Angry at herself for thinking like this. Angry at the police for making no progress. Angry at Pascoe for talking to her here while the real interview was taking place in the next room.

"Let's stop this farce, shall we?" she said.

"Farce?"

"Yes. You don't want a statement from me. What the hell can I state that's any help or even needs recording? All you want is me here so that disgusting Dalziel can chat Daddy up by himself."

Pascoe's face relaxed again at her choice of adjective and this time an answering smile almost broke through.

"Now why should we want that?" he asked politely.

She turned away from him.

"So that he can ask Daddy if what the letter says is true, I suppose. About me not being his child, I mean."

Pascoe seemed to be trapped like a disembodied spirit somewhere in the room where he could see and hear an unemotional policeman, disguised as himself, ask in an absolutely even voice,

"And is it?"

❀ ❀ ❀

"The question's purely biological, I presume, Superintendent?"

"Pardon?"

"You're interested in the narrow question of whether I am physically the girl's father, rather than in my attitudes towards her?"

Christ! another talking like a Sunday Supplement article. Pascoe's bad enough and at least the bugger's on my side. But this...cold fish, Connon. He'd work out which side your balls were hanging before he made his sidestep.

"That's right, Mr Connon. I think. I mean, was young Jenny born as a result of you having intercourse with your wife?"

Connon shrugged. He looked very tired.

"I think so."

"Think!?"

Dalziel took a rapid command of himself so that though the word began as a roar it ended as an almost gentle interrogative.

"I have never had any positive evidence to the contrary. At the same time, I can't point to any proof positive on the other side. There have seemed to me and others to be physical resemblances, but parents and relations in general are notoriously blind in these matters."

"So you admit that it's possible the terms of the letter could be accurate?"

"Not all of them, Superintendent."

Hair-splitting now. Don't answer. Let the sod go on in his own sweet time.

"It's a question of faith, I suppose. I suppose it always is."

"And you didn't have that faith?"

"Once. But it went. Too late to matter as far as Jenny was concerned, I'm glad to say."

"Why did it go? Was there anything in particular, talk, anything like that? Gossip?"

"No. Probably. I never heard, but then I wouldn't. More in your line."

The truth of this simple statement half surprised Dalziel. He ran his mind back over the narrow little track signposted "Mary Connon," but came across no landmarks of interest.

"Well, then..." he said.

"She told me."

"She what?"

"Told me. Several times. She wanted me to give up playing almost from the start. Said it was too much to expect her to cope all week with a baby and then to be left to herself on Saturdays as well. I daresay there was something in it."

"But you didn't."

"You know I didn't. I went on. Every Saturday from September to April. It was important."

"To you?" said Dalziel very softly. He didn't want to disturb his man. He thought he recognized the beginnings of that half-dreamy inward-looking state in which a thought-monologue could easily lead to a confession.

But his soft interjection seemed to blast into Connon's mind like a hand-grenade.

"To me?" he said, laughing. "Of course. But that sounds

selfish, doesn't it? The outskirts of a motive. No, important to us all, the three of us, my wife and child, as well as me."

"But you said she told you. What?"

"She told me that I might as well keep on going to the Club. At least that way I might run into Jenny's father."

"She said that!"

I'd have broken her neck, thought Dalziel. Motive? What better? I'd have broken her bloody neck!

But the thought went on against his will: perhaps that's why she told you by telegram, perhaps that's why you ended up standing stupefied in the lobby of your little semi-detached, reading and re-reading the jumble of words on the buff form. He'd often thought since of his wife in some post-office writing those words down, then passing the form to some clerk to count them up. Had he said anything? Had there been an expression on his face as he counted? Was there a query perhaps?

It must have cost her a packet.

But, he thought now, with a self-irony which had only developed of later years, but, he thought as he looked down at his tightly clenched fist, it had been money wisely spent.

"When was this?"

"Too long ago for a motive. Fourteen, fifteen years."

"What did you do?"

"I forget."

Dalziel let this pass for the moment.

"Did she ever say more?"

"She repeated the claim, twice I think, both times at moments of great anger."

"Did you believe her?"

Connon shrugged.

"I've told you, it's a matter of faith. I knew she'd been with other men before we married. But I believed she loved me. So I had faith."

"And?"

Connon looked at Dalziel with the self-possession the detective found so irritating.

"No 'and,' Superintendent. I think I've said as much as I want to say."

Dalziel infused a threatening rasp into his voice, more from habit than expectation of producing any result.

"You've either said too much or too little, Mr Connon. I need to know more."

"Or less."

"I can't unknow what you've told me."

"No. But you can reduce it to its proper proportions surely. Many years ago my wife implied to me that I was not the father of her daughter. She later withdrew the implication. It's doubtless the kind of nasty thing husbands and wives shout at each other fairly frequently when they're rowing. It didn't worry me, at least not too much. And less as time went on. I never thought of it. Jenny was mine, my daughter, my responsibility, even if you could have proved Genghis Khan was her father. So why should I be bothered? Now my wife's dead and my daughter's had a vicious letter. Now I'm bothered. I'm telling you all this in the hope it might be some help to you to catch the writer of that letter."

"And your wife's murderer?"

Connon nodded wearily.

"If you like. Though I don't see how. And his bit of harm's done, isn't it? This boy's got his still to finish."

Dalziel rose ponderously and belched without effort at concealment. Connon remained seated, looking up at him.

"Good day to you, Mr Connon. Please contact us instantly should any further attempt be made to contact your daughter, by letter or any other means."

"Other?"

"This kind of thing can become a habit. I should try to get to the telephone first in future, for instance."

As if at command, the phone rang.

Connon looked startled, the first unguarded emotion he had shown, then moved rapidly across the room and out into the entrance hall.

Pascoe was standing there with the phone in his hand.

"Hello," he said. "Hello."

Jenny was in the doorway of the lounge.

So he can think too, thought Dalziel.

Pascoe put the receiver down.

"No answer. It must have been a wrong number."

"Surely," said Dalziel. "Well, we'll bid you good day, Mr Connon. Jenny."

He moved to the front door. Behind him he heard Pascoe say in a low voice, obviously not intended for Jenny's ears, "Just one thing further, Mr Connon. Could you let us have a list of the TV programmes you think your wife would have been likely to want to see on that Saturday night? It might help."

"Might it?" said Connon. "But not two lists, surely? I passed that information to your office at Mr Dalziel's request yesterday."

"And," said Dalziel, smiling smugly as they walked to the car together, "I'd have let the girl get to the phone first if I could have managed it. It was probably the only chance we'll ever get of listening in."

"If it was our man."

"Oh yes. I'm sure of that."

Across the road, the curtain fell back into place in a bedroom window.

❀ ❀ ❀

"He asked me if it was true."

"Me too."

"What did you tell him?"

"What I told you when you asked."

Outside they heard the car start up. There was the familiar slap as it brushed against the laburnum tree, then it was on its way. Jenny put the chain on the door and the simple action filled Connon's heart with the grief he had not yet felt.

He had been telling nothing less than the simple truth

when he said that his love for Jenny was in no way dependent on his being her father. But he saw that his own indifference was not shared and he regretted now that he hadn't been absolutely affirmative with her.

What has she done that she must share my doubts? he thought. What have I done that I can expect her to understand my certainties?

The urge to tell her it made no difference was strong in him once more, but he knew it would be a mistake. She must find for herself how little difference it did make. Now all that was necessary was to remind her she wasn't facing a stranger.

"Jenny, love, what about a pot of tea?"

"If you like."

She was pale. Her face had the shape which could take paleness and make it beautiful, but she was too pale.

Connon hated the writer of that letter which had taken his daughter's colour away.

"Will they find him?"

The question slotted so neatly into his thoughts that he was slow in formulating a spoken reply.

"I don't know. He's there somewhere. Out there."

"At the Club?"

"Perhaps. I don't know."

"Have you any idea?"

He moved back along the hallway to the dining-room door. He spoke suddenly with a new resolution in his voice.

"There's a committee meeting tomorrow night. I think I'll go. Will you mind?"

She smiled and his heart split with love and anger.

"If you don't mind, I'll come with you. It's a long time since I showed my face there."

"Right then."

"Right."

Connon turned from the dining-room and moved across to the door opposite.

"We'll have tea in the lounge, shall we?" he said casually.

"All right."

"Then a quiet night. Save our strength for tomorrow."

"Right."

Again he hesitated, looking for words.

"Jenny, I miss your mother. More now somehow. More than I thought."

Then he stepped into the lounge for the first time since Saturday night.

In the kitchen Jenny whistled softly as she made the tea.

Chapter Four

They were dancing in the social room. A record-player shuffled a few simple chords violently together, then dealt them out with heavy emphasis. The upper reaches of the room were vague with cigarette smoke, the lower reaches voluptuous with long legs and round little bottoms.

Dalziel watched with awful lust as the girls twisted and jerked in total self-absorption. A hand squeezed his knee.

"Watch it, Andy, or you'll be spoiling your suit."

Dalziel laughed but didn't turn his eyes to the speaker.

"It's as if they were being rammed by an invisible man," he said.

The music stopped and now he gave the newcomer his full attention.

"They weren't like this in our day, Willie," he said.

Willie Noolan, small, dapper, grey, bank manager and President of the Club, smiled his agreement.

"They were not. We had to earn our wages in those days."

"The wages of sin, eh? Not that it was always difficult, if you knew where to look. Do you recall a little animal called Sheila Cripps? Eh?"

Noolan smiled reminiscently. These two had known each other for well over thirty years, meeting first at school and then finding their paths crossing again and again as they shifted with their respective jobs, till finally they had both come back permanently to the town they started from.

"She's a dried-up old stick now, Andy. Sings in the Methodist choir. I can't believe my memory when I look at her."

"Ay. They don't weather like us, Willie. Even when the shape goes," he said, slapping his belly, "the spirit remains constant. It's a question of dedication. But I'm sorry that little Sheila's been a backslider."

"Oh, she's been that in her time too."

They laughed again, each enjoying the joke, but each with the watchfulness of his profession.

The third man at the table did not join in.

"Careful, Jacko, or you'll have hysterics," said Dalziel.

The long thin mouth was pulled down at the corners like a tragic mask, the eyes were hooded, the shoulders hunched, head bent forward so that the man's gaze seemed fixed on the surface of the table.

God, thought Dalziel as he had frequently thought for the past twenty years, you're the most miserable-looking bugger I ever saw.

"You're like a couple of little lads. Act your age," Jacko said, half snarling.

"John Roberts, Builder" was a familiar sign in the area. He had built the club-house they were sitting in.

He was reputed to have arrived in town at the age of sixteen with a barrow-load of junk and two and ninepence in his pocket. The war was on. He was an evacuee, said some; others that he had absconded from a Borstal. No one took much notice of him then. No one who mattered. It was only when he plunged, wallet-first, into the great post-war building wave that people began to take notice. He lived chancily, moved into many crises, both business and legal, but always emerged from the other side safely—and usually richer, more powerful.

Those who remembered him with his barrow recalled a cheerful, toothy smile, an infectious, confidence-inspiring laugh. Armed with this information, they wouldn't have picked him out on an identity parade.

Dalziel wouldn't need an identity parade if he wanted to worry Jacko. He knew enough about him, had done enough research on his origins and his company, to worry him a great deal. But his knowledge wasn't official. Yet.

He was saving it up for a rainy day.

"How's business, Andy?" asked Noolan. "Putting many away?"

"Not enough. Not near enough."

There was a pause. A new record had started. Slower, softer. Some of the dancers actually came in contact now. Sid Hope was doing the rounds, having a friendly word with those who were late in paying their subscriptions. They were due at the start of the season. Sid gave plenty of leeway, right up to Christmas. But, Christmas past, he was adamant—non-payers were ejected, quietly if possible. But noisily if necessary.

"These two coughed up, have they, Sid?" asked Noolan with a laugh.

"Oh, aye," replied the treasurer as he passed. "See you at the meeting."

"Meeting?" asked Dalziel.

"Yes. The committee. At eight. Just time for another, eh? Jacko?"

"You'll be one short tonight," said Dalziel casually.

"One? We usually are. Oh, you mean Connie? Yes, I expect so. Can't expect anything else in the circumstances. Sad. Very sad."

"Man gets shot of his wife, that's not sad."

"Jacko, my lad, you're lovely."

"Didn't some bastard offer to get them in?"

"That's very kind of you, Jacko," said Dalziel. "Another pint. Please."

Without a word, Roberts rose and headed for the service hatch.

"You've got a way with Jacko, Andy. I've often noticed."

"Observation's anyone's game. Detection's my business, though. Don't start looking too deep."

Make them feel almost a part of it, thought Dalziel. Just a hint's enough.

He's after something, thought Noolan.

"You were saying about Connie."

"Was I? What?"

"About it being sad."

"Well, it was. Very. Not that we'd seen much of Mary lately. In fact I can't remember the last time. It was probably at the bank anyway, not here."

"Bank with you, do they?"

"Yes."

"Interesting account?"

"Not particularly. Just the usual monthlies, and weekly withdrawals for the housekeeping."

"Nothing out of the ordinary, then. Recently? In or out?"

"No. Not a thing."

Dalziel pulled up his trouser-leg and began scratching his ankle.

"Much left at the end of the month?"

"Enough. Not much. But enough to give them a week in Devon."

Dalziel scratched on.

"You're not trying to extract confidential information from me, are you, Andy?"

They both laughed.

"And what the hell's wrong with your ankle?"

"I've got an itch. Nasty inflammation."

"Been putting your foot in it, have you?"

They laughed again.

"Still at it?" grunted Jacko, slamming a tray laden with three tankards on to the table. "Like a couple of bloody tarts."

"Is that the time?" said Noolan. "I'd better go and convene this damn meeting. You'll be here for a while?"

"What do you think?"

"See you later, then. Cheers, Jacko. See you later."

They watched him shoulder his way jovially through the dancers towards the door of the committee room at the far end of the social room.

"A real card," said Jacko, dead-pan.

"He's been a good help to you, Jacko. Saw you through when many wouldn't have."

"Surely," said Jacko. "Beneath these pinstripes hang three balls of brass. Did he tell you owt?"

Dalziel shrugged.

"Nothing helpful."

It was no use playing games with Jacko Roberts, he thought.

But then it was even less use trying to play games with Andy Dalziel—unless he'd invented the rules.

"Was she insured?"

"No. No cover at all as far as we know."

"No cover? That'd be a sight for sore eyes with that one. By God!"

Dalziel put down his tankard in mock amazement.

"Do I detect a note of enthusiasm, Jacko?"

"There's plenty as was. Once."

"Just once? Nothing lately?"

Jacko scowled.

"How the hell would I know?"

Dalziel nodded thoughtfully.

"I'd have heard, too. What about Connie? Has he been having anything on the side?"

"Nothing said. But he moves without you noticing, that one."

On and off the field, thought Dalziel. Yes, it's true. Not inconspicuous, nothing grey about Connie, no blurred edges there. But self-contained. An area of calm.

Like the eye of a storm.

"Jacko," he said.

"Yes."

"If you hear anything..." but as he spoke he became aware

of someone standing behind him and Jacko's gaze was now aligned over his head.

"I didn't know you were bringing the wife," said Jacko.

Dalziel was startled for a moment and twisted round in his chair.

"Hello," said Pascoe.

"I'm going for a run-off," said Jacko.

He stood up, his lean hunched figure making his clothes look a size too large for him. He leaned forward and said softly to Dalziel: "I'll tell you something. Someone's fishing in Arthur Evans's pond. Welsh git."

Pascoe watched him go with interest.

"Tell me, sir. Does he always take his tankard to the loo with him?"

"What the hell are you doing here? I told you, you'd had your go. Now get out."

Pascoe sat down.

"Nothing like that, sir. I'm here socially." He felt in his top pocket and produced a blue card.

"Here you are. I'm a paid-up member. The place interested me. I decided to join. I don't think that your Mr Hope was all that happy, but what could he do?"

"I'm not happy either. And I can do something, Sergeant."

But Pascoe's attention was elsewhere.

"Before you do it, sir, just have a look at who's come through that door."

Dalziel knew who it was before he turned.

Connon, rather pale but perfectly composed, wearing a dark suit and a black tie, stood in the open doorway. His eyes moved swiftly over the scene before him, registering but not acknowledging Pascoe and Dalziel. Then he pulled the door to behind him and moved quickly and efficiently across the floor between the dancers and disappeared into the committee room.

"I bet hardly a soul noticed him," said Pascoe.

"Why should they? Our interest's a bit specialized. And

half these buggers wouldn't recognize him if he came in with a label on. Rugby supporters, pah! They know nothing."

"And we know?"

"At least we know where he is."

Pascoe scratched his nose ruminatively then stopped in horror as he realized who he was imitating.

"Yes, where *he* is. But I wonder where his daughter is? He should have more sense than to leave her alone. These letter boys are sometimes persistent."

Oh do you now? thought Dalziel. Then you should have looked through the door before he closed it behind him. But you worry on a bit longer, lad. Just a bit longer. It's good for the soul.

❀ ❀ ❀

Jenny got half way to the bar before anyone noticed her.

"Well, hell-oh," said a large man as she tried to slip by him with an "excuse-me." He was clutching a pewter tankard with a glass bottom. Now he drained it and squinted at her through the glass. He was still a good two hours from being drunk and even then he would probably manage to drive home without attracting unwanted attention.

There were faint flickers of real recognition at the back of his eyes, but he preferred the mock-lecherous approach.

"What's a nice girl like you doing in a joint like this?"

"I've come about the woodworm. How are you?"

Jenny could only judge the effectiveness of her cool self-possessed act from its results. Inside, it felt so phoney that the merest glimmer of amusement would have sent an embarrassed blush swirling up from her neck to her forehead. The stout man, however, was obviously nonplussed. His own opening gambit made it impossible to take offence.

"Hello, Jenny," said a voice from a side-table.

"Excuse me," said Jenny to the man, who now obviously recognized her and was recomposing his face to a rubbery concern. But he couldn't quite get the mouth right and traces of the leer still showed through. By the time he felt able to add sound effects, Jenny was sitting down at a table with two girls and three youths.

"Hello, Sheila," she said, "Mavis. How's the world wagging?"

"Fine," said Sheila. The other girl in contrast to both Jenny and Sheila was so heavily made up that it was like looking at someone behind a mask. She nodded carefully as though afraid of disturbing it.

The three boys rearranged themselves rather self-consciously.

"You know these creeps, do you? Joe, Colin. And the gooseberry's Stanley."

Jenny smiled.

"Hi. I've seen them around. How's your dad, Stanley?"

"Fine," mumbled the boy.

Jenny smiled again, feeling a kind of desperate brightness sweeping over her, a need to avoid silences.

"Stanley lives in our road. It used to be his main ambition to see my knickers. Stanley the Watcher I used to call him."

She laughed, the others smiled politely. Stanley went very red, then very pale.

"That's a lie. That's a stupid thing to say. I don't know why you..."

He trembled to a stop as the others looked at him in mild surprise.

"You mean you didn't want to see her knickers?" said Sheila. "That's not very complimentary. Why don't you make yourself useful, get Jenny a drink or something? You can't expect her to get them in on a student's grant."

Miaow, thought Jenny as young Curtis stood up awkwardly and set off for the bar, turning after a couple of steps to ask, "What do you want?"

"Bitter, please. Pint."

"Female emancipation," said Sheila. "I can remember doing that for 'O' level history."

"So?"

"Well, so old Wilson used to tell us that lots of men opposed it because they felt it would lead to women in trousers sitting in pubs drinking pints of bitter. It was one of his jokes. He'd laugh if he could see you."

"Perhaps he can," said one of the two remaining boys. "He's dead, so he might be watching."

Something violent happened under the table, and the boy looked startled, then apologetic.

"Look Jenny," said Sheila, "we were all dead sorry to hear about your mother. That was rotten."

They all nodded agreement, Mavis carefully as ever.

"Yes, it was. Thanks," said Jenny. "But life goes on."

"That's one way of looking at it," said Sheila.

"No, that's two ways of looking at it," answered Jenny. "One way, my life goes on despite my mother's death; the other way, someone else's life goes on because of it."

"My, college has made you even sharper," said Sheila with a thin smile.

Jenny sensed she was losing a friend, or rather, cutting the last few strands which held their friendship together. She and Sheila had been very close at school up to the Fifth Form. They had both planned to stop on in the Sixth, then at the last moment, half way through the summer holidays in fact, Sheila had announced she was getting a job.

That had all been more than two years before. They'd seen each other fairly regularly since, but more and more competitively as time went on.

Now it didn't matter who won or lost.

"Thanks, Stanley," she said, taking the pint which had been deposited rather ungraciously before her. "Cheers."

She took a mouthful, coughed and grimaced wryly at Sheila, who smiled back with something of their old affection.

In fact Jenny was really very fond of beer, but she recognized that while an attempt to show off could be tolerated, careless expertise would only antagonize further.

"What're you all up to, then?" she asked.

"We, that is Mavis and me (or I, should I say?) are being entertained by these young gentlemen. Lavishly, as you can see."

"What about you, Stan?"

"He's waiting," interjected one of the boys quickly.

"For what?"

They all laughed. Stanley shrugged and tried to look unconcerned. He made quite a decent job of it too.

"Cheer up. She might be along later," said Sheila.

- "He fancies Gwen Evans." It was Mavis who spoke. Jenny remembered that the joke had always stopped at Mavis.

"All the men fancy Gwen," said Sheila.

But not all the women, eh? thought Jenny. She knew Gwen Evans only slightly; she had seen her at the funeral, and previous to that a couple of times, but the memory stuck.

"I'd have thought she was a bit old for you, Stanley," she said.

Sheila wrinkled her nose scornfully.

"It's all in the mind anyway. This lot read about all these teenage orgies and think they're missing out somehow."

Joe and Colin grinned unconcernedly.

Now you don't look as if you're missing out, my lads, thought Jenny.

"Anyway," Sheila went on, "it's all happening at the universities and colleges, isn't it, Jenny? The intellectual-sexual bit."

Here we go again.

"Yeah," said Colin with some enthusiasm, "all those wild birds. It's all wiggle-waggle and jiggle-joggle at those places."

"We have our moments," said Jenny. She looked around the room. She wasn't quite sure why she had come here at all, but it certainly wasn't so she could sit and chat with this lot. They were too young for a start. Whoever it was that was menacing her with letters (a letter, she corrected herself, but feeling certain there would be more), whoever it was that had anything to do with her mother's death, that person, or those persons, would belong to her father's age-group.

What do I want anyway, she thought. To find out who wrote

that letter? To find out if there was any truth in it? He could have denied it, he could have been positive, but all he did was tell me he loved me, that it didn't matter. Not matter? Something matters. If it doesn't matter, *that* matters. Miss Freud, that's me. Shortly to be Miss Sherlock Holmes. But how to start? What *do* people like Fat Dalziel and Popsy Pascoe do to get things moving? On the telly they just talk to people and find things out. But how do you know who to talk to in the first place?

"There she blows, Stanley," said Joe.

Jenny turned her head. Her first impression was of an exotically beautiful woman lightly covered in a very revealing dress. But this was only for a second. Gwen Evans wore neither less nor more make-up than most other women in the room, her skirt was by no means the shortest there, her dress zipped up the front right up to the collar and she had a cardigan draped casually over her shoulders.

It was the way she moved, the animation of her face, the way she held herself that made her presence so electric, not any ultra-daring revelation of flesh.

Her husband was in close attendance at the moment but Jenny knew he was due at the meeting. The man behind the bar said something to him, probably a reminder, for he nodded, spoke to his wife, then with a quick look round the room, he left.

Gwen too was looking round the room, more slowly, deliberately. Her gaze met Jenny's and paused. Then she smiled an acknowledgment and dropped an eyelid in half a wink. Jenny was surprised to feel herself flattered by this hint of intimacy between them.

"What're you waiting for, Stan?"

Stanley stood up awkwardly.

"Excuse me," he said. "I've got some work to do at home."

He moved across the room and out of the door without a glance at Gwen.

"My!" said Sheila. "Perhaps he's got delusions of grandeur and is playing hard to get."

Jenny suddenly didn't care for her in the least. She downed the remaining beer in her glass in one easy draught.

"I think I'll circulate a bit," she said. "It's been nice having a chat."

"Suit yourself," said Sheila.

"Cheerio."

Near the bar she caught a glimpse of Marcus's round head and began to make her way towards him. When she got a little closer she saw he was talking to the man she'd had the brush with when she first came in, and she hesitated in her progress. Marcus turned at that moment and saw her. His face showed surprise, then pleasure.

"Jenny," he said. "Come and have a drink, love."

She smiled back and squeezed through the intervening people to his side.

"Are you by yourself?" he asked, his eyes probing the further corners of the room.

"Daddy's in the committee meeting."

"Of course. I'm glad he decided to come. It'll do him good to get out and about. You too. Here, what'll you have?"

"I'll have a scotch if you insist."

"Oh, but I do. One scotch. You ready for another, Ted?"

He took the large man's glass without waiting for a reply.

"You know Ted, do you? Ted Morgan. This is Jenny Connon, Connie's daughter. This is Ted. He's the biggest gossip in the Club so be careful what you tell him about me. Won't be a sec."

Marcus turned to the bar and ruthlessly elbowed his way through to the pole position.

Jenny looked at Morgan with interest.

"Look," he said. "I'm sorry if I was rude before. But I didn't recognize you at first. I've only ever seen you a couple of times, with your dad at matches."

His face was set into the perfect sympathetic mould now. But his eyes were still assessing what lay beneath her Marks and Spencer jumper.

Perhaps I should introduce them to him. Now this one on the left is Marks, and this other is Sparks. Say hello nicely.

She grinned at the thought and the solemn angles of Ted's mouth relaxed also.

"I'm sorry if I was rude to you, too, Mr Morgan."

"Call me Ted."

"Is it true what Marcus said? That you're the biggest gossip in the Club?"

"Certainly," said Ted. "Bigger than that, even. There's not much happens here that I don't know."

He nodded with mock-solemnity. Jenny found herself quite liking him.

"And how long have you been a member?"

"Since I was a nipper. My dad didn't like to beat me, so he made me join him."

Jenny laughed with more enthusiasm than the witticism merited.

"Ted hasn't told you one of his jokes, has he? Be careful, Ted, will you? Jenny's not one of your ancient barmaids."

Marcus handed her a goblet of scotch and Ted another pint.

"I'm being entertained very well, thank you, Marcus."

"Good-oh. Well, here's how."

They all drank. A loud outburst of laughter came from the bar. Jenny glanced over. The source was the group round Gwen Evans. Beyond them, just coming in through the door, she saw Pascoe. He edged his way through the standing drinkers and for a moment she thought he was going to join her, but he merely nodded and drifted down the room, taking up a position by the wall where he seemed to become engrossed in watching the efforts of a group of youngsters on the one-armed bandit.

I shouldn't be at all surprised if he didn't fancy me, thought Jenny. Perhaps not though, I seem to fancy every man I meet fancies me at the moment. Either I'm at the height of my powers or I'm suffering from delusions of grandeur. Like poor Stanley. Gwen Evans wouldn't bother with a kid like that, not when she could have the pick of the men in this room. Or any of the other rooms either.

And her heart gave just a little kick of worry as she turned to Ted Morgan again.

❀ ❀ ❀

Clickity, clickity, clickity, click. A lemon, a bell and a cherry. Clickity, chickity, clickity, click. Two bells and an orange. Clickity, clickity, clickity. If you had stood as I have done for five hours in a draughty anteroom of a court-house sticking sixpences into one of those things to see how frequently it paid out, you wouldn't be so keen to chuck your money away, son. Couldn't understand it, could he? Two or three jackpots a night in the Club. Anyone'd tell you. My client wonders if the police have been as thorough in their research as they seem to imply. Perhaps the constable who carried out the test was merely having a run of bad luck. It is in the very nature of the entertainment offered by these machines that the results should be irregular, unforecastable. Odds must be measured over weeks, months, not hours. And me with my second-class honours degree, standing there with corns on my hands saying yes sir, no sir, till I made my smart answer, my quick repartee. Then everyone tut-tuts. And they all jump on me from great heights till corns on my hand seem like the fringe benefits of delirious joy. But no joy for Pascoe, nowhere. Little Jenny there, glad she's there, not elsewhere, listening to phone-calls, opening letters; but no joy there for you Pascoe. Not yet. Not ever? She's very friendly with those two, though; Felstead, Marcus, and Morgan, Edward. Lucky them, but not her style, not big Ted. He looks as if the pools have come up for him. And over there, beyond the blue horizon of desire, Gwen, backseat driver. Gwen, change any gears and we're airborne. That brass ring at her neck, attached to the zip all the way down that dress, like the ring you hold on to when you leap from a plane, plunging in free fall till you dare no more, then you pull the ring down, down and float in airy freedom, master of all you survey.

For a CID man you've no head for beer. Another pint and you'd be like those young lads all falling over themselves to make an impression. Or like fat Dalziel. Worse. Please God, don't let me become like fat Dalziel. But he at least is probing, sniffing around, trying to get things moving, not losing himself vainly in mazes of mental erotica. Listen. Look. Look and listen. That's why you're here. And don't just look over there.

"Everything?" said the highly made-up girl on the table behind him, her eyes rounding with interest into O's of mascara.

"Yeah," said one of the two boys at the table, "that's what he told me. He said he reckoned she wanted him to see. You know. Sort of egging him on."

"More wishful thinking," said the other girl scornfully.

"Mebbe. Mebbe not. Anyway, you know what he did?"

"No. And I don't want to. Let's go next door and dance a bit. Coming?"

"Oh, all right then. Off we go."

Even when I eavesdrop I hear nothing but sex, thought Pascoe watching the four of them disappear out of the bar. Now there was that fellow Roberts. Jacko Roberts. He seemed an interesting kind of man. Perhaps worth a word or two.

Dalziel might not like it, of course.

"Dalziel," he murmured audibly enough for the fruit-machine victims to glance his way, "is not bloody well going to get it."

He began to move towards the end of the bar where Jacko Roberts was drinking alone.

❀ ❀ ❀

"Any other business," asked Willie Noolan.

"There's this competitive rugby survey thing that's come round from *The Times*," said Reg Certes, the club secretary.

"Propose that a general meeting of members be convened to discuss the whole question," said Connon.

"Seconded," said Sid Hope.

"Any opposition? Right, carried. What about timing?"

"Week Friday'd be all right," said Certes.

"Agreed? Right. Anything else?"

"Just one thing if I may, Willie."

Noolan glanced at his watch. If it had been anyone other than Connie... but he could hardly choke him off.

"Yes, Connie."

Connon looked round the table for a moment as though choosing his words carefully. But they had been chosen for some little time already.

"Mr President," he said, and the formality of his voice made the others pay him even closer attention. "Yesterday, the day of my late wife's funeral, my daughter received an anonymous letter. I believe it came from someone connected with this Club."

Evans let out a long whistle. The others merely looked stunned. Then Noolan and Sid Hope both spoke at once.

"What grounds have you...?"

"What did it say...?"

They both tailed off.

"Your ball, I think, Willie," said Hope.

"I'll answer you both. Or rather, I won't," interjected Connon. "I won't reveal my grounds. Nor will I tell you what the letter said. The writer already knows. It concerns no one else."

"Well, Connie," said Noolan expansively, "I'm sure we're all very sensible of the strain of your situation and the shock this kind of thing, whatever it said, must have caused both you and Jenny. But I don't think that a committee meeting is the proper or best place to discuss this, do you? Let's close the meeting, then we can talk informally. This isn't the kind of thing we'd want to see in the minutes, is it?"

"Yes," said Connon. "It is. I'd like to propose that the

writer of this letter when known should be barred for life from the Club."

"You're being a bit bloody silly there, aren't you, Connie?" snorted Arthur Evans. "I mean, how can you bar him from the Club if you don't know who it is, then?"

He looked round, acknowledging the triumph of logic by a small rocking movement of the head. The others were looking at Connon, however, each doubtful what to say. Certes, the first team secretary and the youngest there, the man most likely to succeed Hurst as captain, had a rather different problem. He was the least well acquainted with Connon and had no intention of saying anything at the moment. His problem was knowing what to write. His pen rested, unmoving, on his notebook.

"Connie," said Noolan finally, "I don't think this is an admissible proposition. Firstly, Arthur's right. We can't bar someone we don't know."

"I didn't say I didn't know him," said Connon. Now jump, you buggers. Now stare in wild surmise. This is that thing called change. Things will never be the same again. Till I let them.

Noolan was the only one who did not react.

"Then it is your plain duty to inform the police of your knowledge."

"Haven't I just done that, Willie?"

Now there's one in the breadbasket for you, you old goat, thought Evans. That's got you nonplussed. Spend all your life hanging around on the edge of the scrum and it comes as a bit of a shock to get a pair of fingers up your nostrils.

"Our discussions at these meetings are minuted, Connie, and as such are published to our members."

"I know. I haven't noticed Reg writing much for the past few minutes, though. Have you made a note of my proposition, Reg?"

Still without speaking, Certes began to scribble.

"Very well, Connie," said Noolan resignedly. "We have a motion proposed by Mr Connon. Is there a seconder?"

The blare of music from the social room came in very loud. Connon felt a drum start beating in his head. The edge of pain began to intrude between the muffled notes. He put up his hand and began to massage his temple.

"Are you all right, Connie?" asked Hurst.

"Yes, fine. Just a headache."

The wheels were turning now. He hadn't felt anything for three days now. But it was back. McManus would have to do something. Old fool. Long past it. What can he know about...

"I'll second it."

Well, that's scuppered you, Willie.

It was Arthur Evans's distinctive lilt.

"In that case, unless there's any further discussion we'll take a vote."

"Just one point," said Hurst. "What does it mean if we pass this motion?"

"Nothing until they catch this fellow, whoever he is. Then if he's in the Club, he gets thrown out. If he's not in, he can't get in."

"We're still very much in the dark though, Connie. Can you assure us that the contents of this letter were such as make such action reasonable?"

"You know my daughter? They caused her very real distress. Actionable assertions were made."

"Right-oh. Go on, Willie."

"Let's have a vote then. Those in favour?"

Firmly, Arthur's hand went up. Hurst's. Certes's. More slowly Hope's.

"And you, of course, Connie."

"Of course. And you, Willie?"

"It's not part of my function to vote here, unless the meeting is deadlocked. Carried unanimously. Anything else? No? Then I declare the meeting closed."

They sat still for a second, then Evans stood up and pushed his chair back and the others followed.

"Let's get a drink," said Evans.

"Just hang on a moment," said Certes. "I've got the tickets we ordered for the Welsh match at Twickenham next month. They're a bit scattered around—we must have been near the bottom of the pile, I'm afraid."

"Bloody inefficiency," said Evans. "It wasn't like this when I was secretary. Eh, Sid?"

"Too true. The nearest we ever got to Twickenham was Cardiff."

Certes grinned amiably.

"Anyway, I've sorted them out so we can all sit next to our nearest and dearest."

"With the best seats for committee members, of course?"

"But of course. Here you are Sid. Three it was, eh? One for you, Peter. Two for you, Willie."

He hesitated and a note of uncertainty came into his voice.

"And you too, Connie. There's two here for you."

"Two?" said Connon.

"Let's go and have that drink," said Noolan over-loudly. "All this talking!"

"That's right," said Connon, reaching over and taking the tickets. "It was my turn to get Marcus's this year. I hope we can see this time. I was behind a post last year and the Irish scored three tries right on the other side of it."

"Trust the bloody Irish. Second only to the Welsh in low cunning," said Hurst.

"Are you sure you're OK, Connie?" he whispered to Connon as the others went ahead through the door.

"Yes. Just a bit of a head, that's all. I don't think I'll go through just yet, Pete. I'll catch you up in a minute or two."

"OK, Connie. See you do. It's good to see you around again. We missed you at the selection meeting earlier. There's copies of the teams on the board there. I'd be interested to hear what you think."

"I'll have a look."

"Right. Don't linger too long, though. There's not much drinking time left."

From the far end of the social room, Superintendent Dalziel noted with interest the order of emergence from the committee meeting.

"Sit down, Willie," he said to Noolan who was so deep in thought he'd almost walked past the table. "What kept you so long?"

❀ ❀ ❀

Pascoe found Jacko Roberts fascinating and Roberts himself seemed to be almost obsessively interested in the (to him) paradoxical situation of a well-educated man joining the police-force.

"You went to college, did you?" he asked again.

"Yes. University."

"Like them posh-talking bastards over there in the corner?"

"Yes. That's right. Beneath this rough exterior lies the education of a posh-talking bastard."

"But they'd make you a sergeant straightaway? No uniform or anything?"

"No. I had to spend the usual time on the beat, in uniform."

"Directing traffic?"

"Yes. That too."

"That's what your boss should be. Directing traffic. I can understand him, but *you!*"

"What's a nice guy like me doing in a dirty job like this? Well, I'm trying to get information out of you for a start."

For a while as Jacko's interest grew, Pascoe had seen the outline of a softer, happier, younger face beneath the deeply etched misanthropy of his usual expression. But now the mask returned—or the illusion faded.

"It's your round."

Pascoe brought Roberts two pints.

"It'll save time."

"What do you want to know?"

"Simple questions, really. Who'd want to harm Mary Connon?"

"Next question?"

"Who'd want to harm Connon?"

"Next?"

"Who's knocking off Gwen Evans?"

He jerked his head slightly towards the other end of the bar where someone was describing to the lady in question some event which seemed to involve a great deal of grappling with her unresisting frame. It could have been anything from a dance routine to a loose maul.

"Anything else?"

"That'll do for starters."

Another half-pint gulp.

"I'm no bloody oracle. And I don't see why I should help you. But I'm big-hearted. That's why I'm so poor. Last first. That thing along the bar there, there's so many trying it's hard to say who's succeeding. But I'll tell you who Evans has elected front runner."

"Yes?"

"Connon. That's right. The boy wonder. And that answers two of your questions, doesn't it?"

Perhaps, thought Pascoe. Perhaps it answers three. More likely it doesn't answer any. Not a word of this before, not a hint; surely there'd have been a hint, a nod, a wink? Surely Dalziel would have known?

Perhaps Dalziel did know.

Or perhaps there was nothing to know. Perhaps Gwen Evans was as pure as the driven snow. Perhaps.

But it didn't matter. No woman could look like that without *someone* starting a rumour about her and *someone*. But there had been no mention of Connon exercising his talents there.

Of course, there wouldn't be. You didn't mention that kind of thing to a detective investigating the death of a fellow club-member's wife. Especially when he was the best fly-half the club had ever had. No, it just wasn't done. Not unless you were a jumped-up bastard like Jacko Roberts.

Or a woman. He hadn't talked to any women down here.

But the place seemed full of them. Camp-followers. Regulars as regular in their attendance as any man. He'd have to pick one out. They had a different scale of loyalties.

"Do you believe it?" he asked.

"Me? I'd believe anything bad about anybody, if I didn't know they were all a load of bloody liars."

"Evans, now. I thought he was an old mate of Connon's?"

"The first people you suspect are always your friends. Usually you're right."

"Is Evans right?"

Jacko looked him in the eyes for the first time since they'd met. His head, ill-constructed out of sharp edges and loosely-hung skin, rested against the wall, out of place between two framed photographs of past successful teams, young men, glowing with health.

"Welshmen weren't born to be right. They were born to be bloody tragic."

He finished the second pint with a definitive swallow and the backward movement of his head shifted one of the pictures.

Pascoe reached forward to straighten it. The fifteen young men smiled brightly at him. One face, happier than the others, caught his attention. He looked at the names underneath.

"Aye, that's him. In his Golden Boy days."

"Connon?"

He looked closer. Yes, unmistakable now. Connon's face looked back at him.

"He looks as if he'd been made King of the Harem."

Now Jacko peered closely, this time at the date.

"He had," he said. "Twenty years old. Happy in the day-time, happier in the night-time. Just picked for the first trial. Six weeks later he's bust his ankle and put this girl in the club. He wakes up one morning and though he doesn't know it, he must suspect it—the party's over. And no one's ever going to ask him to another."

"Never?"

"Never. From now on he's a gatecrasher."

Jacko nodded sagaciously and rattled his glasses together. Pascoe smiled and shook his head.

"No thanks, Mr Roberts. I'll be getting on, I think. Thank you for the chat. Cheerio!"

Let me find some nice little girl, with someone else's drink swilling inside her nice flat little belly, who'll talk and talk and talk, and be nice to look at. Or even just one who's nice to look at. I wonder where Jenny is?

But when he turned to look, she was gone and Marcus was talking to someone else.

Ted Morgan had gone too.

❊ ❊ ❊

The price of information was too high, decided Jenny. So far she had got no information and she had come dangerously near to paying the price.

Ted Morgan's car was parked high above the town about five yards down a narrow cart-track which led on the road between two steeply sloping fields. Jenny was heartily relieved that the recent bad weather had made the track so muddy that even the passionate and rather drunk Ted had not dared go any further.

They were not really out of the town. The hill, or knoll, they were on was almost completely surrounded below by two horns of suburb. The gossip was that the farmer who owned the land was merely hanging on till the price came up to his requirements, then some builder would carve out of the hillside a super executive-type estate, with views for fifteen miles and mortgages for fifty years.

The only bit of information Jenny had got out of Morgan was that he "knew" the builder was Jacko Roberts.

It was obviously a popular site, if not for builders, then certainly for lovers. Four or five sets of headlights had blazed rudely into the neck of the lane, then turned in disappointment away.

The sudden illumination did not seem to inhibit Ted, but Jenny found it comforting. She'd also refused to transfer from the front seat and the gear-lever, hand-brake and steering-wheel were welcome allies.

At the moment there was a truce. She lit her second cigarette. She didn't really smoke, but it was time-consuming and also provided a potential weapon.

Ted puffed energetically at his, uncertain yet whether to congratulate himself on being parked up here with this very attractive young girl, or to commiserate with himself for his failure to make more than token progress.

"Ted," said Jenny brightly, "how long have you known my father?"

Morgan shifted uneasily. He didn't like any of the implications of the question.

"Oh, a good few years."

"Are you one of his special friends?"

"I wouldn't say that. Not really. Not like Marcus. Or Arthur."

"Gwen's very pretty, isn't she?"

"So-so," said Ted casually.

Jenny laughed and started coughing.

"Don't be so offhand," she spluttered. "You wouldn't say no, would you?"

He grinned.

"No, I don't suppose I would. Chance'd be a fine thing."

"I suppose there's a lot of competition for a pretty woman?"

How the hell do you get a man to gossip about your dead mother? she thought. I bet Pascoe could.

Ted grew enthusiastic.

"You bet there is. It can be fun."

"Fun?"

"Depends whether you join it, or watch it. Me, I weighed up my chances and decided to watch it. Then it's fun."

He's still talking about Gwen, she thought disappointedly. But what can I expect? If he knew what I wanted he'd be out of the car and away in a flash of shock. But I can't sit here all night. It'll be time for round two soon. Come on, my girl, you're supposed to be a budding teacher. Skilful questioning of the child can make him tap sources of knowledge he didn't know he had. But it'd be easier to give him a work-card.

"Tell me, Ted," she began, but he wasn't finished yet. Like the good gossip he was, he had merely been marshalling the various elements of his anecdote to their best advantage.

"You should have been there last Saturday night. Arthur starts looking at his watch about seven. She should have been there by then. He doesn't go home after the game, you see, not worth it, has his tea here and starts straight in on the beer. Well, I was there, behind the bar, standing in for Marcus, for a few minutes he said, more like two hours, so I saw it all develop. He'd look at his watch, then at the clock on the wall, then at his watch. Finally about quarter to eight he shoots through to the other room and finds Dick and Joy Hardy there, they were supposed to be picking Gwen up and bringing her round. But it turns out she wasn't in. So he comes back through trying to look unconcerned. But he's shooting some pretty piercing glances around, I tell you. I let him see me there bright and clear!"

He paused to chuckle.

"Why?" asked Jenny in puzzlement.

Ted sighed at the stupidity of women.

"Because those who were there couldn't be where his old woman was, could they?"

"And who wasn't there?"

Suddenly the impetus of Ted's narrative seemed to fail.

"Oh, lots," he said without enthusiasm. "I mean, I couldn't see, could I?"

"But you were behind the bar? That means Uncle Marcus wasn't there."

Ted cheered up.

"That's right. He wasn't. Though I can't imagine Marcus… anyway it doesn't matter."

He reached over and put his arm round her shoulders, more paternalistically than passionately.

"Is that the end of the story, then? It's a bit pathetic."

"Pathetic? Yes, I suppose it is. You've got to feel sorry for him, haven't you? I'm sure there's nothing to any of it, really. Anyway, let's talk about something interesting, like you and me."

Poor Ted, she thought. He's just remembered what happened last Saturday night. But it's more than that, isn't it? He's remembered that Daddy wasn't there either; he's remembered who he's talking to and he's just sober enough to mind his p's and q's. Does he really know something about Daddy and Gwen? I wonder. Or is it all in that cotton-wool mind?

She half turned to look at the figure beside her and this proved a near fatal mistake.

Ted mistook the move completely and his other arm came round with an enthusiasm which had nothing paternal in it. Jenny found herself dragged uncomfortably over the gear-stick and hand-brake, her left cheek was pressed in against her teeth by the pressure of an ardent but misdirected kiss and she felt a button on her cardigan give with a violence which boded ill for Marks and Sparks cowering beneath.

Round two, she thought, and I didn't even hear the bell. Now this long metal rod with the knob on the end which is doing God knows what damage to my pelvis is the gear-lever. From the freedom of play it seems to have in relation to my belly it must be in neutral. This other more rigid lever which is gouging a hole in the knee of my tights must be the hand-brake. Therefore if I move my hand down there, poor Ted, he's shifting out of the way, God knows what he imagines I'm going to do, there we are, rather stiff, but there she goes, I think.

It took Ted several seconds to realize the car was moving. Jenny clung to him tightly, partly to delay his attempts to remedy the situation, partly to buffer herself against any possible impact.

By the time he got his foot to the brake pedal they were down among the mud and the car slid on for several yards before coming to a halt.

Below them the lights of the town twinkled unconcernedly on. Jenny had a very poor topographical imagination and needed to apply herself with great concentration to the task of relating the main lines of street lights to her own knowledge of the town. It was a task she devoted herself to while Ted with a most ungentlemanly violence of language put the car into reverse and tried to back up the lane.

The wheels spun in the mud-lined cart-tracks. Jenny let them spin on for a while; but she was above all things a sensible girl and had no desire to find herself irretrievably stuck. That would be jumping out of the frying-pan into a raging inferno.

"Why don't you," she said in the ultra-kind voice she reserved for very recalcitrant children, "get out, put some branches or stones or something under the wheels, then start pushing? I will drive. I do have a licence and I'm really quite good."

Without a word, Ted climbed out of the car and began pulling at the hedgerow. Jenny felt quite sorry for him.

She wound down the window.

"I think we'll need some more branches," she said.

❋ ❋ ❋

Dave and Alice Fernie were walking like a couple of children down the private side of Boundary Drive. They were hand in hand, about a yard apart, swinging their joined hands high and indulging in a tug-of-war every time they encountered a lamp-post or a tree.

Alice screamed with laughter as Fernie gave her a jerk which pulled her forward so hard that her left shoe stayed behind, its heel bedded deep in the grass verge.

"Oh-Dave-you-silly!" she half-panted, half-laughed, hopping towards him as he retreated, holding her at arm's length, but didn't finish for he let her catch up, caught all her weight to his body and kissed her passionately.

It had just been an ordinary night, starting like a hundred others. They had walked to the local pub, about half a mile into the estate, to have a couple of drinks with a handful of old acquaintances. But things had gone absolutely right from the start, contrary to usage. Perhaps the Christmas decorations in the pub had helped. Dave had had just the right amount to drink, he hadn't been tempted to display his superior knowledge in argument; he hadn't produced any slanderous gossip, he hadn't felt it necessary to demonstrate his virility by being over-attentive to someone else's wife. He had irritated no one, offended no one; he had been moderate in speech, witty in comment, generous in purchase and was now obviously amorous in intent.

There was a sharp edge of frost in the air. Above, clouds ragged as crows' wings beat across the sky, turning the moon into a pale flower drifting beneath the sea. When for a moment it floated into a clear patch of the sky, it turned to silver the branches and few tenacious leaves of the tree against which they now leaned. There had been nights like this years ago, when they were younger, before there was a house and a television set, before they were married. Memories real as the rough bark pressing against the back of her hands came crowding into her mind. But she did not speak them. Dave did not like the past and she was not going to risk losing any part of the present.

The wind rose suddenly and her foot began to feel the cold. Gently she pulled away.

"I'll get my shoe, Dave, and we'll get on home," she said.

"Right, love."

His arm was round her waist now as they walked on, quietly, anticipatingly.

It was darker on this side of the road. The trees, the older less efficient lamp-posts, all contributed. Ahead they could see the telephone-box which stood almost outside their gate. "They didn't need one till the *hoi polloi* came," Fernie had once commented. When he was in the mood, everything appeared as evidence of the difference between "us" and "them."

Now it looks like a beacon, welcoming us home, thought Alice, though not without a wry glance at her own romanticism.

They were nearly there and she turned to cross the road. But he pulled her back and leaned her against another tree.

"Dave!" she said.

He kissed her again.

"Afraid of the neighbours?"

"Of course not. I'm afraid of me. There're some things you can't do out on the street."

"Why not?" he whispered. "It'd be fun."

"Oh, you fool," she murmured.

They kissed once more.

"Let's go in now," he said, eagerly.

As they stepped out from behind the tree, a figure, walking rapidly and glancing back over his shoulder, stepped off the pavement a few yards up and came at them on a collision course. There was an urgency about the way he moved which caught Alice's attention, but it was her husband who spoke first.

"Hey, Stanley! What's up, then?"

The figure stopped dead and saw them obviously for the first time.

"Mr Fernie. It's you."

Then no more.

It was Stanley Curtis, his face rather pale, breathing deeply, quickly.

"Is something wrong, Stan?" asked Alice.

"No. Well, yes. It's just that, well, I was passing Mr Connon's house and I just looked over the hedge and I saw someone. Someone there."

He stopped again.

"Where, boy?" asked Fernie, sharply. "What doing?"

"In the garden. Just prowling around. Then he disappeared up the side of the house. I thought it might be…"

"Yes, Stanley?"

"…the man who killed Mrs Connon."

Fernie nodded vigorously, not so much, it seemed to Alice, at what Stan had said, but rather at some thought going through his own head.

"Right. Come on, lad. Alice, you stay here."

"Dave! What are you going to do?"

"To have a look. What else? There's two of us. Come on, Stan."

But Stanley made no movement. Poor kid, thought Alice, he's scared stiff.

She moved to him and put her arm over his shoulders. He was shivering violently.

"Don't be a fool, Dave," she said sharply. "Stan's not coming with you. And you're not going either. There's the phone-box. Get on to the police straightaway."

Fernie stood irresolutely for a moment. Alice glanced round. The Curtis house was in darkness. Maisie and her husband were obviously out.

"I'm taking Stan inside," she said. "You come on in when you've talked to the police. You can watch in comfort then."

So much for the perfect end to a perfect night, she thought resignedly as she walked up the path. All that buildup gone to waste. It'd have been better if I'd told him to go ahead up against the tree. We might have missed Stanley. And he was too scared to notice us. But he'd have called the police anyway and they might really have caught us at it. Against a tree!

The thought made her smile. Alice Fernie was a woman of indomitable spirit.

Behind her, her husband stepped into the telephone-box and began to dial.

❋ ❋ ❋

"Connie," said Hurst, "I've brought you a drink. You're not going to hide in here all night, are you?"

Connon recognized the half-jocular, half-sympathetic note in Hurst's voice. It was a tone he was growing familiar with. Condolences first. Then afterwards talk as if nothing had happened, but inject enough sympathy into your voice to show you're still aware that something has.

He hadn't meant to sit so long by himself. He had come down to the Club that night with a real purpose, a purpose only half of which had been carried out at the meeting. The sight of Dalziel and Pascoe had disconcerted him more than he had cared to show. He felt illogically that somehow he was responsible for introducing a dissonant element into the Club. It was a rugby club. He had long been disturbed by the growing diversification of the Club's interests. And therefore of the Club's membership.

But he put these thoughts to the back of his mind now, with a silent promise that they would be uttered one day soon.

"I've been glancing through the teams, Peter," he said. "What's happened to Jim Davies?"

"He knocked his knee on Saturday. Seemed all right at first, but came up like a balloon over the weekend."

"So you brought in Gerald on the open side. He'll never hold the place, will he? Did you think of any of the youngsters? Joe Walsh? Or Stan Curtis?"

Hurst laughed.

"You might almost have been eavesdropping, Connie. Yes, both of them. But Joe's best-manning at a wedding on Saturday so he's not available. Though he'd come along, white carnation, wedding-ring and all, I reckon, if he was asked to play for the Firsts. But we couldn't do that. And young Curtis has been a bit under the weather, missed training this week, so he's out. Anything else?"

"Yes. I see Marcus's name's missing from the Fourths."

"Time marches on, Connie! He's asked not to be considered, for a while at least. Feeling his age, he says."

"Considered!" smiled Connon. "You don't get considered for the Fourths. You get press-ganged. He'll have to join the great gang of us who move around in disguise on Saturdays till half an hour after kickoff time. You'll be one of us soon, Peter."

Hurst nodded and started to pin the team-sheets back up on the board.

Then he seemed to make his mind up about something.

"Connie, that letter. I was desperately sorry to hear about it."

"Yes?"

It was a calm, simple interrogative, inviting but not pleading for a continuation.

"I'd like to see it if I might," said Hurst.

"Why?"

"I might be able to help. Might, perhaps; there's just something; that's why I asked at the meeting, but I'd have to see the letter first, partly to see what's in it, partly just to see it."

"Well now, Mr Hurst. I think that might be arranged. We'll get in touch with you tomorrow shall we?"

In the doorway stood the solid bulk of Dalziel. Hurst flushed an angry red. But Connon remained as cool and unmoved as he had been while listening to Hurst.

"He'd have to know, Peter," he said calmly. "The police have the letter. Did you want to speak to me, Superintendent?"

"That's right. I didn't come just to eavesdrop. We've had a report on an intruder on your premises. The station just phoned me here. I've told them to observe, but keep off till I get there. I'd like you to come too, if you would."

"Of course. Who reported this?"

"Your friend Fernie. He seems to spend most of his spare time keeping an eye on your house."

Connon smiled thoughtfully.

"Yes, he does, doesn't he? Good night, Peter. Perhaps we can talk again tomorrow."

They moved out into the social room. As they passed through the dancers, Connon noticed Pascoe moving slowly around with an attractive young girl. Sheila, he thought. I saw you last Saturday. It seems like a thousand years.

Dalziel noticed him also and made a motion of the head. Pascoe didn't seem to notice and carried on dancing. But as they walked towards the car park, buttoning up their coats against the frost, footsteps came up quickly behind and Pascoe joined them.

"Jenny," said Connon suddenly.

"She left," said Pascoe laconically. A cold fear gripped Connon's stomach.

"Where?" he asked. There was no reason why they should know the answer, but he felt sure they would.

"It's all right," said Pascoe. "Not home, I shouldn't think. She left with Ted Morgan."

Connon tried not to let his relief show. Ted Morgan was manageable. Ted was forecastable. As far as anyone was forecastable, that was. And perhaps that was not very far at all.

He reached into his pocket for his car keys. The frost on his windscreen was merely dampness still and after four or five sweeps of the wiper-blades he began to see more clearly. Dalziel's car was waiting for him by the exit. Carefully he began to follow it out on to the main road.

❀ ❀ ❀

It was a silent drive back down into the town. Ted lived with his mother, an arrangement which, while it lacked many of the usual tragi-comedy trappings of such situations, did present certain problems. Ted was not altogether happy at the prospect of explaining to her how he came to be covered with mud down the front of his suit.

Jenny had put Ted quite out of her mind and was threshing over problems and questions she would not have believed could have existed a week ago.

She felt very lonely. There was only her father. She loved him deeply, but their relationship had generally been tacit; there had never been a need for definition, explanations, analyses. Love didn't need these things. But now she needed someone to talk to, with; at, if you liked. She needed someone to take her thoughts and rethink them. Look at them in a new way.

She had thoughts she did not wish her father to look at.

And she was certain that whatever was going on in his mind, only the sheltered, leeward aspect would be revealed to her.

I don't want to be protected, she thought angrily. I want to be consulted, listened to, argued with. I'll make him talk to me, I'll force him. I know I can. I know!

But even in her anger she also knew she could not add anything more to the heavy burden of worry and doubt she had seen her father was already carrying.

"Is it right here?" asked Ted in the voice of one speaking only through dire necessity.

"That's right."

Poor Ted. He'd had a bit of a raw deal. And to slip in the mud must have been the last straw. If Daddy was home, she'd invite him in for a coffee and a clean-up. But only if Daddy was at home.

"This side of the road, just before that phone-box," she said.

There seemed to be a lot of cars parked in the street tonight. Without lights. Like taxis. Or...

She rubbed the side-window and peered out. She had been right. That was her father's car.

"Stop here," she cried.

They were almost at the house and Ted was already braking. But her sudden command made him stand violently on the pedal and they were both jerked forward against their seat-belts.

Jenny smacked the release button sharply, opened the door and stepped out.

Connon came trotting up the pavement towards her.

"Daddy," she said, her voice full of relief. "What's happening? What's the matter?"

"No need to worry, my dear," said Dalziel, coming up behind her.

She ignored him and looked expectantly at her father.

"Someone's been seen prowling round the house. Or at least Mr Fernie believes he saw someone."

"You have too little faith in Fernie," said Dalziel. "A man who feels his civic responsibilities more than some. Still, we'll soon see. My ferrets are in. We'll see what they nip out."

Connon put his arm over his daughter's shoulder as she shivered at Dalziel's imagery. There was some kind of sound made remote and distant by the night.

"Ah, action, I think," said Dalziel. "Let's have a look, shall we?"

He strode out energetically towards the gate. Connon and Jenny followed. Jenny was curiously reluctant to come face to face with this intruder whoever it was.

A small group of men were coming down the path. Some were uniformed policemen. One silhouette she thought she recognized as Pascoe's. And another outline looked strangely familiar.

"My dear officers," said a rather breathless but still well-modulated voice, "of what am I accused that you should treat me like the nucleus of a civil rights demonstration? Is this the effect television-watching is having upon the constabulary? Have a care—my father sells meat to the wife of a prospective Liberal candidate."

"Antony," she said with delight. "Daddy, it's Antony."

The group stopped before them.

"Oh, there you are, Jenny. I cannot say how touched I am at the warmth of the reception you have arranged for me."

Even dishevelled as after a slight struggle and with his arms firmly gripped by two impassive policemen, he looked elegantly in control of the situation.

"Do you know this man, miss?" asked Dalziel.

"Of course I do. Please let him go at once. How bloody stupid can you get?"

Dalziel nodded at the policemen, who released Antony's arms.

"I think we had better go inside for some explanations," he said with a sigh. "If you don't mind, Mr Connon."

Connon nodded and set off up the drive. Jenny put her arm protectively round Antony's waist and led him after her father, the uniformed police still in close attendance

Dalziel looked around. At Ted Morgan who stood against

his car, hardly able to take in what was happening. At Dave Fernie who was coming over the road. At Alice Fernie and Stanley Curtis who stood at the Fernies' gate.

"You look after matters out here, will you, Sergeant? Make a thorough job of it, eh?"

He too went up the driveway into the house.

Pascoe looked after the vanishing figure. Then turned back to those remaining, letting his eyes run coldly over them, finally coming to rest on Morgan's mudstained suit.

Yes, he thought, I'll make a thorough job of it, never fear. Sir.

Chapter Five

Connon came up out of blackness into a dream. It was as if he had fainted in his sleep and the recovery from the faint made the level of sleep seem reality by comparison. There stretched before him a great expanse of mud-trodden grass, gleaming brokenly like water viewed from a height in the summer sun. Immeasurably distant on the horizon stood a pair of rugby posts, so high that they were clearly visible despite the miles that seemed to separate them from him. He set off running towards them, smoothly at first, balanced, feeling all the old confidence in his muscles, the ability to shift his weight at will in any direction, to stop dead, accelerate, turn, sidestep. He knew when he felt like this that, given a yard to move in, no man on earth could stop him.

But here there was no one to try to stop him.

Nevertheless he made a few feints out of sheer exuberance, suggested a turn with his hips, moved at right-angles to his forward path with no loss of speed, changed step three times in successive strides, kicking hard on the last change and accelerating away in the joy of being able to run for ever.

The posts did not get nearer.

Suddenly he felt a change. His stride shortened; his legs felt leaden; his breathing, till now perceptible only in a slight flaring of the nostrils, became harsh and ragged, his mouth wide open, his teeth biting desperately at the intangible air.

The sun exploded into whiteness and the muddy grass turned to sand so fine that he sank in it ankle-deep as he ran.

I am in the desert, he thought. At last I am in the desert. And I shall die if I do not reach that rock.

The rock towered on the horizon where the posts had been. The sun sat on top of it like the flame on a black candle.

Desperately, failingly, he ran towards the sun.

Out of the rock's foot grew a shadow so dark that it contained all colours. Its edges, at first three-dimensionally sharp and rigid, after a while began to waver and shimmer on the red heat of the sand. Soon the undulation spread to the whole shadow and the blackness curved smoothly away from the rock. Then at the crest of each polished wave, the blackness broke for a moment into the dark green of very deep water, and the sun shimmered in it like light varnished over.

The shadow stretched towards him like a great shining path. There was a beating in his ears like the roar of a mighty crowd.

He sat up in bed and heard the singing of a solitary bird in the tree outside his window.

Then that noise stopped too and he was not sure if he had heard even that.

It was still dark. The sun came late in December if it came at all. He sat on the edge of the bed and felt for his slippers.

Soon it will be Christmas, he thought. Not more than a week. Season of promises. Vows that this year it will be different. This year those brief moments of feeling, of affection while sharing the task of putting up the decorations, of humility while listening to carol-singers, of joy when waking on Christmas morning, this year these brief moments will spread and grow and shape themselves to fit the whole year, the whole of our life. But there was scarcely enough to colour the greyness of Christmas Day itself. And this year there was no use even in making promises.

Mary is dead, he told himself, and we are to each other for ever what was bearable only in my intuition of its impermanence. Death doesn't change things, then. It merely petrifies things for those who go on living.

He stood up and went out on to the landing. As he passed Jenny's door he paused momentarily, but shook his head at himself and went on down the stairs.

If he is in there, then he is in there, and they might as well bring each other what comfort they can. To know would not help me. To know I know would probably distress Jenny. So I must be careful not to find out. As long as he is capable of tenderness, and I think he is.

He laughed softly to himself.

At least there'll be no shortage of pillow talk with that one. If kids learn by example, he'll turn out whole classfuls of pedants.

At the bottom of the stairs he was surprised to find himself putting on his overcoat. He started to take it off again, then sighed and pulled it back over his shoulders.

My body knows more than my mind, he thought. I might as well get it over with.

Shivering a little he went through into the kitchen and opened the back door. The cold morning air struck damply into his face. A familiar but still timid stray cat peered at him from beneath a blackcurrant bush and howled piteously.

"In a minute," he said.

He stepped across the strip of lawn which separated the side of the house from a small garden shed. Inside the shed it was dark. There was a smell of fertiliser and insecticide. Against the wall opposite the door and clearly visible in the shaft of relative light falling through the doorway was a chair. High-backed, comfortable-looking. His mind a careful blank, he reached to the shelf over it and took down a small plastic bag. Then he turned and went out in the garden again, closing the door behind him.

When he got back into the kitchen the cat, finally coura-
geous in its search for food, was sitting in the corner. It made
a dart for the door as he came in, but he was too quick for it.
Realizing it could not get out, it sat down and started washing
itself.

"That's right," he said. "Breakfast in a minute."

Then he tipped the contents of the plastic bag on to the
kitchen table and began to sort through them.

"Good morning, Mr Connon," said a man's voice, deliberately pitched softly in order not to startle. Connon was a hard
man to startle in any case, as those who knew him well could
vouch. Now he hardly glanced up at the dressing-gowned figure
standing at the door.

"Good morning, Antony," he said. "Sleep well?"

"Like a log," said the boy. "Jenny and I sat up until the early
hours chatting."

"You're up early."

A statement not a question. Connon continued to sort
through the objects before him.

"I'm very good at toast and coffee. May I be permitted...?"

"Go ahead."

Connon now brought his full attention to bear on the
objects before him.

There were four groupings on the table top. The first
group contained seven pennies and three half-pennies. Some of
the coins were almost green with age.

The second group contained pieces of paper. Old bus
tickets, theatre-tickets, a golf score-card, a shopping list, the
items almost unreadable.

He picked this up, and looked at the writing for a moment,
then put it gently down.

The third group contained a variety of items. Hairgrips, a
pencil, a bobbin, a teaspoon with an apostolic head.

The fourth group wasn't really a group at all. There was
just one item. A very small piece of lead, like a tiny cupola with
a lightly-milled edge.

Connon poked at it with his forefinger. It rolled round a semi-circle and came to rest.

"Coffee," said Antony. "Toast follows in a trice."

He put a large mug of steaming black coffee in front of Connon and looked enquiringly at the stuff which littered the table.

Connon picked up the plastic bag, opened it, put it at the edge of the table and swept the items into it with one efficient movement of his hand. Then he tossed the bag lightly on top of a wall-cabinet behind him.

He sniffed.

"Do your habits include burning toast?" he asked.

Antony turned the grill off and looked at the dark brown slices of bread.

"It is only by going too far sometimes," he said, "that we know we have gone far enough."

They drank their coffee and ate their toast (rejuvenated with a sharp knife) in silence at first.

"Is there any more coffee?" asked Connon.

"In a second," said Antony.

"Mr Connon," he said as he busied himself with the kettle and the jar of instant coffee, "I didn't really have a chance last night to explain myself to you very fully. I was too occupied in explaining myself legally to that rather brutal man, Dalziel, then in explaining myself emotionally to Jenny, to have much chance of explaining myself rationally to you. Here's your coffee."

He sat down again.

"Explain away," said Connon.

"I was distressed, as were all her friends, to hear the sad news of Jenny's bereavement. That it was unexpected I knew. I had just been talking with Jenny about her family, yourself and Mrs Connon, that same Saturday night."

"Had you now?" murmured Connon.

"When I read in the newspapers the details of the matter, I was even more distressed. I determined to contact

Jenny, but letters and telephone conversations seemed quite inadequate means of discovering what I wanted to know, that is whether I could be of any use to her. So I vacillated, most uncharacteristically I might add, for several days. Finally I went to the Principal of the college, a sympathetic dame whose ear I have for any amount of services rendered, and told her I had decided that term must end slightly earlier for me than the others. So off I set. My intention was to arrive here during hours of daylight, but the charity of our road-users is not what it used to be. The rest you know. I arrived to find the house empty. I settled down to wait in the passageway between the garage and the house where I was a little protected from the inclemency of the weather and whence I was eventually plucked by the constabulary. More toast?"

"Thank you, no," said Connon, looking reflectively at the youth. "How well do you know Jenny?"

"In terms of time, not well. But in terms of attraction, very well indeed. I am her current beau."

"If the archaism is meant to help me understand you, I don't like the implication," said Connon with a smile. Antony looked apologetic but Connon did not let him speak. "And now you've seen Jenny, have you learned anything that letter or telephone conversation would not have told you?"

"Possibly not. But what I have learned is absolutely clear, which it might not otherwise have been."

"And that is?"

"That I can be of help, that she is delighted to have me here and that my presence can be of great comfort to her during these very trying times. I would like to have your permission to extend my stay, Mr Connon."

"Do I have a choice?" asked Connon. "If I do, which I doubt where Jenny's concerned, then I unhesitatingly offer you my hospitality for as long as you care to accept it. I also noticed Jenny's reaction to your arrival. But make sure your presence remains a comfort to her and doesn't become a complication."

"Is this a private party or can anyone join?" said Jenny's voice from the door.

She was wearing an old dressing-gown, her hair was uncombed, her nose shiny. And her eyes too shone as she looked at the two men sitting there.

Antony rose to his feet and stood gazing intensely at her.

Connon sighed.

"If you're going to stay with us, Antony, you'll have to learn that in this household we don't pay all that much attention to the courtesies. You'll have to break yourself of the habit of bobbing up and down every time my daughter appears, especially when she looks like this."

"It is not a matter of habit this time," replied Antony. "It is a small tribute I offer to beauty."

"Jesus wept!" said Connon, laughing loud.

Jenny sat down, laughing even louder and eventually Antony, a pleasant glow of satisfaction in his mind, sat down laughing also.

In the hall the phone rang.

Jenny, nearest the door, turned in her chair, but Connon was up and out in one smooth movement.

As soon as he went through the door, Antony leaned over and kissed Jenny lightly on the lips. She smiled happily at him and took his hand. They sat looking at each other without speaking. Connon's voice came drifting in from the hall.

"Hello? Connon speaking."

A long pause. The youngsters kissed again.

"Is that all you know? But why?"

Jenny shook her head in mock severity as Antony leaned nearer.

"Yes, of course we must. What? I don't know, do I? You'll have to think that out yourself."

A very short pause.

"All right. Later. Goodbye."

The phone clicked back on to its rest.

Jenny and Antony moved a few inches further apart, then giggled at each other because of the involuntary movement.

Connon came back into the room. One look at his face and Jenny stopped giggling.

"Daddy," she said. "What's the matter? What's happened?"

"I'm not sure," said Connon slowly. "It may be nothing, but the police have picked up Arthur Evans. They've got him down at the station for questioning. About...about last Saturday night."

❁ ❁ ❁

"Listen, Arthur," said Dalziel in his heartiest voice. "We've known each other a long time. All I want's a bit of co-opera-tion. Anything you tell me will be in strict confidence if it's got nothing to do with our enquiries. As I'm sure it hasn't. I give you my word as a public official, and a friend. I can't say fairer."

"Confidence?" said Evans. "You talk of confidence, do you, with laughing boy sitting here with his pencil and paper at the ready? What's he doing, then? Sketching the bloody view, is it?"

Dalziel sighed and looked over at Pascoe who was sitting quietly in the furthermost corner of the room. The sergeant raised his eyebrows interrogatively. Dalziel shook his head fractionally.

"I'm sorry, Arthur. Sergeant Pascoe has to stay. I have to have someone here, you see. It's the regulations. It's in your interest, you see. It's for your protection."

You bloody old hypocrite, thought Pascoe. You'd lie to your own grandmother. Suddenly it's regimental Dalziel, the slave of the rule-book. Poor old Bruiser! If he didn't want me here, I'd be out like a rocket. Though why he does want me here's a bit of a mystery. Why not try the old pals' act, just the two of us together, it'll be off the record? Why not? I'll tell you why not, you half-wit. Because he knows it wouldn't work, that's why not. These two are about as near to being old pals as Judas Iscariot and the Pope. Just look at them. Perhaps Bruiser joined the queue knocking at

Gwen Evans's back door at some time. He's not promising poor old Arthur silence if he co-operates. He's threatening him with lots of noise if he doesn't!

"If it wasn't Sergeant Pascoe here, Arthur," Dalziel continued, "it would have to be someone else. In fact technically I ought to have someone else here as well, but I thought that as the sergeant knew the facts of the enquiry (in fact he was instrumental in getting the information we'd like to question you about), it would keep it in the family so to speak if he acted as my amanuensis, that's the word, isn't it, Sergeant Pascoe?"

Pascoe smiled bleakly at the appeal to his erudition. Dalziel nodded enthusiastically as if he had received encouragement.

"Of course, you're entitled to have your own legal representative present, if we wish to be really formal about things. Would you like that? It's Stubby Barnet, isn't it? It'd be nice to see Stubby again, haven't seen him since last year's Club dinner."

Stubby Barnet! thought Pascoe. Nice to see Stubby again; Good God, the power structure in a town this size was more formidable than politics in New York City. Come on, Arthur, you can't complain, boyo! You're being offered all the protection of the law. We'll keep the crowds back as you wash your dirty linen in public.

"Listen, Dalziel," said Evans, "I don't know what you're getting at, see? This is Saturday morning and I've got things to do. The only reason I came in here was that I was on my way into town when your boys called and they said it would be quicker if I came in to see you. So let's make it quick, shall we?"

"With pleasure, Arthur. Then I'll just ask again the only question you've allowed me to put so far. Would you tell me where you went when you left the Rugby Club about eight-fifteen last Saturday evening?"

"This is to do with Mary Connon, is it?"

"Just answer the question, please, Arthur."

"I went home, then, that's where I bloody well went. Can I go now?"

"Why did you go home?"

"It's where I live, see? That's what home means, don't you remember, Superintendent Dalziel? Ask your bloody amanuensis."

Dalziel was unperturbed by the outburst.

"But why did you leave the Club? You came back later, didn't you? Oh come on, Arthur! You're among friends. We have information. It's no use being coy, there's others who aren't."

"I bet there bloody well is. Old gossiping women dressed up like men. I know them."

"Sergeant. What is our information again, please?"

"Sir!" said Pascoe, sitting to attention. "Our information is that Mr Evans left the Club in order to go and see what was delaying the arrival of his wife whom he had been expecting for some time."

"I see. Is that true, Mr Evans?"

"Yes. Anything wrong with that?"

"Not in the least. Did you try the telephone?"

"Yes."

"But without success."

Evans grunted.

I can't put that down in words, can I? said Pascoe to himself. If I did it would probably read, if someone's rogering your wife on the hearth rug, you can't expect her to answer the phone.

Dalziel was looking happier now.

"You see, it's really all straightforward, isn't it? What happened then?"

"When?"

"When you got home."

"Nothing. I mean, she wasn't there."

Dalziel pushed his right index finger through the small hairs which fringed the cavity of his ear, and wriggled it sensuously about.

"But you knew she wasn't there."

"What?"

"You knew she wasn't there. Your friends Dick and Joy Hardy had already called as arranged and had got no reply. They told you when you asked them at the Club. And you had telephoned yourself without success. So you knew she wasn't there."

He knew she wasn't answering, thought Pascoe. That's what you knew, wasn't it, Arthur?

"I had to be sure."

"In case she'd had an accident or something?" suggested Dalziel sympathetically.

"Yes," replied Evans, hardly bothering to sound convincing.

"Relieved?"

Evans looked up suspiciously, his body tensing, his trunk leaning forward as if he were going to rise.

"Relieved she wasn't there. She hadn't had an accident."

"Yes."

"What did you do then?"

"Well, I came back to the Club, didn't I? You know that bloody well. You just said so."

"Straight back."

"Yes."

"So you left the Club about ten past eight, went home, found all was well, and went straight back?"

"That's right. Yes. Though," he added slowly as if thinking something out, "I didn't leave the house straightaway, mind you. I probably sat around there for, oh, about twenty, perhaps thirty minutes, I shouldn't wonder. Yes. That's right."

Dalziel clapped his hands together as though a tricky point had been made simple.

"Good!" he said. "That's why you didn't get back till after nine-fifteen. It's only five minutes' drive, isn't it?"

Now Evans did stand up.

"Yes," he said. "Is that all then? I don't see the point, but if it helps you, you're welcome. And I'll be on my way."

Dalziel shook his head with a sad smile.

"Don't be silly, Arthur. You're not daft. You know that's not all. I'm just giving you a chance to tell us, that's all. If you don't want your chance, then just sit down again, and we'll tell you."

Slowly Arthur Evans resumed his seat.

"Sergeant, just refresh us with your information again."

"Certainly, sir." Pascoe rippled through the pages of his notebook, stopped, coughed and began to speak in an impersonal monotone as before.

"Information given to us states that Mr Evans's motor-car was seen parked in Glenfair Road just before its junction with Boundary Drive at about eight-forty p.m. on the evening of Saturday last."

He raised his eyes from the page. He might have done this a good deal earlier if he had wanted, for it was completely blank.

His interviews the previous night had been done with all his customary thoroughness, but the most productive one had been not the Fernies or young Curtis, those most directly concerned with the incidents which had taken him to Boundary Drive, but with Ted Morgan whom there was really no reason to interview at all.

Except that he had had mud down his suit. Anyone who came back covered with mud after an evening with Jenny Connon had some answering to do, Pascoe had decided, surprised at his own concern.

Or jealousy.

Me jealous? he thought. Nonsense. I'm questioning this man because he might be able to help us. Not jealous. Just zealous.

But whatever his motives, he soon realised that he had tapped a very useful vein of information in Ted Morgan.

Ted had been a little belligerent at first but a couple of hints that Pascoe had seen him drinking in the Club earlier and an oblique reference to the breathalyser test had calmed him down and made him most co-operative.

Once he got started, like all the best gossips, there was no stopping him. Ten minutes with Morgan was more informative than all the rest of his questioning put together.

What he said about Evans's movements and behaviour on Saturday evening plus his confirmation of Jacko Roberts's placing of Connon high on the Evans suspect list had set Pascoe's mind racing. He knew that the constable on patrol in Boundary Drive had noticed no strange cars parked in the road that night as he passed along. Now he checked with the policeman whose beat took him down Glenfair Road, the main thoroughfare into which Boundary Drive ran. The list of car numbers he had noted that evening for one reason or another was unproductive. Evans's was not among them. But after much thought the constable did vaguely recall noticing a car parked very near to the corner of Boundary Drive, not near enough to constitute a danger, but near enough for him to notice it.

"I didn't make a note," he had said defensively. "Why should I? There was no offence being committed. Nothing suspicious."

But his vague memory was of a white or cream Hillman. Evans drove a white Hillman Minx.

It had all been so flimsy that Pascoe had hesitated about presenting it to Dalziel. But in the end, he knew he had to. The superintendent's reaction had been unexpected. He had been as near to complimentary as Pascoe could recall.

"I've been wanting a chat with Arthur," he had said gleefully. "I'm worried about that wife of his. A woman like that's a... one of those things that helps other things to get started?"

"A catalyst," said Pascoe.

"Right. A catalyst to violence."

"You can't question a man because his wife's well built!" protested Pascoe.

"I once questioned a vicar because his choir was too big. Other churches were complaining, he was poaching their kids. It turned out he was paying well over the odds. But it didn't stop at singing. Let's have him in first thing."

"All right," he said. "So I was there. What of it?"

"Where is 'there,' Mr Evans?" asked Dalziel.

"There. At Connon's. You know. I'm damned if I know

why I didn't tell you in the first place, back when all this started happening. Must look a bit odd, I suppose."

"Perhaps. Perhaps not. Lies, evasions, we get 'em all the time, Arthur. I sometimes use them myself," he said, chuckling.

"I've noticed," said Evans drily.

"Tell us about it then, Arthur," invited Dalziel.

Evans grunted again, then started talking. Having made up his mind to talk, he spoke rapidly and fluently and Pascoe's pen flew over the paper as he took shorthand notes. He was so occupied with the accuracy of his record that he scarcely had time to pay attention to the narrative as a whole and it wasn't until Evans fell silent that the statement jelled in his mind.

The Welshman had set off home in a cold fury. He was convinced that his wife was with another man. He was almost as convinced that this man was Connon. He went right through the house when he arrived home but there was no sign of Gwen; nor of anyone else. Connon had left the Club early, he remembered, saying he was going home. Now Evans got back into his car and drove round to Connon's house. He had not parked in front of the house because he had no desire to draw attention to himself. All he wanted to do was to see if Connon's car was in the garage. The only sign of life he could see in the house was the white light from a television screen shining through a chink in the living-room curtains. He went as silently as he could up the drive and peered into the garage. The car was there. Still unconvinced, he considered ringing the bell and inventing some pretext for coming to see Connon if Mary Connon answered the door. Instead, not wanting to risk a scene without more evidence of his suspicions, he went back to his car and drove back to the Club, stopping briefly at a couple of pubs on the way to see if Gwen was in either. But when he reached the Club she was there already.

It's a reasonable story, thought Pascoe. And if he had rung the bell at Connon's what reason would he have had to kill Mary?

"And *did* you find out where Gwen had been, Arthur?" asked Dalziel softly.

"She said she thought Dick and Joy had forgotten they were to pick her up, so she set off to catch the bus."

"It must have been a slow bus."

It was a flat, totally unaccented statement.

"She just missed one, so she dropped in at our local for some fags, and stayed to have a drink."

"And did she?"

Evans was having difficulty in controlling his voice.

"I do not go around public houses asking if my wife is telling me the truth. That's more in your line."

"Oh it is. Quite right," said Dalziel with equanimity. "We'll ask, never fear. But we won't bother you with our findings if you feel that way."

A touch of the knife, thought Pascoe. Just a hint, a reminder.

Dalziel wasn't finished.

"Why do you suspect Connon of...whatever you suspect him of?"

"Don't be mealy-mouthed, Bruiser."

"All right. Of having it away with your wife. Why Connon?"

Evans spoke softly now so that Pascoe had to strain to catch his words.

"Nothing positive. Things she let slip. We had a row. She said I should pay her more attention, I was always round at the Club with my drinking mates. I said at least I knew where I was with them. I could trust the men I drank with. So she laughed at that, see. Said, 'oh yes?' I asked what she meant. She said that not all of them were overgrown boys like me. One at least, she said, was a man. Still waters run deep, she said."

He fell silent.

"That's little enough to go on."

"Oh, there's other things. I've seen 'em talking. Seeing her looking at him. And when she goes missing like she did last Saturday he's usually not around either. But I wasn't certain, see? That's why I didn't ring the bell."

"You were certain enough last Saturday afternoon when you put the boot in," said Pascoe casually from his corner.

Evans flushed and looked far more embarrassed than he had done at any stage so far.

"What? Oh, that. How do you know? Oh, I don't know what made me do that, rotten thing to do, that was. I was really sorry afterwards. I'd got him to play, see? We were short anyway, always are, and I thought, right Connie, I'll know where you are this afternoon at any rate. Then he went down in this loose scrum, shouldn't have been there, but he was always a bit of a hero, and I put my foot in looking for the ball and there he was. I couldn't have missed him, but I could have slowed down a bit. But I didn't. Silly really, I've never done anything like it before. Never. Hard, you know, but never malicious. I was really sorry. Might have killed him. I thought I had for a moment."

I wish he wouldn't get so blasted Welsh when he's excited, thought Pascoe. My shorthand doesn't have the right symbols somehow. I'll never be able to read it back.

"But I didn't, did I?" Evans went on. "And I didn't kill his missis either, if that's what all this is about, which is all I can think."

"No one has suggested such a thing, I hope?" said Dalziel, shocked. "Your value to us, Arthur, is that you were there. In the road. Up at the house. At a significant time. We want to know what you saw. Tell us again what you saw."

Half way through the third telling, Pascoe was called out to the phone. He returned a minute later looking thoughtful.

"Now look," said Evans. "I've got to be going. Gwen will be thinking I've been put in a dungeon. And I've got to catch the team bus at twelve-forty-five. We're away today. So unless you've got ways of keeping me here you haven't revealed yet, I'm off."

"Arthur," said Dalziel reproachfully. "You've been free to go any time. We've no way of holding you."

"No," agreed Evans, rising.

"Except perhaps for obstructing the police by not revealing all this a lot earlier."

Ouch! thought Pascoe.

"Early or late, I've revealed it now. And it'll go no further, I hope."

"Not unless needed, Arthur. We're always a little doubtful about statements that have to be forced out of witnesses by revealing the extent of our prior information."

Evans laughed, the first merry sound he'd made since his arrival.

"Information nothing. It's piss-all information you had. I volunteered my statement because I wanted to volunteer, not because of your pathetic bluff. When you sort out your notes, Sergeant, you might include in them the additional information that my car was parked at the other end of Boundary Drive, the end furthest away from Glenfair Road, see? So it's purely voluntary isn't it? And now I'm going to volunteer to go home. Good day to you both."

Dalziel and Pascoe looked at each other for a long moment after the door had slammed behind Evans. Then they both began to grin, and finally laughed out loud.

It was their first moment of spontaneous shared amusement that Pascoe could remember.

"Well now, boyo," said Dalziel in a dreadful parody of a Welsh accent, "you'd better watch your bloody self, see? Telling such lies to an honest citizen."

"It might have been his car," said Pascoe. "White Hillman. I mean, why not? It didn't seem absolutely out of the question. By the way, we had a phone call,"

"From?"

"Connon. He was worried about Arthur. Wanted us to go easy on the thumbscrews, I think."

"Did he now? And he asked for you?"

"Why yes. I expect so."

"I see. Thinks I haven't got any better feelings to appeal to, does he? Well, go on."

"There's nothing to go on with. I assured him we were only asking Mr Evans one or two questions that might or might not be connected with the case. And I suggested he should contact Evans himself for full details."

"That was naughty. You didn't ask then?"

"Ask what? Sir?"

Dalziel looked pleadingly up to heaven. Pascoe sighed inwardly.

The party's over then, he thought. Like Christmas, a brief moment of good will and fellowship, then back to normal. You've spent your allowance, Bruiser. What're you going to do at the end of next week?

"You didn't ask who he got his information from. About Evans's being here."

He's right. I should have asked. That's another of his blasted troubles. He keeps on being right.

"No, sir. I didn't. Sorry. I'll get back on to him, shall I?"

"Don't bother," said Dalziel. "If he doesn't want to tell us (and the minute you ask, he won't) there's no way of finding out. From him. But the possible sources aren't many, are they?"

"No, sir."

"Our bobbies. A couple of nosey neighbours. Or the fair Gwen herself. Who's got your money, Sergeant?"

Pascoe's mind was racing.

"That'd mean, or might mean, that Evans is not altogether wrong. And if he's not altogether wrong, then Connon suddenly gets a great big motive."

"Motive? What motive?"

"Why, she, Mary Connon that is, finds out."

"How?"

"Accidentally by finding something," said Pascoe impatiently. "Or is deliberately told. Anonymous friend, a telephone call, that kind of thing. We've got one around that doesn't like Connie much, we know that."

"So. She knows. What then?"

"She tells him, that night. Gets nasty. Says some more unpleasant things about his daughter. Connon sees red. He's had that crack on the head remember. He grabs..." Pascoe paused.

"What does he grab, Sergeant?"

"How do I know? Something odd enough in shape not to be a normal part of living-room furniture. Something, *anything*, he can use as a club. And swings it at her."

"At his own wife? Sitting in his own lounge? Connon?"

Pascoe sighed.

"I didn't know the lady as well as you, sir, but she seems in all particulars to have been a pretty clubbable woman."

"No, I didn't mean her. I mean Connon. It's out of character. You've met him. Sudden violence doesn't fit."

The fat sod's fair, thought Pascoe. You've got to admit he's fair. I'm sure he'd like it to be Connon, but he doesn't try to bend matters.

"Perhaps the whole thing's a fake then, sir. Perhaps there was no concussion, no quarrel, no heat of the moment. Perhaps Connon decided he would like to marry Gwen Evans, or just unmarry Mary Connon. So he goes quietly home, sits and watches the telly with her a while; then, in the commercial break perhaps, he leans forward, taps her on the head with whatever he has selected for the job, waits a couple of hours, then rings us."

Dalziel was scratching with both hands, one on his inner right thigh, the other under his chin. One movement was clockwise, Pascoe noted, the other anti. Difficult.

"That sounds better. But not by much."

Well, let's have your ideas, for God's sake. You're the great detective!

Pascoe kept back his exasperation with difficulty and put his thoughts as mildly as he could manage.

"What do you think then, sir? An intruder?"

Dalziel laughed without much merriment.

"You and your damned intruder. No, be sure of one thing, there wasn't any intruder, my lad. The answer's nearer home. Your intruders'll all turn out to be like that laddo last night. Bit of a disappointment that, eh? Christ, he could talk! Made even you sound like a board-school lad at the pit-face. But he seemed nice enough. He'll be good company for that kid of Connon's. He's not exactly the laughing cavalier, is he?"

Pascoe stood up.

He's going to try to get the knife in, he thought. Just a little wriggle this time.

"Will that be all then? I'd better try to tidy my desk up a bit."

"Mind you," continued Dalziel, ignoring him, "it wasn't all waste, was it? I mean, Ted Morgan turned out to be a real find, didn't he? The eyes and ears of the world. You must have leaned upon him pretty hard."

"Not really," said Pascoe.

Dalziel leered at him across the desk.

"It's not a crime to take Jenny Connon out, you know. Eh? Now don't be offended. Just take care that fancying her doesn't make you go too soft on the rest of the family, or too hard on anyone else. I glanced at the stuff from young Curtis and the Fernies. Nothing much there, eh?"

Pascoe shook his head.

"Though the Fernies do seem to be around a lot, don't you think? And I met Mrs Curtis—she came in to see what it was all about. She'd just got in, and her husband. Do you know them?"

"No," said Dalziel without interest. But Pascoe ploughed on.

"He's nothing, a little silent man, not much there, I think. She's a talker, gab, gab, gab. The Fernies got rid of her when I left and she walked me to the front gate. Made Ted Morgan seem like an amateur. But one thing she did say was that our friend Fernie is going around telling everyone Connon killed his wife. And claiming he knows how."

Dalziel was now immersed in some papers and didn't even glance up.

"There's always plenty of them, isn't there?"

"I wouldn't know, sir. Is it worth a word with him?"

"I shouldn't think so. There hasn't been a complaint? See him if you want, though, but it'll be a waste of time."

He glanced at his watch, opened the top drawer of his desk and swept the papers in.

"Come on," he said. "We'll be able to get a drink in a moment. You'll be wanting an early lunch, won't you?"

"Will I?" asked Pascoe, trying to conceal from himself the effort he had to make to keep up with Dalziel down the corridor.

"Why?"

"The rugby, Sergeant. Remember?"

"We're going to watch?" asked Pascoe, puzzled.

Dalziel sighed.

"I might watch. But the game you're concerned with is Arthur Evans. You heard what he said, his coach goes at twelve-forty-five. So you get round to his house at one. Have a chat. Stop a while. Who knows? Friend Connon might even turn up to keep you company. That'd be nice. You in your small corner, Gwen curled up on the mat and Connon taking his ease in Arthur's rocking chair."

The thought obviously amused him. They were out in the street now. Dalziel was well known, hailing and being hailed by nearly every second person they passed, it seemed to Pascoe. Though he noticed there were some who spoke to the superintendent and were completely ignored, while others looked as if they would have preferred to creep past unknown.

Again there came to him a sense of how small a town of some eighty-five thousand people really was.

"Talking of chairs," said Dalziel, "there was a report from forensic, wasn't there, on that chair of Connon's? Nothing useful, I suppose?"

Pascoe was never quite certain just how genuine his superior's casual contempt for science was. Had he really not even looked at the report? He felt tempted to find out by inventing a number of startling discoveries made through lab tests on the chair. But instead, as always, he thought, I'll play the game.

"No. Nothing. No indication that anyone had been killed

in it or done anything else in it but sit in it. It went back to Connon's yesterday. He made them put it in the garden shed."

"Did he now? Bit of degree work for you there, Pascoe! The psychology of the criminal."

They came to a halt at a busy road crossing. The town was full of Saturday morning shoppers, more than usual even; there was only one more Saturday before Christmas.

"Sir, what about Hurst and the letter? You mentioned last night…"

"Did I? No, I didn't, Sergeant. I'm not senile. Who did?"

Pascoe looked a little shamefaced.

"Well, Connon actually, on the phone. He asked if anything had been done."

Dalziel slapped his inside pocket.

"It's here. I'll be seeing him before the match. Any other little reminders to me, Sergeant? Anything else I might have forgotten? No? Then what are we standing here for? Let's move on before some young copper picks us up for soliciting. Now, where did you say you were going to take me for that drink?"

❀ ❀ ❀

Jenny and Antony looked at each other, brown eyes unblinkingly fixed on blue, over the rims of their upraised pint pots.

"Umh," said Antony appreciatively, putting his glass down and nodding his head, "not bad at all. Unpretentious, with a pleasant touch of wit, should travel quite well. There is perhaps a slight tendency towards making one drunk."

They were sitting near a huge open fire in the lounge of a pub of that kind of indeterminate oldness which is the sign of constant use and development over many years. The fireplace was obviously very old indeed. It was large, and had once been larger. The table they sat at was wrought iron, with a bright brass guard-rail running round the top of it, more of a danger to glasses than anything else. In the ceiling there was visible what might have been an original oak cross-beam, but it had been unceremoniously distempered with the rest.

"I like it here," said Antony. "They have attempted neither to freeze the past, nor anticipate the future. Nor indeed to impress the present upon us with framed photographs of actors and actresses, cricketers and jockeys, the semi-famous sub-world, with duplicated scrawls of spurious well-wishings stamped across their corners."

"I just like the beer," said Jenny.

"It was nice of your father to chase us off together as he did," said Antony.

"He's a nice man."

"Yes, I'm sure he is. Well, Jenny, now we have got over the initial emotionalism of our reunion, perhaps one or two points might be clarified for me. Your father has extended to me the hospitality of his house for as long as I care to take it, or until he grows sick of the sight of me. It did not escape my notice, however, that you were accompanied last night by a rather large, rather muddy man who, I gathered from hints dropped from various quarters, had been your escort that evening. Competition I do not mind. I thrive on it. But we Wilkeses were never dogs in mangers. A word will be enough."

"Which word is that?" asked Jenny.

"If you don't know it, then I shall not teach you it. Good. I'm glad that's out of the way."

"I didn't know it was."

"Well, isn't it?"

"Of course, you fool. Didn't you get a good look at him? I was after information, that's all."

"Information?"

Quickly Jenny explained about Ted Morgan. At least it started off as a quick explanation, but without hardly noticing, she was soon telling Antony everything she had felt or feared in the past week.

He listened gravely without interrupting her. When she finished, he went to the bar and refilled their glasses.

"There are evidently some very nasty people in this little town of yours," he said reflectively.

"And some very nice ones," said Jenny with instinctive indignation.

He grinned at her and took her hand.

"But what goes on on the terraces seems to be very simple and almost harmless compared with that Rugby Club of yours."

The look of strain which had been missing from Jenny's face most of the morning returned.

"You think it's all something to do with the Club too, do you? Daddy does, I'm sure. And I think fat Dalziel does too. Oh, I wish it was something simple, some burglar, a tramp or something, who broke in and did it. It would still be as horrid, but it'd end there at least. Instead of which it seems to be going on and on and I'm finding myself going round playing at stupid amateur detectives. And what it's doing to Daddy, I just don't know."

"Hey, cool it, baby."

The shock of hearing such an expression in the accents of Hollywood gangsterese come from Antony's lips pulled her up sharply. He was smiling at her, but there was concern in his eyes.

"Thanks," she said. "I was going on a bit."

"Nonsense," he said. "Of course you're concerned about everything. But there's nothing wrong with playing games to ease your concern, whether it's playing detective or playing rugby. That's what games are, recreational. They give us a space in the business of life to re-create ourselves. Don't you think I would teach R. E. extremely well? And talking of detectives, aren't those two gentlemen, who have just come in like Laurel and Hardy, of that ilk?"

They were Dalziel and Pascoe. They looked around the room.

"See that? All good detectives look around the room," murmured Antony. Jenny giggled and kicked his ankle.

Dalziel saw them and waved. Pascoe glanced over and nodded almost imperceptibly.

"You know," said Antony, "I think that Laurel there fancies you."

"Don't be silly," replied Jenny, feeling the fringe of a blush caressing her cheek.

"Silly? Am I then so esoteric in my taste as to be the only man in the world who fancies you?"

Jenny finished her second pint with a swallow that reminded Pascoe, who was watching her surreptitiously through the bar mirror, of Jacko Roberts.

"Come on," she said. "I've got to get home and make the dinner."

"Right," he said. "And this afternoon?"

"Well," she said, "I wondered if you'd mind going out with Daddy. Get him off to the rugby match or something."

"Of course. But what are you going to do?"

"I want to clear out their, his, bedroom. Of Mummy's things, I mean. I've been meaning to do it, he doesn't seem to have the will, and it's more my job, I think. All her clothes and everything. I must do it now. He's been sleeping in the spare room, you see, but when you turned up last night, he moved back in. I think that's why he was up so early this morning."

"I'm sorry," said Antony. "I didn't realize."

"Why should you? Anyway, I'd like to do it. I know he's been through her papers and that, not that there was much. But the police asked, in case there was anything there to help. So if I can get rid of the rest..."

"Of course. Well, let's be on our way. I haven't really tasted your cooking yet, have I? I mean, I did in fact make my own breakfast. Not at all what I am used to."

Jenny grinned, that wide, slightly toothy grin which she tried so hard to avoid, and which filled her whole face with an animation and glow that turned Antony's heart upside down.

He laughed back at her and they left the pub hand in hand.

Dalziel looked meaningfully at Pascoe, but said nothing. Pascoe felt the cold beer fill his mouth and listened to the landlord's radio distantly above playing "White Christmas."

It was twelve o'clock.

"Time for another," he said.

❀ ❀ ❀

Gwen Evans wasn't being very helpful. At least, not in any sense that had any bearing on the case.

But Pascoe found her a great deal of help in restoring his rather worn manly pride. She was not a coquette, he had decided. She did not deliberately set out to make herself interesting to men. There was nothing self-conscious about the way she moved, stood, sat down, or talked to a man. There was nothing suggestive about her, she gave no hints of interest or invitation. She was dressed in a sloppy brown sweater and an old pair of slacks.

Whoever else she might be expecting, he had thought on arrival, it surely can't be her lover.

But the overall effect of two minutes in her presence had been to fill him with an all powerful sense of her sex.

The beer helped, he assured himself. Three pints heightened most men's receptivity.

But what the hell! he added. I don't just want her. I like her! She's a nice woman. A nice, pleasant, unfairly sexy woman.

But she wasn't any help at all as far as Evans was concerned.

Yes, she knew he was jealous of Connon.

No, there was nothing in his suspicion.

No, there hadn't been anything odd about the previous Saturday, either about her husband or about her own behaviour.

She repeated what he had heard already from the lips of Evans. She had decided that her friends had forgotten to pick her up. Had set off to catch the bus. Missed it. Dropped into the local, the Blue Bell, to get some cigarettes. Stayed to have a drink.

No, she hadn't talked to anyone in there. It had been quite crowded, but she had sat quietly in the corner with a drink.

No, she could not remember who had served her.

"And what the hell business of yours is all this anyway, Sergeant?"

She spoke without animosity and Pascoe smiled at her apologetically.

"None, of course, in all probability. We never know what's our business, and what isn't, till we get the answers."

He could afford not to press, he thought. All he had to do to check on her story was to ask at the pub. If she'd been there, no matter how quietly, someone would remember. You couldn't go around looking like Gwen Evans and hope to remain anonymous.

"Would you like a drink, Sergeant? Or a coffee?"

The beer was just beginning to turn a little sour in his stomach, and his bladder felt very full. Coffee would help one, but not the other.

"Coffee would be very nice," he said. "May I use your bathroom?"

She rose from the furry white armchair which he was sure was her choice. The thing he was sitting in felt hard and lumpy, almost certainly an Evans family hand-me-down.

"First left up the stairs," she said in the hallway and went into the kitchen.

He had just shut the door, locking it from ingrained habit, when the front-door bell rang.

With a longing look at the gleaming white bowl, he hastily opened the door again and stepped on to the landing.

Through the railings overlooking the small entrance hall, he saw Gwen appear from the kitchen. She didn't even glance up the stairs.

Not much sign of guilt there, he thought. Perhaps it's just the baker.

He heard the door being opened. All he could see was Gwen's back from the waist down. It was a sight worth dwelling on, but not much use for present purposes. He wanted to see faces if this were Connon.

"Hello Gwen."

A man's voice. Familiar. But not Connon's.

"Hello Marcus," said Gwen evenly, with just a touch of surprise. "I'm afraid you've missed Arthur. In fact I think you've probably missed the coach as well."

There was a pause.

"The coach? Oh, damn. I'd forgotten. No, I'm not playing this week. I'd forgotten it was an away game."

"Anything I can do?"

"No. I'll see him tonight. It was just that, well, I heard he'd been down at the police station this morning. I suppose I'm just being nosey, but I was worried. It's not nice this business. Anyway, I'd had a drink in the Club, that's where I heard. They were talking, you know how it is. So I thought I'd call in before Arthur got down there, just to see what was what. And to warn him the long knives were out. Some of them are like a lot of old women."

"Thanks, Marcus. But don't worry. It was nothing at all really."

It would be diplomatic, I suppose, thought Pascoe, to stay up here till she'd disposed of Marcus. If he sees me here, trouble will be confirmed. And if he is more nosey than friendly, then the rumours will fly. But, as Bruiser might say, if God had wanted me to be a diplomat, he'd have painted pinstripes down my backside. Which he didn't. So here goes.

He stepped back into the bathroom, pressed the little gleaming chrome lever, and moved hurriedly away from the sound of the rushing water.

Gwen looked as if she were about to shut the door.

"Mr Felstead," said Pascoe with a note of surprise more genuine, he felt, than anything Dalziel could produce. "How pleasant to meet you again. Not playing today? You haven't been dropped, I hope?"

God, it sounded bad. Perhaps he wasn't much better than Dalziel.

"No, I'm not, Sergeant. But not dropped," he added with a grin which made him look like the prototype jovial monk. "You've got to die to be dropped from our Fourths, and then it's best to be cremated just to be on the safe side. No, I'm retired, temporarily at least. I'll leave it to the young men, like yourself. Do you play?"

"Not rugger. No, I used to kick a rounder ball in a less violent game, but now I'm kept far too busy."

"Even on Saturday afternoons?" asked Marcus, raising his eyebrows quizzically in Gwen's direction.

"Even then," agreed Pascoe. "Though it is not without its compensations."

Gwen yawned unconcernedly at the compliment. From the kitchen came a high whistle.

"Coffee," she said. "Marcus, would you care to step in and take a cup?"

"Of kindness yet, for the sake of auld lang syne," ran absurdly through Pascoe's mind.

"No, I won't, thank you, Gwen. I'll get along. Cheerio. Cheerio, Sergeant."

Pascoe followed Gwen into the kitchen.

"He didn't seem very interested in why I was here, Mrs Evans."

She heaped a teaspoonful of instant coffee into a couple of beakers and poured a steaming jet of water on to it.

"No? Why should he be?"

"Because he seemed fairly interested in the police when he arrived."

Silly twit, he thought as she turned to him, faintly amused.

"So you had a listen, did you? Well, well. It must be second nature."

He smiled back and shook his head.

"I'm sorry. But it's not second nature. No."

"No?"

"No. It required an act of will. In fact, now you've rumbled me, may I, would you mind if I postponed the coffee just a few moments more?"

He heard her laughing with real amusement as he went up the stairs once more.

❊ ❊ ❊

Dalziel wasn't getting much co-operation either. He seemed to have been elected the most avoidable man in the club-house. Willie Noolan gave him a distant wave; Ted Morgan did an almost military about-turn when he spotted him and disappeared through the door; even Jacko Roberts seemed to consider his offer of a drink with more sardonic suspicion than usual.

"You've been found out," he said.

"Found out?"

"That's right. The myth of rugby veteran, dirty story teller, hail-fellow-well-met Bruiser Dalziel's been knackered and they're seeing you as what you are."

"What's that?"

"A nasty, nosey, nobody's-friend copper."

Dalziel finished his drink and stood up. Peter Hurst had just come into the room, dressed in his track suit though there was some time yet till kick-off.

"Fat bugger," said Jacko to the policeman's retreating back. Then he wondered if Dalziel had heard, and wished he didn't care.

Hurst doesn't look as if he's very delighted to see me, either, thought Dalziel.

He had always thought he had no illusions about the artificiality of people's reactions to him, but some must have taken root unaware. Tender young plants as yet, and all the more vulnerable to sudden blasts of cold.

"I've got that letter," he said as jovially as he could manage.

"Oh yes."

"Yes. Shall we go into the committee room?"

Hurst looked reluctant to go anywhere.

"Look, Superintendent," he began.

"Andy," interrupted Dalziel. "We're in the Club, aren't we? This is unofficial."

"That's it," said Hurst. "What I said to Connie last night

was unofficial as well, between the two of us. I'd no idea you were listening."

"Listen, Peter," said Dalziel sympathetically. "If you've got any information, you've got to give it to me. It's your duty."

"Suddenly it's become official again, has it?"

Hurst's voice had risen a little, but he dropped it again as he realized that several pairs of eyes were watching them with interest.

Dalziel's mind gave the equivalent of a shrug.

These people never realize that I can stand a row better than any of them, he thought. They think a bit of sound and fury against me confirms something. It's like water off a duck's back.

"Mr Hurst," he said formally, "I have reason to believe you can help me with an enquiry. Now you can do that now. Or you can do it tonight. Or you can do it next week. But be sure of one thing. If you want to be out on that pitch when the referee blows his whistle, you'd better do it now."

"Andy. Peter. For heaven's sake! Remember where you are!"

It was Noolan, attracted by the waves of interest emanating from all sides of the room.

"The committee room?" said Dalziel with a smile.

He put his arm over Hurst's shoulder as they went through the door, but removed it before the door was quite closed.

"Now, Mr Hurst," he said. "You wanted to look at the letter Jenny Connon received the day before yesterday. I have that letter here. Before I show it to you, however, I want to know your reason for wanting to see it."

Hurst looked angrily at him, then questioningly at Noolan who had followed them in.

The bank manager nodded.

"Tell him, Peter."

"So," said Dalziel. "Another in the plot? Don't say you've taken to concealing information as well, Willie?"

"No, Andy. Peter saw me last night after you'd left. Peter. Tell him."

Hurst played with the zip on his track-suit top, moving it up and down.

Like a nervous tart on her first job, thought Dalziel. Will the man never start?

"It's nothing really," said Hurst. "It's just that a few days ago I heard one of our members say something about Connie. It was just after we'd heard about Mary. We'd been saying how awful it was, how sorry we were for Connie. And this chap said that we might well be sorry for Connie, but not to overdo it. He said that there were things about Connie that he wouldn't like his daughter to know."

"And?"

"Nothing really. We'd all had a few drinks. Someone said there were things about himself he wouldn't like his wife to know, we all laughed and went off happy. It kind of broke the gloomy atmosphere."

"Exit on a joke. Is that *all?*"

"No. On Wednesday after the selection committee meeting, I realized I'd left my fountain pen in here. I came in to get it and found this same person using it. He finished off quickly as I came in, apologized when he realized it was my pen, and that was an end to it. But I got a distinct impression he didn't want me to see what he was writing. He folded it up and tucked it away very quickly."

"Again, is that all? It's not much, is it? And why do you want to see the letter?"

Hurst obviously did not like what was happening. But he feels he ought to dislike it even more than he does, thought Dalziel. Jesus, it's all do-it-yourself public relations now. Everyone's sweating on their image.

"Whatever he was writing," said Hurst slowly, "he was writing in block capitals. I saw that much."

"One block capital looks much like another, upside down, from a distance," sneered Dalziel. "Is that all?"

"No. It would be written with my pen, you see, if it was that letter. And that day my pen was filled with green ink. I'd run out and borrowed some from my boy. You know what kids are. Anything exotic. It happened to be green."

Carefully Dalziel reached into his inside pocket and took from it a large envelope. Out of this he drew a Cellophane packet. Framed in it they could see a letter. He held it up to the light to give a clearer view.

The ink was black.

Hurst sighed deeply.

"I'm glad," he said.

"Who was it you saw?" asked Dalziel.

"Why? Is that necessary," he asked, turning to Noolan.

"You'd have named him if he seemed guilty. It seems odd not to do so when he is innocent. Eh, Willie?"

"It was Arthur Evans that Peter saw. We heard he was down at the station this morning. Peter wondered..."

"...if we in our own bumbling way had caught up with him? No. Well, thank you both very much indeed for your time."

"Not at all," said Noolan. "I'm sorry yours has been wasted."

Hurst left without a word.

"Andy," said Noolan. "Don't make such a big noise round the Club, eh? You put me in an embarrassing position."

"I shall be so quiet you'll never notice me. In fact, with your permission, I'll start now and stop here for a while. All the best fictional detectives do it. Have long thinks, I mean."

"Be our guest," said Noolan and went back into the social room leaving the large figure, head wreathed in cigarette smoke, seated at the top of the big committee-sized table.

He was still there two hours later when the whistle went for no-side.

❋ ❋ ❋

"A curious game," said Antony as they drove away from the ground. "Especially when seen through a glass, distantly."

They hadn't cared to join the small crowd of spectators in

the old stand, but had remained in the car parked about twenty-five yards behind one of the goals.

"A poor game," replied Connon, "seen from no matter what distance."

"Why?" asked Antony, with a polite interest which ten minutes later had turned into the real thing.

Whatever else you know, Jenny's father, he thought, you certainly know your rugby. At least I think that if I knew my rugby, I would be in a good position to acknowledge that you know yours.

But he knew enough about the game to recognize the scope and justice of Connon's analysis.

"Now I feel I could watch the game again," he said when Connon finished.

"Nothing is repeatable," said the older man. "Not even the moments that we relive a thousand times."

Connon fell silent and Antony, great talker though he was, knew when conversation was not being invited. The rest of the drive home passed in almost complete silence.

But I like him, thought Antony as they got out of the car. He might do for me very well. I could not bear a dull father-in-law. And Jenny, now Jenny, there's the find of the century.

He went towards the front door with pleasurable anticipation. But there was no reply to his enthusiastic bell-ringing and Connon, coming from closing the garage, had to get his key out to open the door.

The house was quiet and felt empty.

"Jenny! Jenny!" called Connon.

There was no reply.

"She can't have gone far," said Connon. "She'll be back in a minute I expect. Probably gone round the corner to the shops."

Probably, thought Antony, but he didn't feel happy.

He went upstairs to change out of the heavy boots he had (unnecessarily) decided were good rugby-watching gear.

As he passed Jenny's bedroom door, he saw it was ajar. He pushed it gently open and looked in.

The room was quite empty. He looked at the furnishings, the pictures, the bed with its rich crimson bedspread. Seated on top of it was a fluffy white dog, its red tongue grotesquely hanging out, its head lolling to the side. It was a nightgown case and his eyes lit up as he saw it.

Quickly he moved into his own room, grabbed his pyjama top and returned. His intention was simple, to substitute this for whatever garment he found in the dog.

But as he went across the room to the bed, something on the dressing-table caught his eye. It was a large sheet of paper with writing all over it.

Antony was a man with considerable respect for individual privacy. Looking at other people's letters was not something that attracted him. But something about the sheet of paper, lying with its contents reflected unreadably in the mirror, drew him towards it.

He picked it up.

"Dear Christ," he said.

He read it again.

"Dear mother of God!" he said.

His pyjama-top dropped from his hand.

"Antony? Anything wrong?"

Connon stood in the door.

"I found this. On her dressing-table."

He reached out the letter.

Connon read it with one sweep of the eyes. Then without a word he turned and ran downstairs. Antony walking out of the room to the landing heard him dialling the telephone.

Three numbers only.

"Give me the police," he said. "Quick."

❊ ❊ ❊

"As obscene letters go," said Dalziel, "I've seen worse."

"Is that supposed to be some consolation?" asked Connon.

"It's pretty graphic I should have thought," remarked

Antony, trying to hide his tremendous concern under a calm exterior.

"Oh yes. It's graphic. It's that all right. Crudely so. But it's not perverted. This is all good straightforward stuff."

"For God's sake, Dalziel!" exploded Connon. "Can we cut the expert critical review and get on with the job of finding out where Jenny is!"

Dalziel made squelchy soothing noises in his throat.

"Take it easy," he said. "We have her description out. Every policeman in town's on the look out for her. I'm sure she'll have come to no harm."

"Thanks," said Connon. "You realize there was no envelope with this thing. And there's only one post on Saturday and this had arrived well before I left?"

"Yes, sir. We realize that. So now you're imagining that he, whoever he is, popped this through the letter-box, waited till she had had time to read it, then rang the bell and invited her to take a stroll with him. Now is that likely?"

"Only if," said Connon slowly, "only if it was someone she knew well."

The same thought had crossed Dalziel's mind much earlier, but he still found it hard to believe. In his experience those who wrote letters like this were unlikely to follow them up, at least so rapidly.

But there was something disturbing about the letter. Not just in its contents. He had been speaking nothing less than the truth when he put it well down the list of those he had seen.

No, there was something else.

The door of the lounge opened, and Pascoe came in. They all looked at him, Dalziel interrogatively, Antony hopefully, Connon fearfully.

A single shake of the head did for them all. He went across the room to Dalziel.

"Nothing yet, sir. We've got everything on it we can."

He was plainly as concerned as anyone else there, really concerned, not just professionally.

Antony found himself quite liking Laurel after all.

He went up to the two detectives and coughed delicately.

"Forgive me for my effrontery," he said. "But my father always taught me never to be afraid of pointing out the obvious. I'm sure you have noticed the implication of the letter, that the writer has in fact observed Jenny undressing for bed? I just wondered if you also knew, as I'm sure you do, that her bedroom's at the rear of the house?"

"So?" said Dalziel.

"Well, as I know from personal experience it's almost impossible to get to the rear of this house from the front when the door at the end of the passageway between the garage and the house wall is locked. There is a very stout trellis on the other side of the house, with an equally well-barred door in it."

"Through someone else's garden?" said Pascoe.

"From my brief observation of Mr Connon's hedges, he seems to have a peculiar fondness for a near lethal mixture of African thorn, briar rose, and bramble."

"May we, Mr Connon?" said Dalziel, setting off without waiting for an answer.

They all stood in the rapidly darkening garden, most of them glad to have even the illusion of activity to take their minds off the unchanging situation.

It was a long garden, the kind of length which only generous pre-war builders gave to house-buyers.

There'd be a two-bedroom bungalow tucked away there on a modern estate, thought Pascoe. Not that it bothers me. A bachelor gay.

The hedges were as Antony had described them. The door to the garage passage was bolted and locked, as was the door in the trellis work on the other side.

"You always keep these locked?" asked Dalziel.

"Always at night," said Connon. "It's habit. One of us, Mary and me I mean, always checked. Sometimes both. It was a bit of a joke."

It was growing very cold in the garden. There was frost

in the air. None of them was wearing an overcoat and Antony shivered violently.

"Over the tree?" suggested Pascoe.

A large sycamore tree growing in the front garden had branches which stretched along the side of the house over the trellis.

"I don't know," said Dalziel. "Possible, but I don't see why. He could hardly know he was going to get a show for his efforts, could he?"

"No," said Pascoe, glancing at Connon and Antony. "I don't suppose he could. Shall we go back in? It's a bit chilly out here."

Connon took a last look back at the gathering gloom before he stepped into the house.

I know what he's thinking, Pascoe told himself. If they don't find her before it's dark...

He didn't much like the thought himself.

Dalziel still wasn't happy about the letter. He let the others go on, sat down on a kitchen stool and took it out of his pocket. Pascoe stepped back into the kitchen.

"There you are," he said.

"You checked the house?" asked Dalziel, not raising his eyes from the sheet of paper he held gingerly before him.

"Yes. She's not tucked away here."

"Then she'll probably be all right. Sergeant, read this letter again."

Silently Pascoe looked over his chief's shoulder and read. He felt again the anger which had gripped him when he first saw it.

"Any comment?"

"Well, sir, it's not really the same kind of vein as the last one, is it? I don't know if we can tell really much about such things, but I'd have said it wasn't from the same man."

"I think you're right. But something else too. You're our expert here. Making allowances for the natural exaggeration of this kind of mind and the rather stereotyped language, does that sound to you like Jenny Connon?"

Pascoe was puzzled.

"Well, I don't know," he began, but Dalziel wasn't finished.

"And look at this paper. Look at the way it's folded. You know what I think..."

But he didn't finish. Outside in the hall they heard the front door open, footsteps pattered along the polished parquet floor and a light high voice cried, "Daddy? Antony? Are you there?"

Pascoe's stomach did a quick flip-over, he beat Dalziel to the door by a full two yards and almost fell into the lounge.

Jenny was being embraced by her father and Antony looked as if he was standing in the queue.

"Welcome home, Jenny," said Dalziel. "We were worried about you."

She turned and saw them. Her face lost some of its animation.

"Hello," she said. "You're here."

"Jenny, what happened?" said her father. "Why did you go out when you got the letter? You should have phoned us at the Club."

"Got the letter?" she said. "Oh, the letter. You found it?"

Dalziel held it up gravely. Her face suddenly lit up with understanding.

"And you thought...oh, I see. Daddy, I'm so sorry."

She put her arms around him again. Antony still stood patiently in the background. Connon looked puzzled.

"Sorry? What for, dear?" he asked.

Dalziel answered.

"Jenny is sorry she inadvertently misled us all, I think. You see, *she* didn't receive the letter. It wasn't meant for her. She found it. I think."

"Among your mother's things!" said Antony with sudden understanding.

Connon's grip on his daughter relaxed.

"You mean, that letter was sent to Mary?" he said, incredulous. "To Mary? No! She would have told me. You don't receive a letter like that and not..."

His voice trailed off and he sat down heavily on the arm of a chair.

"Where did you find it, Jenny?" asked Pascoe gently.

There were tears in the girl's eyes now.

"In the wallet pocket of one of Mummy's old handbags. I thought I'd better turn everything out, you see, and then this came up. I just glanced at it, I didn't want to pry, but I had to look to see if it was important. I felt ill when I read it. It wasn't what it said, I mean I've read books and heard jokes just as bad, it was just the thought of Mummy getting it. I went into my own bedroom and sat on the bed for a few minutes. But then, I don't know, I got a bit frightened. The telephone rang, but I didn't answer it. I just got my coat and went out. I didn't want to talk to anyone, you know, but I wanted to be near people. So I got a bus into town. I thought I'd walk down to the Club and see you and Antony there, Daddy, but there were so many people, I could hardly move. I'd almost forgotten it was so near Christmas. Anyway I realized I'd have missed you at the Club, so I turned round and set off back. It took me ages. I'm sorry. I should have phoned. I didn't want you to find the letter before I'd told you about it."

She was crying hard now, tears coursing down her face over the pale curve of her cheeks.

"Sergeant," said Dalziel, "perhaps you'd take Miss Connon upstairs and ask her to show you where she found the letter."

He waited till the door closed behind them.

"Now Mr Connon, I'll want to talk at length to you about this, you realize. But quickly now while Jenny's upstairs, do you have any knowledge, any suspicion even of the source of the letter?"

"None. Nor did I even suspect its existence," said Connon. "Superintendent, could this have anything to do with Mary's death?"

"I don't know. I really don't know."

The door opened again and Pascoe came in alone. He

motioned with his head to Antony, who nodded and went swiftly out of the room and up the stairs.

"Well, Sergeant?"

Pascoe held up a large envelope.

"I've put them in here. Three more in all, sir. In the same place. Jenny must have just got hold of the first. And, sir."

"Yes."

"Mrs Connon's bedroom is at the front."

Chapter Six

"It'll soon be Christmas," said Pascoe inconsequently.

Dalziel's gaze wandered suspiciously round the room as if seeking signs that someone had had the effrontery to deface the slightly peeling wall with festive decoration.

"What do you want, Sergeant? A present?" he asked sourly.

It's getting him down, thought Pascoe with a frisson of pleasure for which he was instantly and heartily ashamed.

It was, after all, his job too.

But the past few days *had* been depressing. Things had seemed to be opening up. For a while there had been a feeling that they were asking the right questions and that at any moment the individual answers would shuffle themselves into a significant total. But they remained ragged, unfinished, unproductive. The enquiry's initial impetus was being lost and now they were all groping. Other matters, important and routine, had arisen. New demands on time and men were being made all the time.

"Yes, I suppose it will," said Dalziel.

"Will what?"

"Soon be Christmas."

"Thanks," acknowledged Pascoe satirically, but for once Dalziel ignored him.

"Something'll happen soon. Something pretty big. We're stretched as it is. Something will happen that will almost snap us. It always does," he ended with sour satisfaction. "Just before Christmas."

"What had you in mind?'

"Anything. Have you never noticed? Look, there's good reasons. People need more money at Christmas, even crooks. And there's more about. In the shops; in the wage-packets; moving to and from the banks. Right?"

"Right."

"And it's darker. Gloomier. Half the bloody day. Makes it all seem easier. Darkness encourages other things too. Children have to come home in it. Women in lonely places are there more in the dark than at any other time of the year. Or if you want something else, the weather's rotten as well. Cars crash easier. Trains hit ice on the rails. Planes lose themselves in fog and drop out of the sky into city centres.

"But most often there doesn't seem to be any good reason. Things happen just because it's Christmas. Life showing its arse at the universal party."

"It's the other way round, isn't it, sir? Things are just more striking if they happen against the background of Christmas. Now I bet if you looked at it statistically..."

The very word, as Pascoe had half intended, was enough to jerk Dalziel out of his reverie back to his normal state of being.

"Statistically!" he sneered. "if you're not superstitious yet, son, you bloody well get superstitious. And stuff your statistics!"

"Up life's arse at the universal party?" enquired Pascoe politely.

Dalziel laughed, almost sheepishly for him.

"I said that? It must be the high-class company I keep. But I mean what I say. Get superstitious. One of us had better get lucky soon."

Pascoe looked ruefully at the piles of paper which had accumulated since the enquiry started.

"No, sir," he said, "I can't agree. It's not luck we want now. It's a computer. The answer, or at least, an answer, is in here somewhere."

"We're just waiting for it to rise to the surface are we, Sergeant? Have you noticed in the detective books how there's always something bothering the private-eye's subconscious? Some little oddity of behaviour or event which, when he recalls it, will prove the key to the whole problem. But it's not like that, is it, Sergeant? Nothing is odd because there's no norm. Or everything's odd. I mean, look at this lot we've got ourselves mixed up with. All of them, known and unknown, thrashing around in uncontrolled sexual activity like midnight at a Roman orgy."

"It's like midnight all right. It's catching them at it that's difficult. If only we knew! Is there anything going on between Connon and Gwen Evans? That gives us some kind of motive if there is, but there's damn' little evidence. She might have phoned him up when we brought Evans in. It seems likely she did, but we don't know for sure. He might have gone to see her that Saturday night. Fernie saw him going into the house. Evans says the car was there when he went round. But the only person who could tell us whether Connon was in or not is Mary Connon, and she's dead."

"Gwen Evans isn't."

"No, but she says she was round at the local. The landlord knows her well, but couldn't remember seeing her that night. He said he'd ask the staff when they got in. He hasn't contacted me, so I assume no one saw her. But she could still have been there."

Dalziel took a noisy sip from the cup in front of him and pulled a wry face.

"It's gone cold. Carry on Sergeant, do. I'm stuck for something else to do at this minute, so I might as well listen."

Pascoe inclined his head in acknowledgment of the favour.

"Thank you for your enthusiastic reception. Then there's this letter writer, or rather, these letter writers. We're no further forward with either. You got no help on the first at the Club, and anyone from a dirty old man to a randy adolescent could have written the others."

"They did suggest a combination of experience and athleticism," smirked Dalziel. He must have caught a shade of disapproval in his sergeant's poker-face for he added, "Don't be so strait-laced, Sergeant. They're just so much pornography and none of us turn up our noses at a bit of that now and then. They probably haven't anything at all to do with the case. And if it's that girl you're thinking of, forget it. They're tough nowadays. You heard her. It's a bloody permissive society."

"Yes, sir," said Pascoe. But he could not dismiss the thought of Jenny Connon so easily. He had never been short of girl-friends, not at university anyway. But he had discovered that joining the police had, for one reason or another, cut him off very largely from his old source of supply. The reaction of several members of his old student circle had surprised him. There had been nothing dramatic, no great debate, just a lot of jokes and heavy irony to start with, then a gradual, gentle separation.

Plus, of course, he admitted to himself wryly, the fact that the hours and the work don't make me the ideal boy-friend, let alone husband. Still, there's always that little bit of vitality Sheila whatsit, Lennox, that's it, down at the Club. Now she'd shown an interest. Young perhaps. But Jenny's age at least. *And* enthusiastic. If Dalziel found out he'd laugh for seven days.

"To get back to the letters, sir," he said.

"We'd left them had we? Daydream on your day off, will you."

"Sir. Well, I've read them pretty closely and though there's no date or any positive indication in them of the order in which they were written, there does seem to be a progression of a sort. I mean, two of them seem as if they are referring back to something which has happened since the first two."

Dalziel was interested.

"You mean, they'd met. Or something like that?"

"No, nothing as positive as that. It's as though the show had become somehow more spectacular. All the time he's writing as if he'd seen her undressing, but there's something just a bit more theatrical about the last two."

"You're being vague again, Sergeant. We'll get no further on with vagueness. We need something positive."

There was a knock on the door and the station sergeant stuck his head round.

"Excuse me, sir. There's a Mr Wilkes here to see Sergeant Pascoe."

"Is there now? Wheel him in here, then."

"And there's a telephone call for you, sir. From a Mr Roberts."

"Christ, I ask for something positive and they come shooting at us from all angles. Right, Sergeant, you take your boy elsewhere and I'll see what jolly Jacko, the life and soul of the party, wants."

Pascoe got up and went out. He saw Antony standing talking animatedly to a rather bewildered looking police constable who looked relieved to get away.

"Hello there, Sergeant," he said brightly. "I was just enquiring of that officer whether in fact he was formally trained in deliberateness of manner. Perhaps you as a graduate in Social Sciences and a policeman could tell me?"

"I'm afraid I can't help you, sir," said Pascoe woodenly.

"There you go!" said Antony. "And the reason why I asked to see you rather than your superintendent was that you looked capable of rising above it."

"What did you want to see me about, Mr Wilkes?"

"I'm sorry. Have I been offensive? It's just sheer nervousness, I assure you. It's like coming into a hospital."

Pascoe looked closely at the smiling youth. Suddenly he believed him. He was nervous. No one could appear as self-confident as this boy and not be nervous. Almost no one.

"Come in here," he said. "Sit down."

"Here" was an empty interview room.

"What do you want to say to me?"

Antony perched himself comfortably on the edge of the table.

"It's about the letters. A piece of impudence on my part, really, but I have a strong sense of civic duty. Mr Connon when I arrived told me about the letter Jenny received and also about your warning to him that there might be phone-calls also. This made me think. I wondered if perhaps the letters Mrs Connon had received could have been associated with phone-calls as well."

Pascoe sighed at the arrogance of youth in general and this youth in particular.

"The thought had occurred to us, sir. There's little chance of checking up on it. We did ask Mr Connon if he recalled any unusual telephone calls—any that he answered, I mean, when the caller just rang off. He said no. And it would be curious if Mrs Connon took one while he was there and said nothing of it."

"Or even when he was not there. But she hadn't mentioned the letters."

"No, sir. Well, if that's all..."

He moved to the door.

"Oh please, Sergeant. I would not presume to try to do your job. No, I haven't come down here with suggestions—that would be presumptuous—but with information, or what might be. This chap had obviously been watching Mrs Connon in her bedroom, from the street almost certainly, or the garden. When I was waiting at the Connons the other night before you all so efficiently arrested me, I had occasion to use the phone-box almost opposite the house. I rang my parents to say where I was. I also took the opportunity of giving them Mr Connon's phone number so they could contact me if they wished. To do this, I had to look in the directory."

"And?"

"And it was heavily underlined."

Pascoe's mind was racing so fast he had to make an effort

of will to bring it under control. Two or three small elements on the edge of the puzzle seemed to be coming together. But whether they were related directly to the main body of the puzzle was not yet clear. But it was a possibility. But that's all it is, he told himself. A possibility has been suggested to you. Nothing more. A theory.

But he could hardly wait to get rid of Antony so that he could test it.

"It seemed odd at the time," the youth went on, unconscious of his sudden undesirability. "Why should anyone want the telephone number of a house only twenty yards away?"

"I can think of a dozen good reasons," smiled Pascoe. "But I'm very grateful to you, Mr Wilkes. Thank you for coming. If there's ever anything else you would like to tell me, please call in."

"Do I detect a note of irony?" asked Antony cheerfully. "Then I will be off. I am a sensitive plant. Like asparagus, I take a long time to grow and am easily killed off."

"But you have a most delicate flavour all of your own," said Pascoe as he ushered him out.

"Saucy," said Antony. " 'Bye!"

Dalziel was still on the phone. Pascoe began sorting rapidly through the papers on his desk.

Dalziel put the phone down with a ping that rippled violently across the room.

"Roberts," he said.

"I know," said Pascoe. "Tell me, why do I have to pay my informants a quid or more a time while you have snouts who could buy and sell both of us and who rush to buy you drinks whenever you appear?"

"Beauty," said Dalziel. "I have a beautiful soul. What're you doing?"

"Just reading a report."

Quickly he told Dalziel what he had just learned from Antony and of the train of thought this had started in his mind.

When he finished Dalziel nodded appreciatively.

"I like that," he said. Then, almost modestly he added, "I've got a little something too. Perhaps there is a God."

He rolled his eyes at the ceiling.

There isn't a God, thought Pascoe. No one capable of creating kangaroos could have resisted hitting him in the face with a divine custard pie.

"What did he give you?"

"Nothing much, really. Some odds and ends. But one interesting thing about a gentleman we may have overlooked. Mr Felstead."

"Tubby little Marcus?" laughed Pascoe. "Well, he is over-lookable."

"Don't underestimate him. He's a man of parts, used to be a very nippy little scrum-half and he's still a very enthusiastic wing-forward."

"Was," amended Pascoe. "He seems to have given up. That's what he said on Saturday. What about him anyway?"

"Well, his best service to the Club at the moment is perhaps in the club-house. He's not married, he's keen, reliable, and he has a lot of time. So he helps a hell of a lot. With the bar, that kind of thing."

"So."

"He was on the bar the night Mary Connon was killed."

"I know. It's in here somewhere."

Pascoe struck his papers with the palm of his hand. A little dust drifted up.

"So was Sid Hope."

"Yes."

"So, from his own graphic account of the exit and re-entry of Evans that night, was Ted Morgan. But you never asked him why."

"Well, he did begin to go on about it being unusual for him to be that side of the bar, but I told him to get on with it."

"Not bullying him, I hope, Sergeant," he said reproachfully.

It was Pascoe's turn to roll his eyes at the heavens.

"Anyway," said Dalziel, "Morgan was on because Felstead was off."

"Off?"

"For almost two hours. Off. No one knows where." He stood up and reached for his hat.

"What's worse, no one has *asked* where."

Pascoe stood up too.

"Would you like me to...?"

"No thank you, Sergeant. I'll have a chat. Tonight. You'll be out yourself, won't you? Drop in at the Club later and exchange notes."

He put his hat on, flung his coat over his arm and went to the door.

"And Sergeant," he said, as he closed it behind him. "Marcus Felstead has a car. A cream-coloured Hillman. See you later."

❁ ❁ ❁

Dave Fernie was shouting at his wife. Alice Fernie was shouting at her husband.

The room was in a state of some disorder, but as yet, the little cool area at the back of Alice's mind told her, no permanent damage had been done.

The evening paper flung aside violently and scattering into its separate half-dozen sheets accounted for a good fifty per cent of the chaos. A coffee cup had been knocked off the arm of Fernie's chair, but there wasn't much left in it and the stain would be easily removable. The saucer had broken, however.

A single cushion had been hurled across the room and it lay on the edge of the fireplace. She would have to move it before it singed. It had struck the wall and disturbed a line of three china ducks. The middle one looked as if it had been shot and was going into its final dive. Even as she observed this, it did just that, slithered off the nail which supported it and plunged headfirst into the deep blue of the mantelpiece.

That was no great loss, either. She'd never liked them much; in fact she had only kept them up so long because Mary Connon long ago, almost on her first visit to the house, had been openly patronizing about them. It was a kind of V-sign, ever present, to keep them there.

But now that reason was gone, and the memory that remained of it seemed rather mean and cheap. It was time they were down.

All these thoughts and observations co-existed with the words she was hurling across at her husband.

"You'll end up in jail!" she yelled. "Or you'll be paying damages for the rest of your life!"

"It's a free country!" he shouted. "I'll say what I bloody well think. I'm as good as he is. There's one law for us all!"

"You were lucky last time!" she screamed. "He didn't care for the law. He just worked you over a bit, put you in hospital, big man!"

"Let him try that! Bloody rugby players! Bloody cream-puff. I'll take him apart."

"Can't you see, Dave? Are you blind? You'll just get us all in trouble. We've had enough. Can't you leave it alone?"

The note of appeal in her voice was obviously analysed as a sign of weakness.

"Leave it alone? Why should I, for God's sake? I reckon the man's knocked off his wife and he's getting away with it! Someone's got to say something. The bloody law won't!"

There was a brief pause, Alice silent in despair, Fernie for want of breath.

Through the silence rang a bell as if signalling the end of a round in a boxing match.

"Who the hell's this?" snarled Fernie.

Alice didn't answer. She was moving round the room at great speed for so heavily built a woman. The newspaper resumed its normal shape, the broken duck and the pieces of saucer were dropped in the coal scuttle, Fernie got the cushion back hard in his chest.

The bell rang again.

Smoothing back her hair, Alice went to the front door and opened it.

Pascoe stood there.

"Hello, Mrs Fernie. I was beginning to think the bell was broken."

"Who the hell is it?" asked Fernie again from the living-room.

Pascoe walked in with a smile.

"It's only the bloody law, Mr Fernie."

Fernie glowered at him, corrugating his eyebrows to aggressive bristles.

"You've been listening at keyholes, have you? What a job!"

"Dave," hissed Alice.

Pascoe was unconcerned.

"Not necessary, Mr Fernie. Anyone passing could hear you loud and clear."

"We're not worried about what people hear, Sergeant," said Alice fiercely.

"No? You sounded worried, Mrs Fernie. And I think you've got cause to worry."

Alice's angry flush faded to pale anxiety.

"Is that why you're here?"

"Not primarily, but now it's come up we might as well talk about it. Mr Fernie, I gather you've been making certain allegations about your neighbour, Mr Connon."

"Neighbour? He's no neighbour of mine. Neighbours are on this side of the road only in this street. And what if I have anyway? What's it to you?"

"Nothing officially, yet. If we think that what anyone says is likely to cause a breach of the peace, then we'll act. I gather you have said things in the past which caused a breach of the peace?"

"Mind your own bloody business!"

"Dave thought someone was running around with a neighbour's wife," said Alice quietly. "He said so. Often. Someone beat him up one night. They never got anyone."

"But you think it was something to do with the slander?" asked Pascoe.

"Slander? What's this about slander?"

"Nothing yet, Mr Fernie. Slander normally involves a civil action. If you say a man has killed his wife, you are damaging his reputation and he is entitled to damages which could be considerable. Your only defence would be that you did not publish the slander, which in this case would be very difficult, I feel. Or you might plead that it was not slanderous because it was true. Even this is not always an acceptable defence, I should add. The truth can often be slanderous if it is put in certain ways. But still, it would be your best bet."

"Best bet? But there isn't a case, is there? He wouldn't dare!"

"Why are you so certain of this, Mr Fernie? What proof have you got of your allegations?"

There was a long uncomfortable silence in which Pascoe noticed the missing duck, the broken china in the scuttle, and Alice noticed him noticing.

"You have no proof, do you, Mr Fernie?"

Fernie said nothing. Alice put her hand over his.

"You have nothing more than a dislike of Mr Connon and a very nasty twist in your mind which is going to get you into very serious trouble indeed. If I hear of one more occasion on which you make these allegations I shall feel it my duty to pass them on to Connon myself. Do I make myself clear?"

Fernie still said nothing.

"Very clear, Sergeant," said Alice quietly.

Pascoe ignored her.

"I say you have no reason other than a dislike of Connon, Mr Fernie. I hope this is your only reason for wanting to accuse him?"

Fernie shifted uncomfortably. The anger seemed to have gone out of him.

"It stands to reason, doesn't it?" he argued. "I mean, her, with her always flaunting herself."

"What other reason, Sergeant?" asked Alice. "What other reason could there be?"

"Mrs Fernie, I'd like to speak to your husband alone if I may."

Alice looked from Pascoe to Dave, her face tense with worry.

"Why?" she asked.

"What's this then, Sergeant?" said Fernie.

"I won't go," said Alice, with sudden determination. "We've got nothing to hide from each other."

Pascoe shrugged.

"All right. Mr Fernie, you said that Mary Connon was always 'flaunting herself.' Those were your words, I think?"

"That's right."

"What did you mean?"

"Mean? Well, I meant she was, well, always showing herself off, you know, putting on the style. Mutton dressed as lamb."

"Was that all?" asked Pascoe.

Fernie looked around the room, not quite focusing on anything. Alice felt a little knot of fear tying itself in her belly.

"Yeah, that's all. What else?"

Pascoe reached in his pocket and pulled out a notebook.

"Mr Fernie, Detective-Constable Edwards who interviewed you on the morning after Mrs Connon was killed, said in his very comprehensive report that you had noticed the police arrive the previous night. You knew something was up."

"That's right. Make enough bloody noise, don't you?"

"To the best of my recollection, very little was made that night. In any case, according to Edwards, reference was made to you standing looking out of your front window for some time. Is that true?"

"No. Well, yes. I don't know. What's some time? I can look out of my own window, can't I?"

"Of course. What were you looking at? Or waiting for?"

Alice Fernie had taken enough of this. She leaned forward angrily.

"Come on, Sergeant. What are you getting at? Are you trying to suggest Dave *knew* something was going to happen?"

"Did you, Mr Fernie? Did you know? Or were you just hoping for something?"

Fernie was obviously in some distress. He looked at his wife, then at Pascoe, picked up the newspaper and began fiddling with it.

"Know? How could I know? Of course not. No, it was just that…"

Suggest an accusation of the larger to get an admission of the smaller, thought Pascoe smugly. But never forget, he admonished himself, that this is no proof that the larger isn't accountable also.

"Something to do with Mary Connon? Flaunting herself," he prompted.

Fernie was now talking to his wife, rapidly, with just a hint of pleading.

"It was just that a couple of times I'd been looking out, or I'd just glance up as I passed, and, well, I'd seen her there. The light blazing, curtains not drawn. Well, Christ, of course I looked. What man wouldn't? I mean you could see everything. Everything. I'd have said something to you, love, but she was your friend."

Alice just looked at him speculatively.

"Not very nice, really," said Pascoe. "Being a peeping Tom."

Fernie grew indignant.

"Peeping Tom nothing! All I did was look. I wasn't hiding or anything. And make no mistake about it, she knew I was there. She knew she had an audience. That's what I meant by flaunting. She'd yawn, you know, like they do to show off, stretch her arms right back so that her…"

He glanced anxiously at his wife.

"Breasts?" she suggested amiably.

"…stuck right out. Right out," he repeated.

"She had a big figure," said Alice, as though some explanation was needed.

"Mr Fernie," said Pascoe, "do you ever use the phone-box outside in the street?"

Fernie looked puzzled.

"Yes, I've used it. I phoned your lot from it the other night. Why?"

"Did you ever ring the Connons' house from it?"

"No," said Fernie. "Why should I?"

He looked even more puzzled but Pascoe could see from Alice's face that she was beginning to get the picture.

"Did you ever write a letter to Mrs Connon?"

"No. Never. What the hell's all this about?"

"Sergeant," said Alice, "had someone been phoning Mary? And writing to her?"

Pascoe nodded.

"Phoning her perhaps. Writing to her certainly. Did she ever say anything to you?"

Alice put her finger to her brow in the classic pose of thought. It did not look affected on her.

"No, nothing," she said. "But are you trying to say that Dave here might have been the man writing?"

Fernie's face lit up with amazement, followed by red indignation.

Could anyone really be that slow on the uptake? wondered Pascoe. Even complete innocence? Perhaps complete egotism could.

Fernie was on his feet now.

He's going to shout again, thought Pascoe.

"Now listen here, you, I don't know what you're up to, but I don't have to sit in my own house and…"

"Sit down and be quiet, Dave," said Alice.

He obeyed instantly.

"Thank you, Mrs Fernie," said Pascoe.

"Sergeant," she said. "These letters. Do you have them with you?"

"Not the originals," he said. "They've got to be carefully looked after and tested. Ink, paper, that kind of thing. Fingerprints. I'd like to take your husband's prints if I may. I've brought the stuff."

He knew that only a few not very helpful smudges had been found after Mary Connon's prints, taken from the dead woman's fingers at the post-mortem, had been eliminated. But it was always worth putting a scare into people.

Fernie looked as if he was ready to explode again, but Alice nodded and he subsided.

"I've got a photostat copy of one of them, though," he went on. "Why?"

"May I see it?" she asked.

He looked dubiously at her.

"I'm a big girl now," she said. "I stopped reading fairy tales years ago."

"Right," he said. "Here you are."

He handed it over. She read through it quickly once. Then more slowly a second time.

To his surprise a smile began to tug at her cheeks and when she finished the second reading she laughed aloud as though in relief.

"Is there something funny?" he asked politely.

"Not to you, Sergeant. But to me. It's the thought of my Dave writing this.

"I'm no psychiatrist but I'll tell you one thing. That letter was written by some poor, unhappy, twisted, frustrated man with a rather scanty knowledge of women. My Dave may be a bit short on mouth control, he may talk too much, he may not know how to make friends and influence people..."

"Alice!" interjected her husband, outraged. But she went on as if he wasn't there.

"...but whatever else he is, he's not frustrated. If he sees a woman undressing in a window, he'll stop and have a look. Who wouldn't? You would!"

Oh yes, thought Pascoe, yes, I would.

"Especially if she's like Mary Connon. She was a big woman.

But I'm no nymphet myself," she said proudly. "Anything she had, I had too, and it was thirteen years younger, and readily available to my husband as, when, and how he liked to use it. Any man can be unfaithful, but it takes special circumstances to write a letter like that."

She finished, slightly flushed, but looking him defiantly straight in the eye. Fernie was regarding her with some awe.

"You may be right, Mrs Fernie," said Pascoe. "Now, if I can just take your prints, Mr Fernie, I won't bother you any more."

"Do you think whoever wrote those letters killed poor Mary?" she asked as she saw, him out of the door.

"Perhaps," said Pascoe.

"You can cut Dave right out," she said with a smile. "He couldn't hurt anyone. He goes queasy at those doctor programmes on the telly."

Pascoe felt inclined to agree with her as he drove along Boundary Drive. Still, it was as well to keep an open mind. But all that had really happened that evening, he thought, was that he had developed something that was very nearly envy of Dave Fernie.

❀ ❀ ❀

Dalziel's superiors would not have been happy to see him. He had already been seen once that day. A progress report had been requested. He had asked if what was wanted was a detailed account of the whole course of the investigation so far or a brief statement of what was known.

The Assistant Chief Constable had mentally spoken a prayer for self-control and asked for a brief statement.

"Enquiries are proceeding, sir."

"Is that *all*?"

"I have sent in full and detailed reports of every aspect of the investigation, sir. Do you also require a digest of them?"

The Assistant Chief Constable had squirmed in his seat

with irritation but, like the good golfer he was, he kept his head quite still.

"No thank you, Superintendent. I would like to suggest, however, that you might tread a little more carefully in certain places."

"Like, sir?"

"Like the Rugby Club. If you go there as an investigating officer either do it more subtly or use the full paraphernalia of your office."

"You mean dress up, sir?"

"I mean act either as a policeman, or a member. Don't try to be both at once."

"But I am both at once, sir. All the time."

The Assistant Chief Constable sighed.

"There have been one or two…"

"Complaints?"

"No. Words, gently dropped. But from a height. How important is this Club in your investigations?"

Dalziel thought a little, his hand working inside the waist-line of his trousers.

If only he wouldn't *scratch*, thought his superior.

"Central," said Dalziel finally. "Will that be all?"

"For the moment. Keep me informed."

"As always, sir."

"And please. If you want to interview any more members of this Club, do it quietly, at the station preferably."

"Sir!"

And here he was not many hours later sitting with Marcus Felstead in a relatively quiet corner of the club-house, twisting the guts out of him, though Marcus did not know it yet.

"Not bad beer here, is it?"

Marcus sipped his pint as if to make sure.

"No, not bad."

"Many storage problems?"

"Not really," said Marcus, a little surprised. "It's all kegs nowa-days, so as long as you keep it fairly cool, it comes up smiling."

"How's the Club fixed for money now?"

Again surprise.

"I don't really know. Better ask Sid."

"No, I don't mean figures. I just wondered if there was any thought of getting a permanent steward?"

"Not that I know of. It seems an unnecessary expense. There's plenty of us to do the work."

Dalziel took a long pull at his pint and sighed happily.

"You do quite a lot, don't you, Marcus?"

"I do my share."

"No; more, I'm certain. Just about every Saturday night."

"Not every. But pretty frequently."

"You were on the night Mary Connon died."

That's a shot across your bows, my lad. Field that any way you like, thought Dalziel, observing his man closely.

Marcus's hand might have gripped the handle of his glass a little more tightly, but that was all.

"I think I was."

Now a long pause. Let him wonder if it was just a casual remark. Let him try to organize his defences. Then let him relax.

"Hello, Willie!"

He waved his glass casually at Noolan, who smiled and waved back as he went to join a small group standing by the bar.

"Yes," he said, returning his attention to Marcus. "Yes. You were here all that night, weren't you?"

"I don't recall," said Marcus, definitely a little ill at ease now.

"Oh, you were. We checked. All night. Except for the two hours when you went out and drove round to Boundary Drive."

Marcus went white. He pushed the beer away from him with his rather small girlish hand.

"Don't be stupid," he said. "I never went anywhere near Boundary Drive."

Dalziel laughed in a friendly fashion.

"Come off it, Marcus," he said. "Your car was seen. What's the matter? It's no crime, is it? That's what they usually say to me."

"I never went near Boundary Drive," repeated Marcus, a little recovered now. "You must be mistaken. It can't have been my car."

"No? Well, there's a simple way to settle this, seeing as you're so worried."

"What's that?"

Dalziel leaned across the table, pushing Marcus's glass back at him.

"Tell us where you really were, then."

"Why the hell should I?"

Oh dear, thought Dalziel resignedly. He's going to start shouting. Time for us to go.

"Listen, Marcus, my lad," he whispered confidentially. "There's obviously some kind of misunderstanding here. We can't discuss it properly here in the Club. Why don't we take a drive down to the station to talk things out? Less embarrassing than shouting at each other in front of all these people."

He waved his hand airily around, realizing as he did so that all these people now included Connon.

Marcus saw him too and nodded his head.

Connon didn't acknowledge the greeting but just continued to stare at them.

"Coming?" said Dalziel, smiling still for the benefit of the onlookers, but infusing a new grimness into his voice.

"For God's sake, Superintendent, sit down. Look, if it means that much to you where I was…"

"Oh, it does, it does," said Dalziel.

Marcus stared into his beer broodingly for a long minute.

What's he hatching? wondered Dalziel. Have I hit the jackpot? Jesus, that'd be a laugh, Connon's best mate bashing his wife's head in.

But there was still a large doubt sitting hugely at the back of his mind. What possible motive could this round, friendly, most amiable of men have for murder? It was no use going by appearances, but a man who reminded him so strongly of Winnie the Pooh…

Marcus seemed to have made up his mind.

"Come on," said Dalziel. "It's either the truth or a very complicated lie."

"It's the truth," said Marcus. "But first, I must have your assurance that this is in the most absolute confidence."

"As long as it has no bearing on the case."

"It hasn't."

"Then you have my word."

The fingers he was scratching under his arm with were crossed. Dalziel preserved many of his old childhood superstitions.

"Well, look." He was almost whispering and Dalziel had to lean even further forward to catch the words.

"Hello, Marcus, boy!"

Evans's heavy hand smacked down on the small man's shoulder. Marcus went white and jerked round sharply to look at the figure behind him. Even Dalziel, who was facing him, had not noticed his arrival, so intent had he been on catching Marcus's words.

"Give you a fright, did I? What're you two hatching anyway? You've got to be careful who you drink with these days, Marcus. Might lose your good name."

"Evening, Arthur," said Dalziel as unwelcoming as he could be in the limits of politeness. "Gwen not with you?"

That should get rid of him, he thought with malice. He won't fancy a needling match on these terms.

But Evans merely grinned and helped himself to a stool from under a neighbouring table.

"She's in the loo making herself lovely for you, Bruiser. Marcus, boy, it's you I wanted to see. Listen, I'm having a hell of a job holding this team together. You know how important it is, a club's known by the quality of its fourth side. Now you drop out, one of the regulars. It's a big hole to fill. You should have seen us last Saturday. Walking bloody wounded! Couldn't you hang on till the end of the season?"

He's not listening to you, Arthur, thought Dalziel. He

was going to tell me something, now he's having another little think. He's very worried. That's how I like them, worried. You'll have to go, Arthur. If you won't take a hint, I'll put it to you in terms even a thick-skinned Welshman can understand.

But before Dalziel could begin his dismissal operation, Marcus forestalled him.

"My round, I think," he said. "Arthur, will you have one? A pint? Right."

He swept Dalziel's glass from under his nose and set off to the bar at the quick march. Dalziel watched him go in amused exasperation. But it was merely a postponement.

"Here, Arthur," he said. "When Marcus comes back, piss off for a bit, will you? We're having a bit of a serious talk."

"Are you now? It can't be more serious than the Fourths, can it? After all, this is a rugby club."

Oh, they're all getting in on the act, are they? thought Dalziel. All dropping their little words in the direction of my bosses. But yours don't come from very on high, Arthur.

"In any case," said Evans, "what makes you think he's coming back? He seems to have bloody well disappeared altogether. And his round too!"

Dalziel looked sharply round at the bar. Noolan and his group were still there. Connon was standing a little apart from them, still looking across at the superintendent's table.

But of Marcus Felstead there was no sign.

❀ ❀ ❀

Pascoe had pulled into the Club car park close behind the Evanses' car. He had not got out immediately, but sat and watched the broad Welshman and his wife pick their way carefully over the already frosted surface towards the club-house.

They looked just like any other couple, he reflected. Comfortable. Affectionate. Evans had taken Gwen's arm to help her circumnavigate a frozen puddle. She said something to him and he seemed to laugh. Then they disappeared through the door.

Perhaps it was all a mistake, thought Pascoe. Perhaps it was just in Evans's mind, this other man. It would be impossible to live with a woman like Gwen and not know that other men envied you, would like to fish in your pond. And a temperament a lot less volatile than Arthur's could easily come to believe this was exactly what was happening.

What would it prove anyway if it turned out that there was a man and that man was Connon? A motive, he had said earlier to Dalziel. It would prove a motive. Or rather it would give a possible base for the possible erection of two or three possible motives. Lots of possibles. No probables. Probables versus possibles. And a young man, certain of his own strength and skill, running with balanced ease round all opposition as he made for the line.

I'm beginning to think in their imagery, he admonished himself, and lit a cigarette, somehow reluctant to leave his car and go in search of Dalziel. Or perhaps it was because Sheila Lennox might be there. He had had to stand her up on their second date. Nothing dramatically urgent to season an apology with; no startling new development, breathtaking chase, or a second murder. Just pressure of paper and organizational routine.

Her voice on the phone had been cold. His suggestion of another meeting ignored. Perhaps it was for the best. She was only a child. Nearly nineteen. That meant eighteen. And he was nearly twenty-nine. That meant thirty. But they grew up early these days. Or at least they seemed to. She had promised a wealth of experience on their exploratory first date. But it had been mostly verbal. What lay behind it he would probably never know.

He opened the car door and dropped his cigarette end on to the concreted surface where it glowed with vulgar ruddiness on the silver sharpness of the frost till he ground it under his foot as he stepped out.

Then, half in, half out of the car, he suddenly became very still.

The club-house door had opened and a man came carefully out. He was unrecognizable at this distance, but the woman who followed him a moment later only had to take a couple of steps for Pascoe to know that this was Gwen Evans again. She had taken her coat off. He could see her bare arms gleam whitely for a moment as she too disappeared into the shadow down the side of the building.

Pascoe watched them out of sight. Then he slipped his hand into the glove compartment of his car till his finger rested on the heavy rubber casing of a torch. With this in hand and keeping low, he now stepped out of the car and closed the door quietly behind him, certain he was unobserved. He had long ago severed the connection between the door and the interior courtesy light. Three hours' extremely cold and tedious observation had been ruined by the sudden flash of this light several years earlier. Pascoe was a man who learned from his mistakes.

Silently he moved across to the club-house and made his way along the side wall. At first in the shadow of the wall it seemed pitch black, but his eyes rapidly adjusted to the light, or lack of it.

There was no one there.

He moved swiftly down the line of the wall, slowing as he neared its end. It was lighter here. A faint glow came through an opaque window which must belong to one of the cloakrooms.

He stopped beneath it. From round the corner came voices.

First Gwen's. Anxious. Tense. An edge of panic.

"Darling, darling. What're we to do? What's going to happen?"

Then a man's. Reassuring, but also anxious beneath. And familiar.

"It'll be all right, Gwen. I'll have to tell him. He'll want to talk to you. But we can still keep it quiet."

"Quiet!" Almost a sob now. "Quiet! I'm tired of it all.

I'm tired of being quiet. I can't see where it's leading. I can't, I can't!"

The voices lowered to an indistinguishable mixture of near-sobbing and reassuring murmurs.

Pascoe took another step forward.

And trod on something.

A plastic coated cardboard cup, his trained ear told him. Or an empty ice-cream carton.

It cracked like a beechwood fire.

The talking stopped.

Oh dear, thought Pascoe. Well, here we go.

He switched on his torch and stepped round the corner. They were close in each other's arms and the beam of the torch was enough to catch them both.

"Good evening, Mrs Evans," he said apologetically, trying to keep the note of astonishment out of his voice. "And good evening to you too, Mr Felstead. You'll catch your deaths out here if you're not careful."

❀ ❀ ❀

"I thought he'd made a bolt for it," said Dalziel. "He looked bloody scared."

"I daresay he was," grinned Pascoe. "I mean, imagine you are about to confess you're knocking off Arthur Evans's wife and suddenly his great hand comes down on your shoulder. Anyone'd be scared. On the other hand he carried it off well. When he came back in, I mean. Did Evans notice anything?"

Dalziel nodded his great bull's head.

"Oh yes. He noticed something. I mean, I moved quite quickly when I saw Felstead had gone. But Connon stopped me, said Marcus had asked him to order while he went to the bog, and thrust a pint into my hand. You can't give pursuit under those conditions. Anyway, by the time he came back, Arthur was getting too impatient for his wife to put in an appearance to pay much attention to anyone else."

"I told her to go into the other room and say she thought he was going to be in there. Not that I needed to coach her, she must have had plenty of practice. But what a turn up, eh?"

"You've never said a truer word, Sergeant. She confirmed everything?"

"Oh yes. They were at it in the house, then in Felstead's car on the way to the Club, all the time he was away from the bar. The way they were hanging on to each other when I caught them, it's very easy to believe."

Easy to believe? Dalziel asked himself, thinking of Marcus Felstead and trying to revise his mental picture of him. The physical reality couldn't be changed! Five feet four or five at the most, looking almost as round as he was high, with a balding pate that rose like a monk's tonsure through an unruly and still retreating fringe.

Then he thought of Gwen Evans. He had always felt he was a bit of an expert on Gwen Evans. He had spent many beery hours just assessing the value of all visible assets, and visualizing the invisible.

That she should spare a first glance, let alone a second, on this man was almost incredible.

But it all fitted. It had been Marcus who turned up at the Evans house on Saturday afternoon when Pascoe was there. He'd played it very cool, they both had. He could imagine the facial contortions, the mouthed warnings, at the front door.

It had also been Marcus who had phoned Connon with the news of Arthur's visit to the police station. And he, of course, had had it direct from Gwen the minute Arthur left the house.

"We were both very worried," Marcus had said. "We've got a very great respect for Arthur."

Dalziel had laughed inwardly when he heard that. Tell that to him when the Celtic red mist's before his eyes and he's kicking your head in in a jealous rage, he thought.

But he hadn't spoken, just gone on listening.

Marcus told everything, reluctantly at first, but more freely after a few minutes. Then when Evans went in to a selection committee meeting, the reason for Connon's presence that night, Dalziel had had a long talk with Gwen.

They were obviously telling the truth about themselves. Too many details fitted. The affair had been going on for nearly two years.

"I bet he's been dying for an audience," Dalziel said to Pascoe. "It must be hell having a woman like Gwen and not to be able to strut around in public possession. Mark you, it might have worked both ways. Perhaps it was the secrecy that made Marcus acceptable to Gwen, eh? Christ, Arthur was no oil-painting, but he was like the Winged Victory compared with *him*!"

And where does that place you in the beauty stakes? thought Pascoe. But what's it matter? Hell, in one day I've been jealous of a sour-faced moron like Dave Fernie and of a little tub of lard like Marcus Felstead!

Dalziel shook his head finally in dismissive amazement at the inscrutability of woman.

"It can't be true," he said. "It's a bloody lie all of it. Only, Marcus wouldn't dare to tell a lie like that unless it was true."

"Irish," said Pascoe.

"You know what I mean," said Dalziel.

"More important," said Pascoe, "is, where does it leave us? Does it put us any further forward?"

"It teaches us humility," said Dalziel pompously. "No other revelation in this case can possibly surprise us after this."

"Not even if it turns out to be an intruder?" asked Pascoe.

"Not even if your intruder turns out to be Jack the Ripper. I'm off to my bed now. I might even go to church in the morning. Good night."

He lumbered away shaking his head. Pascoe watched him go with a feeling he was disgusted to find almost resembled affection.

But as he climbed into his own bed in his little two-roomed flat half a mile from the police station his mind was occupied still with the case. He wished he had one of those "feelings" which Dalziel had so efficiently mocked. But he hadn't.

All he had was the certainty that whatever steps had been taken that day had led them in one direction only.

Backwards.

He switched off the light and fell into an uneasy sleep troubled by dreams in which Gwen Evans, Sheila Lennox and Jenny Connon blended and merged into one.

Chapter Seven

There were three days left till Christmas. The weather was dark, misty. The sky was low and constantly shifting as different layers of grey and black cloud were dragged around by gusty winds. Guiding stars were rarely seen. In any case, no one had much time to look.

The greatest money-spending competition on earth was coming to its climax. The streets were thronged all day with compulsive shoppers, intermittently spattered with hard-driven rain and tinted by the glow of festive lighting. And a constant background to everything was the music: carols, pop, sentimental, classical; now near, now far; on tape, on record, and occasionally even issuing from a real, live, human throat.

It was a strange unsettling atmosphere. No one could remain unaffected by it.

Some were hardened by it.

"I haven't given or received a Christmas present for more than a dozen years," said Dalziel. "Bloody idiots."

Some were softened.

Should I have tried to go home this year? wondered Pascoe guiltily.

Home meant a suburban semi, two hundred miles away, grossly overcrowded for the holiday by his grandmother, his two elder sisters, their unsympathetic husbands and their four even more unsympathetic children, in addition to the normal complement of his parents.

He hadn't spent a Christmas there for three years. It was nearly time to try it again.

But not this year.

Some were worried by it.

"He's looking worse than he did when it all happened," said Jenny. "Perhaps it's Christmas. I think they always made a special effort at Christmas. For my sake as well, I suppose. He looks awful."

"Is he seeing the doctor?" asked Antony.

"No. But I'm going to send for him. He had that knock on his head, I don't think he's recovered from that yet."

"No," said Antony staring out of the window into the front garden.

Some were made hopeful by it.

"Look, girl," said Arthur Evans. "I know we've had some bad times recently and a lot of it's been my fault. But let's make an effort, shall we? It's Christmas, eh? Let's see what we can make of ourselves, eh?"

"Yes," said Gwen. But her eyes did not shift from the book she was looking at.

And the atmosphere of hectic unreality made some resolute. Marcus Felstead whistled a Christmas medley to himself as he carefully packed his suitcase.

But in a house in the heart of the Woodfield Estate there was no whistling as a man searched the streets for the fourth time for his child, then finally, belatedly, picked up a telephone and rang the police.

❀ ❀ ❀

"It's happened," said Dalziel.

"What?" said Pascoe, standing at the threshold of the room.

"Mickey Annan. Aged eight. One hundred and three, Scaur Terrace, Woodfield. Didn't get home from school last night. They broke up yesterday, had a bit of a party. It's the usual story. His parents thought he'd gone to a friend's house in the next street. He usually does on that night. But this time it was different, they were all going off for Christmas as soon as their kid arrived. So Mickey wasn't asked. So he wasn't missed till nearly ten."

Pascoe raised his eyebrows. "That's late."

"They breed 'em hard in Woodfield. Anyway, they always kid themselves. Never admit that anything can be wrong until they've got to."

"What's happening now?"

"The usual. One of his mates thinks he said he might go up to the Common. Someone had told him there might be some snow there. He was mad keen on snow."

"Oh, Christ."

The Common was the local term used to describe an area of several acres on the western boundary of the Woodfield Estate. It was unfit even for grazing purposes and its main function in human terms was that its near edges provided a useful if unofficial dumping ground for anything and everything. The Common contained a disused quarry, two ponds and a steep-sided stream, all of which had been fenced off after years of complaint. But not even a full-time repair unit could keep up with the constant breaching of the fencing.

"We've got a full-scale search going on now. County are standing by with frogmen."

"House-to-house?"

"No point yet. We're stretched as it is talking to every kid in the school now that they're on holiday."

"He might have just taken a walk and got lost," said Pascoe without conviction. "Fell asleep behind a wall or in a shed."

"He should have woken up by now."

"What would you like me to do?"

"Look after the walking boys. It'll take them all morning to cover the kids from the school. By then if nothing's come out of the search, it'll be time to start asking everyone questions."

"Anyone in particular? Streets, I mean?"

Dalziel looked surprised.

"Why, you'll start by asking everyone on the Woodfield Estate, and if we still haven't found him, we'll work our way through the rest of town. There's only eighty-five thousand of them."

"Thanks," said Pascoe.

"Think yourself lucky," replied Dalziel, shaking a newspaper on his desk. "At least they had the plane crash in North Africa this year."

Funny man, thought Pascoe as he went swiftly and efficiently to work. Is it just a cover like we all put up? Or does he really not feel these things? What a man to spend Christmas with! I'd be better off at home with all those kids!

By midday the Common had been turned over with meticulous care, the pools dragged and the frogmen sent down. As far as Mickey Annan was concerned, the result was absolutely negative. But lots of other things were brought up. A list was always made on these occasions and Pascoe glanced quickly down it. A small part of his mind was still on the unidentified weapon in the Connon case. But there was nothing here which rang a bell. The usual household expendables, a suitcase containing some fairly valuable pieces of pewter (dumped by mistake? or stolen and dumped in fear?) and, an item which made Pascoe whistle slightly, two guns. But he had no time for idle speculation. A large-scale map of the Woodfield Estate lay before him. He still had to complete his detectives' schedules.

It was one-thirty before he had any lunch. He ate it alone in the police canteen.

Mickey Annan now went to the back of his mind. He had taken part in the search that morning for a while, talked to some of the children from the school, as well as helping to organize the house-to-house. But he knew it was a routine, automatic business, none the less essential for all that, and nine times out of ten effective. Mickey Annan would probably be found very soon. It was after the finding that the real work began, and Pascoe was not a man given to anticipating events. Except in the line of business.

His thoughts drifted back to the Connons. The missing boy wasn't really interfering with the progress of the Connon case, because the progress only existed in theory. Investigations were still proceeding, but unless Dalziel had some private little line well hidden from everyone else, the phrase was as empty as it sounded.

The only thing that was any clearer to him now than it had been when he started was his picture of the murdered woman. It wasn't a very complete one. She seemed to have been a reasonable kind of mother to Jenny; at least she hadn't stimulated any of the strong resentments which seemed to lie uneasily dormant in most daughters, especially those very fond of their fathers. And she seemed to have made Connon a bearable kind of wife. But she had told him his daughter had been fathered by another man and she had tried to separate him from his main interest in life, the Club. Add to this that she was a vain woman with a streak of snobbery, but one who had made a friend of Alice Fernie (who herself was unlikely to pick her friends haphazardly); that she was a man-hunting, high-life-loving girl who had shown no desire to keep up her connection with her old stamping-grounds; and finally, that she apparently received obscene letters with equanimity, merely folding them up and putting them away like love-letters sentimentally preserved; add all these things together and you had a woman who was as incomprehensible as women traditionally are.

Over his coffee, Pascoe toyed with permutations of possibilities in which Felstead or Evans had written the letter (*all* the letters?), in which Mary Connon had a lover (someone at the Club? Noolan? Jesus! Or what about Bruiser Dalziel? Joke); in which Connon swung a metal bar held like a spear into his wife's forehead (jealous rage? didn't fit. Careful plan? but was he so cold-blooded a man as *that*?).

He'd been along all these paths before. They led nowhere yet, except to fantasy in which Gwen Evans held a crow-bar to Mary's head and Alice Fernie struck it home with a sledge-hammer while Mary, unheeding, watched the television.

He sighed and returned mentally to the canteen. There was other work to be done. Connon would have to wait. Mary was dead. There was still the faintest of chances that Mickey Annan might still be among the living.

❈ ❈ ❈

Connon was angry when the doctor arrived, but even in anger he didn't lose the moderation of speech or manner which Antony now recognized as his main characteristic.

"I didn't send for you, Doctor," he said.

"Just a checking-up call," replied McManus cheerily. "Just because you don't send for me doesn't mean you don't need me any more."

"I'm fine," said Connon. "You've had a wasted journey."

"It's a good way to waste it, then. But I'll be the judge of how fine you are. You don't look so hot to me."

Connon did not look well. He seemed to be visibly losing weight. His cheek-bones were prominent and the paleness of the skin stretched over them was accentuated by the darkness which ran like a stain round his eyes.

"Come along, then, and let's take a look at you," said McManus.

Connon had enough of himself left to give Jenny a sardon-ically accusing glance as he left the room with the doctor.

"He knows it was you," said Antony.

"That doesn't matter. As long as Doctor Mac can do something for him."

"I'm sure he can," said Antony cheerfully. "He'll come up with some witches' brew."

But he could not feel so certain inside that Connon's malady would respond to physical treatment.

"Do you think the police have given up?" asked Jenny.

"I don't know. Do you want them to?"

"I'm not sure. I don't much care now whether they catch someone or not. But I'd just like everyone to know for Daddy's sake that he had nothing to do with it. Do you think they took any notice of what you said about the telephone-box?"

"They must have done. There's a new directory there now. I had a look. But I don't think my amorous rival Pascoe was too delighted to receive advice and assistance from me. As far as the police are concerned I suspect there's a very thin line between public support and amateur interference."

"As if you would interfere in what wasn't your business!" said Jenny with mock indignation.

"I see you've come to know me well," responded Antony. "Come and sit on my knee."

His hand stroked her leg as he kissed her.

I've been here before, thought Jenny. But she was very glad to be there again.

"Talking of interference," said Antony a little while later, removing his lips from the side of her neck.

"Don't be disgusting," she said.

"I think I shall interfere once more. There's something else which keeps on coming back to me which they might possibly be interested in."

Jenny sat upright. "What's that, Sherlock?"

But they heard a footstep on the stairs and Jenny rose swiftly, smoothing down her dress.

The door opened and McManus came in.

"How is he, Doctor?" asked Jenny anxiously.

The old man carefully closed the door behind him. "He's just putting his shirt on. He'll be down in a minute."

He looked enquiringly at Antony.

"It's OK, Doctor," said Jenny. "How is he?"

"Well, physically there's nothing I can put my finger on. He complains of being listless, loss of appetite, that kind of thing. But this we might expect. Also his head still pains him from time to time where he got that knock. But I think this is like his other symptoms. There's nothing wrong. It's purely nervous in origin."

"But he seems to be getting worse, not better," protested Jenny. Antony put his arm comfortingly round her waist.

"Yes. That's true. It's a delayed reaction, not uncommon. A kind of shock. He's been living on his reserves of ner-vous energy for the past couple of weeks. It can't go on for ever."

He struggled into his overcoat which Antony brought him from the hall.

"But don't worry. I've been his doctor for many years, nearly all his life, I suppose. I've seen him like this before, before you were born, when he cracked his ankle the week before the final trial. He went as thin as a rake, and deathly pale then for a couple of weeks. You'd have thought the end had come. But it hadn't. He got back to normal in no time. No, no, it hadn't. It hadn't."

He shook his head and laughed softly to himself at the memory.

Hadn't it? wondered Antony. And in what way could the end come twice?

"Well, I suppose you've told them three times as much as you've told me," said Connon from the door. "I long ago noted that to a doctor keeping confidences means telling your patient nothing and his relatives everything. You should all be struck off."

McManus laughed as he picked up his bag.

"Goodbye, Jenny; and you, young man. I'll call in again, Connie, if you don't call to see me. Take your medicine now and stop worrying your friends."

They watched him get into his car, then returned to the lounge.

"Well," said Jenny, "time for lunch, I think. Antony, make yourself useful for once, love. You'll find a table-cloth in the top drawer of the sideboard. Set the table, if it's not beneath your dignity."

She went out into the kitchen. Antony grinned in resignation at Connon and began searching for the table-cloth.

"It's good of you to stay on with us, Antony," said Connon. "I hope your parents are not too disappointed."

"It would be foolishly modest of me to say they will not be disappointed at all," said Antony, "but they are both very understanding. I hope to introduce Jenny to them very soon, when I think they'll be more understanding still."

"Oh," said Connon. "Do I detect a note of serious intent creeping in?"

Antony pulled out a table-cloth and shook it open with a fine flourish like a bull-fighter showing his cape. Something fluttered to the floor.

"I think it highly probable," he said seriously, "that I shall marry Jenny eventually, with, of course, her consent and your permission."

He bent down to pick up the photograph which was what had fallen.

"In that case," said Connon with equal seriousness, "we must take an early opportunity of reviewing your prospects."

Antony didn't reply. He was looking closely at the picture in his hand. For one brief moment he had thought it was Jenny, absurdly garbed and with a ridiculously short haircut. Then he realized that the only thing of Jenny's which was there was the familiar, wide, all-illuminating grin on the face of the young man in muddy rugby kit who was walking alone in the picture.

Connon took the photograph from him.

"That's the only picture of me playing rugby I ever kept," he said.

"Why this one?" asked Antony.

Connon stared down at the young man in the picture as if he was looking at a stranger and trying to analyse what made him seem vaguely familiar.

"It was the first time I played for the County. I was nineteen. Still in the Army, on a weekend pass. But nearly finished. There was a five-yard scrum. I was standing square over our own line ready for the pass back and the kick to touch. The pass came, I had plenty of time and shaped to kick to the near touch-line. Then I changed my mind. All their backs were coming up like the clappers. So I chipped it into a little space over the scrum, ran round, picked it up and went up the middle of the field. I don't recall beating the full-back. They told me after I ran through him as if he wasn't there. All I could see was the posts and the exact spot centrally between them where I was going to touch down. Nothing else was real till I grounded the ball. Then I started walking back up the field. No one runs up and kisses you in a rugby match. In those days it was considered bad form even to slap you on the back. You just walked back to your position trying to look unconcerned and got your clap from the crowd. I could feel this smile on my face, feel it spreading out to a grin. The crowd all roared like mad. It was the biggest crowd I'd ever played in front of. I bent my head a bit, look, you can see on the picture, but I couldn't stop grinning. It was a grin of pure happiness. It felt as if it was fixed on my face for ever. I think I believed it was."

He stopped talking. Antony for once was stuck for words. He's in the past, he thought, the poor devil's anchored there beyond hope of release. What a state to get into.

A wave of sympathy swept over him, some of which must have shown on his face, for Connon now smiled at him ironically.

"I think you may be misunderstanding me, Antony," he said. "I don't live down memory lane. What this photograph says to me is not that happiness is gone for ever, but that it's repeatable. I've often felt like this since, mostly on occasions connected with Jenny. The picture reminds me of what's possible again, that's all, not of what's gone for ever."

"I'm sorry," said Antony, rather shame-faced. "I didn't mean to…you're very lucky. I'll go and set the table."

He left the room with the cloth cast loosely over his shoulder like the end of a toga.

It suits him, thought Connon. Then he returned his attention to the photograph.

Repeatable? he asked himself. I wonder. Will it ever be possible again?

From the kitchen Jenny's portable radio began to play a selection of brass-band music. This faded almost at once, but then returned louder than before as though the set had been re-tuned.

Connon listened, then a smile moved slowly across his face.

I believe she's leaving it on for me.

❀ ❀ ❀

It was five o'clock and dark and cold and wet. The shops were still crowded. Inside them it was bright and warm. Too warm. The crowds who had jostled close to each other all day, shoulder to ruthless shoulder, thigh to strange thigh, had left their unexpungeable smell. Sweat, scent, tobacco and damp clothing all mistily merged into an observable haze. The best shop-assistants were growing irritable, the worst had long been downright rude. But the artefacts of good cheer had not yet lost their power, the music was as merry as ever, the colours as gay, and nearly everyone was going home.

The festive spirit stalked abroad, reaching out to seize backsliders.

Mickey Annan had still not been found.

And Jacko Roberts was talking on the telephone to Dalziel.

"What the hell do you want, Jacko? I'm busy."

"I wish I was. This weather's no good for my business."

"It doesn't help mine much either. Come on now. Is this social? If it is, piss off. If not, get your finger out."

One day, Jacko promised himself, one day I'll tap him on the head and wall him up in a brick kiln.

It was his perennial New Year resolution.

"A bit of both," he said. "I'm having a little party for a few select friends, tomorrow night. Christmas Eve. I'd like you to come."

Dalziel hesitated. Jacko Roberts rarely entertained but

196 A CLUBBABLE WOMAN

when he did, it was usually lavishly. He regarded it as an investment. Dalziel didn't mind being invested in as long as it was done the right way. A couple of years earlier, Jacko's investment had consisted of the introduction of a group of very willing young ladies to his previously well liquored stag party of civic and other dignitaries.

Dalziel had been sober enough to leave early. He had noticed that the Roberts Building Company got a large share of municipal contracts the following year and had had words with Jacko.

Now he wondered if he had forgotten.

"Don't worry yourself," snarled his prospective host. "It's all respectable. They'll all be there, from Noolan to the Town Clerk. With their wives."

"What time?"

"Any time after eight."

"I can't promise. I'll try to make it."

"Oh, and Bruiser. As you're short of a partner, why not bring that nice sergeant along? Whatsisname?"

"Watch it, Jacko," said Dalziel softly. "There's a notice on my overcoat which says, this is where Christmas stops."

"All right. But I meant it. Ask him anyway. It pleases these old cows to have a virile young man about the place."

Dalziel grunted and thought that Jacko must be doing well at the moment to be in, for him, so light-hearted a mood. He made a mental note to check on what the builder had been up to.

"Right," he said. "You said there was some business. Or is that what we've just been talking about?"

"That's an odd thing to say, super. No, but are you still interested in this Connon business or is it all neatly tied up?"

"Don't play clever buggers with me, Jacko. What have you got? Anything or nothing?"

"I don't know. It's just that Mary Connon and Arthur Evans were seen in close confabulation over a drink the Friday before she died."

Dalziel digested the information for a moment.

"Where?" he asked.

"The Bull, on the coast road."

"Anything else on a connection between them?"

"Not that I've heard."

"It's probably nothing. That all?"

"Unless you're going to thank me."

Dalziel put the phone down hard and sat looking at it. Then he picked up the internal phone and pressed a button.

"Sergeant Pascoe here."

"Dalziel. Busy?"

"Well yes. I've just got in."

"Had your tea?"

"Not yet. I was just going to…"

"Then you can't be all that busy. Step along here for a minute, will you. Bring your coat. I'll probably want you to go out."

Pascoe sighed as he took his sodden riding mac off the radiator. A minute earlier he had been feeling sorry for the men who were still out on house-to-house questioning.

Now he began to wonder if his sympathy was misplaced.

Back in Dalziel's office the phone rang again. He picked it up crossly, but after listening for a few moments, his expression softened and he nodded twice.

"Yes, yes. That's good. I'm glad, very very glad."

Pascoe was surprised to find him looking almost happy when he came through the door.

❋ ❋ ❋

"Jesus H. Christ," muttered Detective-Constable Edwards. It was his private theory that Woodfield Council estate had been built as a series of experiments in wind-tunnelling. Behind him the door of the house whose occupant he had just been interviewing had been closed with considerable firmness. Some attempt had been made to turn the area immediately in front of the door into a rose-arbour by the erection of a bit of trellis work at right angles to the wall, and he crouched behind the little protection this afforded. The wind came howling down the street full of rain and incipient snow. A shoot of the rambler clinging precariously to the trellis whipped round and slashed against his face.

"Jesus," he repeated and turned up his collar and went up the path. As he closed the gate he saw the curtain drop into position in the front window.

"All right. I'm off the premises," he said aloud. What a thing it was to be loved. Not that we deserve it anyway. Bloody half-wits. God, to think how chuffed I was to get out of uniform. Detective! All I've done since seems to be walk around and knock on doors.

First Connon. Now this. Poor little bugger. I wonder where he is?

He turned his mind away from the private conviction that little Mickey Annan was somewhere lying dead; deep beneath bracken on the moors; under an old sack in some outhouse; it didn't matter where. His job at the moment was to ask questions.

Someone must have seen the boy that night.

His heart sank when he saw where his questionings would take him next. It was a little cul-de-sac of some two dozen semi-detached bungalows. Pensioners. Old women. Mostly alone, often lonely. Welcoming, garrulous. He would be pressed to cups of tea, cocoa, Bovril, Horlicks. He tried to harden his heart in advance, but knew it was just a front.

I'm your friendly village-bobby-type, he thought, not your hard-as-nails CID boy. This is going to take hours.

"Mrs Williams? Mrs Ivy Williams?" he said to the large heavily-made-up woman who answered his ring.

"No, that's my mam. What are you after, then?"

"I'm from the police. We're checking on the movements of people in this area last night, Mrs..."

"My name's Girton. Is it about that lad then what's missing? Well, mam can't help you. Never gets out at night, do you, mam?"

An elderly woman had appeared out of the kitchen which

Edwards could see through the half-opened door at the end of the small hallway.

"What's that? What's up?"

"It's a policeman, mam. You weren't out last night, were you, mam?"

"No, I wasn't. Where'd I go?"

"That's right," said Mrs Girton to Edwards. "Where'd she go?"

"Well, thank you. You weren't here yourself last night, were you?"

"No, not me. Mondays and Thursdays are my regular nights. Sorry."

"Will you have a cup of tea, eh?" Mrs Williams was already turning into the kitchen. Her daughter caught the look on Edwards's face and grinned sympathetically.

"Don't be daft, mam. He's got a lot of work to do, haven't you? Got to visit everyone in the road?"

"That's right. Thanks all the same. Good night."

He turned to go.

"Everyone in the road, eh?" shrilled the old woman. "Well, make sure you talk to Mrs Grogan next door, then. She knows something, eh? She'll be able to tell you something if you're from the police."

She disappeared back into the kitchen. Edwards raised his eyebrows quizzically at Mrs Girton, who shrugged.

"You never know. She's getting on now, but she takes good notice of whatever anyone says. I wouldn't pay too much heed myself, though."

"Well, thanks anyway. Good night."

"Good night."

It was now raining in earnest. He glanced at his sodden list under the street-lamp. Mrs Kathleen Grogan, No. 2.

There was a sharp double blast from a horn. Turning, he saw at the end of the cul-de-sac a police-car. He went towards it.

"Hello, Brian," said the uniformed constable cheerily. "Enjoying yourself?"

"Great. What are you doing here?"

"They've found him. Mickey Annan."

Edwards nodded and said, more as assertion than question, "Dead?"

"No. Alive and well. We've come to tell you to jack it in. Hop in and we'll give you a lift back."

Edwards was half into the back seat before he remembered Mrs Grogan.

He hesitated.

"Come on, then."

"Look, John. Could you hang on just a couple of minutes? There's just one more call I'd like to make."

"What're you on about? Playing detectives? I told you, the house-to-house is off..."

"Yes but..."

"Sorry, Brian. I've got to get on. There's at least two other poor sods trudging around in the wet when they could be clocking off and going home. Now hop in and let's go."

Edwards got back out of the car.

"OK, John. You shove off. I'll make my own way back."

"Have it your own way. But you're a silly bugger. Cheers."

Yes, I'm a silly bugger. The silly bugger to end all silly buggers.

"Bugger!" he said aloud as he watched the car's tail-lights disappear into the driving rain. "I must be mad."

He made his way back along the pavement and turned up the narrow path.

❀ ❀ ❀

Pascoe had sat in silence as his superior swiftly and effi-ciently did his part in calling off the search for Mickey Annan. This was the first rule when an operation was over. Get your men back. There were too many working hours for too few police as it was without letting any be wasted unnecessarily.

Finally Dalziel was done.

"What happened?" Pascoe had asked.

"He was out looking for Jesus."

"What?"

"It's these bloody schools. When I was a kid it was two-times tables and the sharp edge of a ruler along your arse if you didn't know them. Now it's all stimulating the imagination. Christ! Show me a kid who ever needed his imagination stimulated! Anyway, little Mickey Annan was a wise man in the school Nativity play and got very interested in guiding stars in the East, and all. Especially when his teacher explained that Jesus was born again for everyone every Christmas and Bethlehem was never far away. How many bloody miles to Bethlehem! His favourite poem! Anyway, to Mickey the East was where his Uncle Dick and Aunt Mavis live at High Burnton out towards the coast."

"How did he get there? He did get there, I take it?"

"Oh yes. Sat on a bus. Told the woman he was sharing a seat with that he'd lost his money. He reckons wise men don't need to bother much with the truth as far as ordinary mortals are concerned. Anyway his uncle had gone off for Christmas with his family, the house was empty. He got in through a half-closed larder window. Very small evidently. Then he bedded down."

"But what's he been doing today, then?"

Dalziel had looked pityingly at his sergeant.

"Wise men don't travel by day," he said. "You can't see any stars by day. You've got to wait till it's night."

"Oh? I suppose you would, really."

"Anyway the woman in the bus saw his picture in this evening's paper, told the local bobby and gave him the boy's uncle's address which the lad had passed on to her the previous evening. He was very chatty, evidently, not a care in the world when she was with him. She never associated him with the missing lad till she saw the picture. Off they went to Uncle Dick's just in time to meet Belshazzar taking off in search of a clear patch of sky. Kids! I hope his father whacks him till he's a confirmed atheist."

Pascoe was still grinning at the story as he rang the doorbell of Arthur Evans's house. There were lights on all over the house but no one seemed in a hurry to answer the door. He hoped it would be Gwen Evans who came, though his business was with her husband. Analysing his emotions, he came to the conclusion that Gwen's affair with Marcus, far from making her more inaccessible, had merely confirmed her accessibility.

He rang the bell once more.

Almost instantly this time the door was flung open. Arthur Evans stood there. He looked distraught, his tie was pulled down and his collar open, his hair was ruffled, but even if he had been neatly dressed and groomed, the bright staring eyes and hectic cheeks would have warned Pascoe that something was amiss. And the smell of whisky.

"What the hell do you want?" demanded Evans, then with a sudden change of tone. "Is anything wrong? Have you found them?"

"Found who?" enquired Pascoe politely.

"Oh, Christ," said Evans, letting his shoulders sag as he turned and walked away from the open door. Pascoe hesitated a moment then followed him, closing the door quietly behind him.

Evans had gone through into the lounge and was standing leaning against the mantelpiece in the classic pose of grief.

But this was no mere pose, Pascoe decided.

"Mr Evans," he said softly, "what has happened?"

Evans looked at him wretchedly.

"What am I to do without her?" he groaned.

"Without Mrs Evans, you mean?" asked Pascoe. "Why, where is she, Mr Evans. What's happened to her?"

He did not go any further into the room but stood in the door keeping a watchful eye on Evans. For all he knew, Gwen was lying upstairs dead and the man in front of him was building up to another outburst.

"She's left me," said Evans with difficulty, mouthing the

words in an exaggerated way as if examining them in disbelief as they came out.

"Left you? How do you know she's left you?" asked Pascoe, still suspicious that he might be listening to the self-deceiving euphemism of murder.

Evans reached into his pocket and pulled out a piece of paper, crumpled as though it had been thrust deeply and desperately out of sight.

Pascoe came carefully forward and took it.

"Dear Arthur," he read, "I am leaving you. Our marriage has been at an end for some time as far as I am concerned. I am sorry, but there's nothing else to be done. Please forgive me. Gwen."

What the hell do I say? Pascoe asked himself. Oh, Bruiser, I wish you were here.

Evans sobbed drily, gulping in great mouthfuls of air, and rocked back and forward against the mantelpiece which was lined with Christmas cards. One rocked and fell. He looked up then and became aware of the others. Soundlessly, he swept his forearm down the whole length of the mantelpiece, scattering cards and ornaments alike.

Pascoe touched his arm.

"Come and sit down," he said. For a moment it looked as if Evans might resist, then he let himself be led to the sofa where he sat down quietly with his head between his hands and began to cry.

Pascoe left him and ran lightly upstairs. It was his business to make sure that Gwen Evans was not still here. Arthur had obviously had the same idea. Every door was open, even wardrobes and cupboards, and all the lights were on.

He looked into the wardrobes and through the drawers in the dressing-table and tallboy.

She had packed well. Hardly a feminine article remained.

The same in the bathroom. Only, there on its side on top of the medicine chest was an unstoppered bottle. He picked it up. It was empty. He read the label, then turned and ran downstairs three at a time.

Arthur Evans was still on the sofa, only now he was sitting limp with his head resting against the arm. His eyes were closed and his breathing noisy.

Pascoe turned back to the hall, picked up the telephone and dialled.

"Ambulance," he said. "Quick."

❀ ❀ ❀

"How was I to know," said Pascoe defensively, "that there were only two tablets in the bottle? Anyway he must have had about half a bottle of whisky."

"You do not pump out a man's stomach because he's drunk half a bottle of scotch," said Dalziel. "If you did, half the top men in this town would be swallowing rubber tubes every weekend. Christ, your common sense should have told you. Evans isn't your romantic suicide type, he's your find-'em-and-mash-'em type. He'll have you on his list now."

"I hope they've gone a long way," said Pascoe. "They seem to have taken everything. Felstead's landlady says he told her that he definitely wouldn't be coming back. They're almost certainly in his car. Is it worth sending out a call?"

Dalziel shook his head emphatically.

"Nothing whatsoever to do with us, Sergeant. If a woman runs away from her husband that's their business. Our only concern is if and when Arthur catches up with them. I can't see him sitting down for a quiet civilized three-cornered discussion."

Like you did? wondered Pascoe. Some hope! You and Evans are brothers under the thick skin.

"What did he say about meeting Mary Connon, that's the important thing," went on Dalziel.

Pascoe tried to stop himself stiffening to a seated attention position and couldn't quite manage it.

"Nothing," he said. "That is, I didn't actually ask him. I mean, how could I? The occasion didn't arise."

He wished his voice didn't sound quite so childishly defensive in his own ears, but Dalziel seemed happy enough with his explanation.

"It'll keep," he said. "Nothing's so important that it won't keep. Or if it is, and you keep it too long, it stops being important, and that's much the same thing. Look at the time! There's nothing more for us here. Come on!"

He stood up and took his coat from the chair over which it had been casually thrown.

"Well, help me on with it, lad," he said to Pascoe. "And hurry up. The most dangerous moment of a policeman's life is the time between getting his coat on and getting out of the station. You never know what's just coming in through the door."

Just coming in through the door at that very minute was Detective-Constable Edwards. He was very wet.

"Where've you been, then?" asked the desk-sergeant aggressively.

"Out," said Edwards with a nerve sharpened by cold and more than an hour in the company of Mrs Kathy Grogan. "Is the super still in?"

Entry to the Grogan household had not been easy. Mrs Grogan had wisely taken note of the many warnings issued to householders, especially the elderly living on their own, to examine carefully the credentials of all callers before admitting them.

It took Edwards's warrant card, two library tickets, a payslip and a snapshot of himself and his fiancée on the beach at Scarborough to win him admittance. The snapshot was the clincher. The girl, Mrs Grogan told him, had the look of her late sister.

Once her doubts had been satisfied and the door unchained and unbolted, her attitude was one of reproachful expectancy.

"So you've come at last," she said. "You take your time don't you?"

"Pardon?" he said.

"Come along in, then. It's draughty out here. Gets right under my skirts if you'll excuse the expression. If I've written to the Council once about that front door, I've written fifty times. I told her next door you'd be coming, but I didn't think you'd be so long about it. If this is what you're like when you are anxious I wouldn't like to wait for you when you're not."

The small living-room she took him into was made even smaller by the amount of stuff she had in there. Every ledge and shelf was crowded with ornaments of one kind or another, most of them bearing some civic inscription ranging geographically from "A gift from Peebles" to "A souvenir of Ilfracombe."

Mrs Grogan, Edwards decided, was strongly attached to the past. He knew very well the dangers of any allusions to any of these articles, but the mere unavoidable act of looking at them was more than enough for his hostess.

He reckoned he had done well to get away with two cups of tea and forty minutes of reminiscence before an opening arose to thrust in a question.

"Mrs Grogan," he said, "you said before that you thought we were anxious to see you…"

"No," she said. "You said that."

"Did I?" he asked, half ready to believe anything.

"Yes. Here. Look, I'll show you."

She dived into a pile of newspapers which lay in an untidy stack beneath her chair and after a short search, triumphantly produced a neatly folded paper which she handed to Edwards.

He looked down at it and found himself reading an account of Mary Connon's death.

Mrs Grogan's gnarled and knuckle-swollen finger was interposed between his eyes and the paper. The meticulously clear and polished nail came to rest on a line near the end of the story.

"The police are anxious to interview anyone who may have walked or driven along Boundary Drive between seven and nine on the night in question."

"But that means," Edwards began to explain, then pulled himself up with a smile.

"I'm sorry we've taken so long to get round to you, Mrs Grogan, but we've been very busy. Now, I understand then that you did take a walk down Boundary Drive on that night?"

"Oh yes. Of course I did. I always do. I go to my nephew's for tea on Saturday afternoons and if the weather's not too bad I get off the bus in Glenfair Road and walk down the Drive. It saves me three-pence on the fare that way. My nephew thinks I stay on the bus right into the estate, but I don't always. It would worry him if he knew. This won't have to come out in court, will it?"

"We'll try to keep it quiet," Edwards assured her.

"Well, I'd just got opposite that poor woman's house, and I glanced up at it. I always look at the houses as I walk by them. It's really interesting. And then I saw the man."

"The man."

"Yes. I saw him quite clearly. A man."

"Mr Connon?" suggested Edwards.

"Oh no. Not him. I saw his picture in the paper. It wasn't him. Someone quite different."

"Evans," interjected Dalziel when Edwards reached this part of his story.

"Probably," agreed Pascoe gloomily.

"Evans?" asked Edwards.

"Yes. Arthur Evans. He was round there that night. I've talked to him about it."

"Oh, I see," said Edwards disappointedly. "I didn't know. I suppose you asked him, sir, what he was doing up the tree?"

"Up the tree? Up what tree?" said Pascoe, his interest revived.

"No. We didn't ask him that, Constable," said Dalziel. "Do go on."

Edwards finished his story rapidly. Mrs Grogan had seen a man half way up the sycamore tree in the Connons' front garden. Despite the darkness and the distance, she claimed she saw him quite distinctly and, taking Edwards to her own window, she gave him a convincing demonstration of the excellence of her eyesight.

"What did you do then?" asked Edwards.

"What should I do? Nothing, of course. It's none of my business. I always look at the houses as I walk past, and I see a lot of things odder than that, but it's not my business, is it? No, it wasn't until I read about the murder in the paper that I thought any more about it. And when it said you were anxious to see me, I've been waiting ever since. I've even missed going out a couple of nights."

"I'm sorry," said Edwards gently. "Next time why don't you come down to see us, to hurry us along a bit? Ask for Mr Dalziel if you do."

But he didn't put that bit in his report.

"What price my intruder now, sir?" asked Pascoe, with some slight jubilation.

"It depends who he is," said Dalziel thoughtfully. "And if he is. It's late now. And dark. Sergeant, first thing in the morning, you exercise your limbs round at Connon's and see what you're like at climbing trees. And I'll do a bit of sick-visiting, and go and talk to my old mate, Arthur, again. But watch yourself. Listen to that wind."

And a few miles away Antony heard the boughs of the sycamore tree sawing together and watched the sinister patterns moved by the wind across the frosted glass of the bathroom window. He put his toothbrush down and rinsed his mouth out. Then moving quietly along the landing in his bare feet, he came to Jenny's bedroom door.

It made a small noise as he opened it and he paused.

"Jenny," he whispered.

There was a little silence, then the sound of movement in the bed as she sat up. He could see her faintly, whitely.

"Come in," she said.

❀ ❀ ❀

They're looking very pleased with themselves this morning, thought Pascoe. Even from this angle.

"This angle" was almost ninety degrees. He had left the comparative safety of the platform of the step-ladder and was now clinging to what felt like a dangerously pliable branch of the tree.

Below him, hand in hand, staring up with lively interest, were Jenny and Antony.

Looking up, it had seemed no height at all. Looking down corrected the illusion, so instead he applied his mind to the business in hand.

If there had been a man up the tree on the night of Mary Connon's death—and a conversation with Kathy Grogan earlier that morning had convinced him, though her interpretation of the written word might be naïvely literal, there was nothing wrong with her senses, then that man could have been there for only one of three purposes.

Unless he was a bird-watcher, he told himself. Joke. No, either he was up here to have a good look through one of the windows. In which case he'd be disappointed. Only if he really craned his neck sideways could he see anything of the front bedroom windows and then not enough to make the effort worthwhile. Or he wanted to get over the fence into the back garden. Which would be easy enough. Oops! Christ, nearly did it myself without trying. Or he was trying to get in through the one window in the house which was approachable from the tree side. The bathroom. Frosted glass. No good for your keen voyeur with an eye for detail, not even with the curtains open, blurred white shapes, very frustrating.

So, decided Pascoe, if it was the window he was after, he was trying to get in.

It was too much to hope that any sign of human presence in the tree would have survived two and a half wintry weeks. Not unless the climber had been wearing hobnailed boots. None the less Pascoe examined the likely branches conscientiously and as always in such cases, the satisfaction of expectation was a disappointment.

Then he selected what looked like the safest route to the

window and edged his way carefully out along the chosen branches. A sharp gust of wind set the whole tree in motion and he clung on desperately like a sailor in the rigging, remembering Dalziel's jocular injunction to "watch himself."

One thing's certain, he told himself, it wasn't fat Dalziel who climbed up this tree. Or anyone built like him. I reckon I'm about the limit. I reckon also I've reached the limit.

He was as near to the window as he felt he could get without falling. There was nothing to be seen. Again he had expected nothing. One of the first things that had been done when the police arrived at the house was to examine all windows and doors for signs of forcible entry. There had been nothing. There still was nothing.

The wind rose again, and again he tried to combine safety with dignity, thinking of the watchers below. And elsewhere. He had seen a few curtains moving in neighbouring houses.

It was time to descend, he decided, and began to move backwards, fixing his eyes on the wall of the house in his determination not to look down. Then he stopped moving and kept on staring. At first he thought it was merely the effect of looking too hard, and he blinked his eyes twice. But it was still there.

Just below the windowsill on the vertical brick there was something which looked like a footprint. Not much of a footprint, more of a toe-print. But it was there. As if someone scrabbling desperately for a hold had used even the little frictional grip that pressure against the vertical could give.

Wind and height forgotten, Pascoe swung down from the tree like a gymnast.

Jenny's hair was blowing wildly all over her face, evading all the effort of her hand to restrain it. She was beautiful.

"Have you found anything, Sergeant?" she asked, pitching her voice high to get over the wind.

"Give us a hand with the steps," he said to Antony. "Over here."

Together they moved the step-ladder right up against the

wall. The earth was soft here and the feet of the ladder began to sink as he ascended.

"Hang on," he grunted to Antony and clambered quickly to the top. The bathroom windowsill was not far above his head. He stood on his toes and peered up towards it.

"Look out!" cried Antony, and the steps lurched violently sideways.

But he was smiling as they helped him out of the herbaceous border.

It was definitely a print, most probably made by the toe of a rubber-soled sports-shoe; a tennis-shoe, perhaps, or basketball boot.

"Are you all right?" asked Jenny anxiously.

"He looks a bit dazed," said Antony. "It was the soil. One of the legs just went down as if it was on quicksand."

"I'm all right," said Pascoe, rather light-heartedly. "Take me to my leader."

Jenny and Antony looked at each other dubiously. "Come inside and have a cup of tea," suggested Jenny. "Or a drop of Daddy's scotch."

She took him by the arm and led him unresistingly into the house.

"Hello," said Connon, looking at the sergeant's earth-stained suit. "Had a fall?"

"Nothing to worry about, sir," replied Pascoe. "Winded me a bit that's all. May I use your phone?"

"Of course. Any luck with your tree?"

"Perhaps," said Pascoe enigmatically, then seeing Jenny's look of enquiry, he relented and added, "I think there may be a footprint."

"On the windowsill?"

"On the wall."

"That's absurd," said Connon. "No one could get in there. And the window was fastened in any case."

Pascoe didn't answer but went out to the phone. Jenny looked worriedly at her father. Today he looked paler than ever.

"I wish they could have left this alone till Christmas was over," she whispered to Antony. He squeezed her shoulder and went out into the hall after Pascoe who was just replacing the receiver.

"He's out," said Pascoe, more to himself than Antony. "He'll ring here when he gets back."

"Sergeant," said Antony. "Forgive me if I seem to be playing the amateur sleuth once again, but something else occurred to me the other day, which might or might not be of interest to you."

"Let's have it," said Pascoe. "Every little helps. Shall we go into the other room?"

"Well no," said Antony. "It would make my explanation easier if we stepped outside."

Two minutes later Antony returned to the lounge.

"Has he gone?" asked Jenny, who was sitting on the arm of her father's chair.

"No. He's in the garden again. But he sent me in to ask you something. You know a girl called Sheila Lennox?"

"Yes."

"He wants to know if you know where she works."

Thirty minutes later the three of them were still sitting in the lounge.

"I hope he's going to pay for his telephone calls," said Jenny.

"It's a little price to pay to see the great detective's great detective at work," said Antony.

Connon sat with his hand pressed to the side of his brow.

"Have you got your headache again, Daddy?" asked Jenny.

"No. Not really. Just a little. It'll pass."

"Oh, I wish..." but the front-door bell interrupted Jenny's wish.

Antony rose, but they heard the door being opened before he left the room.

"How do you do, Sergeant?" boomed a familiar voice.

"Oh God," groaned Jenny, "it's Fat Dalziel."

"The gang's all here," intoned Antony.

In the dining-room, Pascoe was speaking swiftly, persuasively to Dalziel who listened intently.

"All right," he said when the sergeant had finished. "I'll buy it. Let's ask him now, shall we? Where's he work?"

"He doesn't today. It's Christmas Eve, remember? He finished early for Christmas. That's why I left word for you to come here."

"That makes it easier. Come on."

Pascoe hung back, his memories of training thronging his mind.

"Shouldn't we call up a little support? Just in case."

Dalziel laughed contemptuously.

"A strapping young lad like you? Not to mention me, the terror of seven counties. You must be joking. Anyway, it might still be a lot of hogwash. Let's ask."

Jenny heard the front door close.

"That's bloody polite, I must say," she said angrily. "In and out without a by-your-leave, and they don't even say goodbye."

"Perhaps they're not going far," said Antony, peering through the curtains. "In fact, they're not. They're just going across the road."

"Where to?" demanded Jenny, jumping up and rushing to the window.

Connon stood up too and slowly followed her.

Over the road, Dalziel held his thumb down hard on the bell-push.

"Someone knows we're here," he said laconically. "Or there's a big draught behind the curtains."

"Here we are," said Pascoe.

The door opened.

"Good morning, madam," said Dalziel with effusive politeness to the large woman who stood there, still rubbing her sleepy eyes. "We're police officers. I wonder if I might have a word with your son."

Maisie Curtis opened her mouth to say something. From somewhere at the rear of the house came the slam of a door.

"Sergeant," said Dalziel. "The back."

But he was speaking to an already retreating Pascoe.

Stanley Curtis was young, fit, and had a good start. When Pascoe rounded the back of the house, he had already moved across the Fernies' garden and was clearing the next hedge like a trained hurdler. Pascoe made no attempt to follow him but rapidly assessed the situation. While the barriers between the Boundary Drive gardens were uniformly low, the hedges and fences which separated the bottoms of the gardens from those of the houses behind were generally much higher.

Pascoe took this in, turned and ran past Dalziel again without a word.

The Connons saw him leap into his car like a Le Mans driver and accelerate explosively up the street.

Two hundred yards on he brought the car to an equally violent halt.

Stanley Curtis, dragging in great mouthfuls of air through his hugely open mouth, was coming out of someone's gate.

He stopped when he saw the car and made as if to turn back.

Pascoe leaned over and opened the passenger door.

"Come on, Stan," he said. "It's no weather to be out without your jacket."

His chest still rising and falling spasmodically, the youth came across the pavement and climbed into the car.

"Let's get Superintendent Dalziel," said Pascoe, swinging the car in a turn which took him up on to the pavement. "Then we'll go somewhere quiet and have a talk. I expect you're ready for a talk, aren't you?"

Chapter Eight

"I didn't kill her," said Stanley.

"No?" said Pascoe.

They were sitting, the three of them, in Dalziel's room at the station. Mrs Curtis had with some difficulty been persuaded to leave. She had become slightly hysterical and it had taken the intervention of the boy himself to get her out. He had spoken to her with a kindly firmness which seemed to surprise her and she had left without further protest.

Pascoe too had been surprised by the maturity the youth was showing. It was as if the desperate physical effort to get away had burnt off all the panicking, fearful element in him. For the moment anyway.

"Let's start with that," said Stanley firmly. "I didn't kill her."

"I hope we finish with it too," said Pascoe.

Dalziel sat back quietly, apparently happy to leave the talking to the sergeant at this stage.

"I'd been expecting you earlier," Stanley went on.

"Everyone seems to have been expecting us earlier. But why should you?"

"Well, the Club mainly. I'd seen you talking to people

round the Club, and I'd said one or two things to my mates. Just boasting, you know."

"About watching Mrs Connon?"

"That's right. I thought someone would tell you. Sheila perhaps. You got pretty thick with her. Joe wasn't half mad."

Pascoe nodded.

"Yes, she did. But only when I asked. And only today. I'd overheard something once, but it didn't mean anything then. Smoke?"

Curtis shook his head. "Not when I'm in training." He looked anxious suddenly. "Am I still in training? I mean, what'll happen?"

"It depends on what you've done, lad," said Dalziel sternly. "Just speak up and tell us everything."

Pascoe winked fractionally at Stanley, inviting him to join in a laugh at Dalziel's portentous manner.

"Tell us about the letters first, Stanley."

"You found them, then? I hoped you wouldn't."

"But we did. You went back to have another look for them, didn't you?"

"I was going to. I was dead worried. But that lad was there. I nearly died when he moved and I saw him. But he didn't see me, did he?"

"No, Stanley. But he realized that you must have been in the garden to be able to see him where he was sitting. He just realized that today as well."

"Christmas Eve," said Stanley. His eyes suddenly filled with tears.

"Just start at the beginning, lad," boomed Dalziel. "And get a move on, eh? Or it'll soon be Boxing Day."

"All right," said Stanley. "I'll have a fag after all, can I? Bugger training. Thanks."

He took a long draw and then began talking.

"It began accidentally. I mean, I just looked out of my bedroom window one night and I saw her. Her curtains weren't right closed and she was getting undressed. She moved around a bit and sometimes I could see, sometimes not. Like a show. Well, after that I kept my eyes open. I had an old telescope, just a kid's thing that I'd had for years. But it brought things up pretty close. It happened quite often. I got to looking forward to it. I like big women," he said almost apologetically, glancing at Dalziel.

"We all do, lad. But we don't go around making obscene phone calls to them. Get on with it, eh?"

Stanley stubbed his cigarette out.

"That's what I did first, made a call. I'd been watching her. I didn't dare say anything when she answered. I just put the phone down. Then I started writing letters. I didn't mean to send any. But she sort of got into my mind. You know how you sometimes start thinking about women and all, well, it was always her. Finally I sent her one. Nothing happened. So I sent another. And it was as if, well, after that, she seemed to be at the window more often, you know. As if she knew and she was putting on a real show. So I wrote again. And I telephoned her when I knew Mr Connon was out. It was stupid really but I got a kick out of it. I mean, I wouldn't have done it if it was frightening her, I wouldn't frighten her, believe me. But she seemed to join in. She laughed on the phone and told me to go on, to say more. I used to work out things to say to her, new things, you know."

"You used to ring from the box in the street outside your house?"

"That's right. That was daft too, I suppose. But being able to see the house made it more exciting somehow. Anyway, I got into the box one night, but before I could pick up the phone, it rang. I nearly dropped dead. But it kept on ringing so I answered it. It was her. 'Hello, Stanley,' she said, laughing, you know. 'What have you got for me tonight?' She'd found out somehow. Though, Christ, I suppose it was easy enough, really. I mean, I wasn't very clever. She might even have recognized my voice. I tried to disguise it a bit at first, but then it didn't seem to matter. But it was different now. It stopped being a game."

He fell silent. Pascoe shifted his position in his chair and asked, "How do you mean, Stanley?"

"Well, she started getting me to do things for her. Like run messages. Go and get her cigarettes. Or just stupid things like walk three times round the telephone box. Or sit for an hour at my window in my overcoat and Dad's trilby."

"How do you mean, she started *getting* you to do things, Stanley?" asked Pascoe.

"I mean, she had those letters, see? And she said she'd show them. To my parents, to Mr Connon, to the police. I don't know who she wasn't going to show them to."

"So what happened?"

"Well, in the end I told her I wasn't going to play any more. I'd had enough."

"Told her?" queried Dalziel.

"On the phone. She made me phone her regularly. We never actually met, except by accident outside and then she just smiled at me and said good-morning or whatever. Anyway she said that was up to me. If she didn't hear from me in five days, she'd start showing the letters. I just put the phone down. I mean, it seemed daft. I didn't see how she could without making herself look silly. So I wasn't bothered much at first. But as the time got nearer, the Sunday, I mean, when the five days were up, I began to really worry. Then on the Saturday, I had a couple of pints after the game and I got this idea. It seemed dead simple really. I just had to get the letters back and I'd be all right. Then there was nothing she could do. Nothing at all. I knew she had them in her bedroom, she'd told me often enough. So I got this idea that I'd just get in the house somehow, pick up the letters and be away without anyone knowing a thing about it. It seemed really funny. I thought I might even ring her afterwards for a laugh. You know, ask her to make sure the letters were safe, and all. It seemed a real giggle."

"Was it?" asked Pascoe gently. "Was it a giggle, Stanley?"

"Was it hell!" the boy said. "I nearly killed myself getting in for a start. I went up the tree and through the bathroom window. I made enough noise to raise the dead, I thought, but I knew they had the telly on downstairs. It was real loud. I couldn't wait till later, see, because it was the bedroom I wanted to get into. Can I have another cigarette, please?"

Pascoe handed one over again and lit it. The boy was frowning with the effort of recollection. He had a rather long, thin face, intelligent-looking, just beginning to fill out slightly, and firm into adulthood; but still with the fragility and the remnants of the mild acne which is often the stigma of adolescence.

He's just on the turn, really, thought Pascoe. Eighteen years old, a foot in both camps. She got him just at the turn.

"Go on, Stanley," he said.

"I stopped in the bathroom for ages. At least it seemed like that. Then I thought, 'you stupid twit, if anyone does come up here for any reason, chances are this is the room they'll be heading for.' So I got out then. The telly was still going strong below. It was easy to work out which must be the bedroom door, so I headed along the landing towards it. The door was open. I took a step in. Then I nearly died! Someone made a noise. A sort of groan. Then this figure moved on the bed. I hadn't noticed it before, it was so dark. Then he sort of pushed himself up."

"Who was it, Stanley? Did you know him?" asked Pascoe.

"It was Mr Connon, I think. I'm pretty certain, but I didn't stop to look closer. I just ran. I was so terrified I didn't head back for the bathroom, I went the other way to the stairs. There was still a hell of a noise down below..."

"What kind of noise?" snapped Dalziel.

"Voices. And laughing. And music. It might all have been the telly, I don't know, I didn't have time to find out, did I? I just set off down the stairs. I was half way down when the lounge door burst open and Mrs Connon came out. She saw me and screamed."

"Did she recognize you, Stanley? Surely she'd recognize you?"

Stanley looked rather shamefaced.

"Well, no. She wouldn't. I mean, I'd put this thing, a stocking, over my head, like they do, you know!"

"Oh Christ!" groaned Dalziel.

"What happened then?" said Pascoe.

"She just stood there. She only screamed once. Then this man..."

"Which man?"

"The man in the lounge with her."

"Did you see him? Do you know him?"

"No. I mean I didn't see him. Not really. I heard him say something like, 'What's the matter?' or something like that. And I sort of half saw him coming up behind her. But I wasn't going to wait, was I? I just threw my...this...something at her, you know, not to hurt, just in panic, and she stepped back and must have bumped into him, and I shot past and out of the front door. I don't even remember opening it."

"What did you do then, Stanley?"

"There wasn't anyone in the road, luckily. I dragged the stocking off as I got out of the gate and ran all the way up to the main road. Then I just walked about for a bit, had a drink. I was scared stiff, I didn't know what to do. I went back home after about an hour, I suppose. I wanted to see what was happening. But it was all quiet. I watched from my bedroom for ages. Then about eleven o'clock, the police came, to Mr Connon's house, I mean. I couldn't understand why they'd taken so long. I mean, I thought it was about me, you see. I didn't find out about Mrs Connon till the next morning."

"Why didn't you come and tell us all this, Stanley?"

The boy wrinkled his nose as if at the stupidity of the question.

"I was scared. I was so frightened I was sick. I couldn't go to work for most of that week. I just hoped that things would get quiet, that it would all blow over. But it didn't."

His shoulders sagged hopelessly.

Pascoe leaned forward and spoke sympathetically.

"Just one more thing, Stanley," he said. "What was it you threw at Mrs Connon?"

Stanley stopped sagging and looked alert, uneasy.

"Why, nothing," he said. "Just something I picked up, I suppose. I don't know."

"Wasn't it something you took into the house with you, Stanley? Wasn't it something belonging to you?"

A look of stubborn obstinacy came over the youth's face. Dalziel stood up and moved swiftly behind him. His hands came down like a pair of great clamps on his shoulders.

"Listen, my lad," he hissed close to his ear. "When Sergeant Pascoe asks you a question, he deserves an answer. He's bloody well going to get an answer, isn't he?"

Stanley twisted free.

"What's it matter anyway?" he cried. "All right. It was a gun. Not a gun really, a pistol, an air-pistol. It was just an old thing, I hadn't used it for years. It was old when I got it as well. I just took it along for...I don't know why I took it! I wouldn't have used it, I mean, it didn't work anyway, did it?"

"How should we know, Stanley?" said Pascoe. "Where is it now?"

"I don't know. I left it. I didn't go back and ask for it."

The boy crumpled again. Pascoe stood up and went to the door.

"Excuse me a second, sir," he said.

"Go ahead," said Dalziel gloomily looking down at Stanley.

"You're in trouble, lad," he said. "Even if you're telling the truth, you're in trouble. You know that. But if you're not, then you're really in it. Just have a think. A long, long think and see if there's anything else you haven't told us."

They were both still bowed in contemplative silence when Pascoe returned. He was carrying a box.

"Stanley," he said. "Open the box."

The youth reached forward and took the lid off, one-handed, then froze as he saw what was inside.

"Stanley, is that yours?" asked Pascoe.

The boy peered closer, then nodded.

"Yes. That's it. That's mine. But look at it. It's old and rusty. It couldn't hurt anyone, that."

Pascoe reached into the box and took out the pistol.

"You're right," he said. "I don't suppose it could."

He looked at Dalziel and raised his eyebrows.

Dalziel shook his head.

Pascoe went to the door again.

"Constable," he said to the uniformed man outside, "take Mr Curtis along to the interview room, will you? Both his parents are there now. He can talk to them, but be present all the time. And watch him. He's a nippy runner."

He smiled cheerfully at Stanley as he left the room and the boy managed a wan grin in reply.

"You managed that quite well, Sergeant," said the superintendent.

"Thank you, sir."

"Now suppose you let me into your confidence and tell me where you've been hiding this."

A great paw was waved at the pistol. Pascoe held it up and squinted along the barrel. It was, as Stanley had said, old and rusty, but it still looked formidably solid, eight inches of steel tube pointing menacingly at Dalziel.

"I haven't been hiding it. It was hidden though, in a pond up on the Common. It was brought back to daylight only yesterday, when they were looking for Mickey Annan. I noticed it on the list."

"But didn't connect it with the Connon case at the time I hope?"

"Of course not, sir. I'd have mentioned it, wouldn't I? But there was a connection there for us to see, if we'd known. In the chair."

"The chair."

"The chair she was killed on. There was a list of things they found in it. Ordinary things, money and the like. It's all back with Connon now."

"I saw it. Wait. Of course, there was a pellet."

"That's right, one air-gun pellet."

"But what's this leading to, Sergeant? You're not suggesting she was clubbed to death with the barrel of that thing? How the hell would you hold it if you were trying to produce something like that effect?"

"Like this," said Pascoe.

He held the pistol up between them twisting his hand so they both had a side view.

And he pressed the trigger.

A six-inch cylinder of steel crashed out of the barrel, extending its length to over a foot.

"Now we load it," said Pascoe, putting the end against the wall and forcing the internal cylinder back into the shorter barrel.

"Then we fire it again."

This time he held it close to the frame of the window.

"Hell," he said, nursing his wrist.

There was a circular dent nearly half-an-inch deep in the wood.

"That's public property," observed Dalziel. "Also you're making forensic's job more difficult."

Pascoe returned the gun to the box.

"I've told them it'll be coming down."

"That's a nasty bit of machinery," said Dalziel.

"It's an old-fashioned bit. I don't know if they make them like that any more. It's years since I had an air-pistol. What now, sir?"

Dalziel scratched his navel.

"I think we'd better have another talk with Connon."

"Do you believe young Curtis?"

"Yes," said Dalziel, and added surprisingly, "and I sympathize with him a bit. When you're that age, it's all sex, isn't it? I've seen him hanging around Gwen Evans at the Club too, wishing he dared. He does like 'em big, doesn't he? I think we all discovered the comic-obscene possibilities of the telephone in our teens, didn't we? If Mary Connon had shouted at him, told her husband, started drawing her curtains, that would have been an end to it. But she wasn't like that, Mary. She always liked to be controlling people."

"What about this other man? Lover? Or what?"

"How the hell should I know? But you're not the only one who's been out detecting today, Sergeant. I had a long talk with Evans, remember?"

I think he's really hurt I didn't ask, thought Pascoe.

"What did he say?"

"He said he met Mary Connon at her invitation. He said she wanted to discuss with him the relationship between his wife and her husband which was causing her considerable distress."

Pascoe shook his head in amazement.

"That woman. I'm beginning to be glad I didn't know her."

"Not much chance of that now anyway, lad. It's the living we're after. I've got a man sitting outside Evans's door. He won't go far. But there's a few questions Mr Connon's got to answer first of all. Let's hope he's co-operative or we'll never get to Jacko's party."

❀ ❀ ❀

The television was on in Connon's lounge when they arrived. It was Christmas Eve fare, a selection from the old silent film comedies. Antony had turned the sound down to cut out the nauseating superimposed American commentary and the only sound for the past half hour had been his and Jenny's chuckles.

Even Connon had smiled from time to time, Jenny had observed with pleasure.

The doorbell's chime was an unwelcome interruption. Nor were the visitors it harbingered any the more welcome.

"Privately, please," said Dalziel. "We'd like to see you alone, Mr Connon. Perhaps we can leave these two young people to their television."

Jenny rolled her eyes at the unctuous condescension of Dalziel's tone. Pascoe laughed as the Keystone police-waggon lost another half dozen incumbents.

"Come into the dining-room," said Connon.

He and Pascoe sat opposite each other at the dining-table. Dalziel stood in the bay, blocking out the light.

"Superintendent," said Connon.

"Yes?"

"Stan Curtis. We saw what happened earlier. What has he got to do with my wife's death?"

"Should he have anything?"

"I cannot imagine so for one moment. Where is he?"

"He's at the station at the moment, sir, helping us with our enquiries."

"How?"

"He has admitted being illegally present in your house on the night of your wife's death. More serious charges against him are at present under review."

Nasty old Dalziel, thought Pascoe. What a little liar he is.

"No," said Connon. "No. Not Stanley. It was Stanley who was here?"

He sounded amazed.

"That's right. Why not?"

"I didn't think..."

Connon tailed off.

"Didn't think what? Never mind. There'll be time for that later."

Connon was rubbing the side of his head. Dalziel suddenly wheeled round, sat down beside Connon and began speaking urgently, in a low voice to him.

"Come on, Connie. Tell us about it. Make it easy, boy. It's got to come out now. Got to. Just fill in the gaps."

Connon sat silent. He looked really ill.

"For God's sake!" exploded Dalziel. "Don't you believe us? We don't know it all, but we know enough. All we want are the little things. Why did you clean up the bathroom windowsill and close the window, for instance? And drop the pistol into the pond on the Common? What were they doing when you came downstairs? What were they up to? Making love?"

Tut tut, thought Pascoe. He's at it again. He read the pathologist's report as closely as I did.

"Come on, Mr Connon," he said. "It'll help everyone to get it out in the open. You. And Jenny. Who was it downstairs? Arthur Evans?"

Connon sat looking blankly ahead. Outside the telephone rang. The door opened and Jenny came in.

"It's for you," she said to Pascoe. "Daddy, are you all right? What's going on anyway?"

Pascoe went out to the phone.

It was the desk-sergeant down town.

"Pete?" he said. "Alan here. Sorry to interrupt whatever I'm interrupting but you did say you wanted anything new at once. Well, it's probably nothing, but a chap called Johnson just rang up for you. Landlord of a boozer, the Blue Bell. He said you'd been asking about Gwen Evans, whether she'd been in on the sixth. None of his lot could remember her, he said, and then it had gone out of his mind, till they started talking about her leaving her husband. News gets round. Then he mentioned it again and one of his women, a temp, only comes in at weekends, says she was definitely in that night, for at least an hour. She served her twice. She remembers clearly she says, because she went sick on the Sunday after and was laid up for the next two weekends."

"What's she doing there now then? It's not a weekend."

"It's Christmas Eve. Remember? Lots of people actually go out and enjoy themselves. Big crowds in pubs. Merry Christmas."

"You too, Alan. Thanks."

So Gwen had been in the Blue Bell that night as she said at first, not lying spread out on the counterpane as she was willing to admit later. Later, when Dalziel had had a go at...

He went quickly back into the lounge. He'd been dimly

aware of background noises as he took his call. Now they stopped, but the little tableau that greeted him—Jenny, flushed, standing with her hands on her father's shoulders; Antony, concerned, just behind her; Connon, blank, staring at the empty rose-bowl in the centre of the table; and Dalziel, hands spread out in front of him, with his injured, professional footballer's what-have-I-done expression on his large face—this was enough to tell him there had been some kind of row.

He didn't need to be a detective to guess the details. But he was a detective, and he was too near the truth now to be deterred by considerations of health, feeling, or sentiment.

"Tell me, Mr Connon," he said harshly. "Tell me, why had Mr Felstead come to see your wife that night?"

The tableau remained the same. Only the expressions changed.

But it was Connon's alone that he watched. For a second it froze into an even greater withdrawal, a kind of desperation. Then slowly it dissolved, the life and movement came back, and something very like relief rose to the surface of the eyes.

He let out a long sigh and glanced round at his daughter and Antony.

"May they stay?" he asked.

"If you wish it," said Dalziel.

"Yes. It's best. I'll do my best to be brief."

"No need to hurry, Mr Connon," said Pascoe.

He smiled.

"Once you decide to have a tooth out, Sergeant, don't you want to run to the dentist? It's not all that complicated really, not any more than human beings are, anyway. Though that's enough I suppose. What happened was this. Everything I told you about my going home and passing out was true. Only I woke up again much earlier. Shortly after eight I should think. I went out on to the landing. There seemed to be some kind of disturbance downstairs, but I was still too dazed to pay much attention. I went into the bathroom and bathed my face in cold water. That woke me up a little. I noticed the window was wide open and the fresh air helped clear my head as well. Then I set off downstairs."

"How long had this taken?" asked Dalziel. Jenny looked at him angrily.

"Five minutes. Longer. I don't know. Anyway, I came downstairs and opened the lounge door. The television was still on, no other lights. Mary was still in the chair with its back to me. In front of her stood Marcus. He had this pistol in his hand. I could hear Mary laughing, it was as if something very funny had happened. The pistol was sort of hanging loose. Now Marcus raised it up. Mary stretched out her hand and seemed to pull it towards her. I couldn't see properly because of the chair."

"What did Mr Felstead look like?" asked Pascoe.

"Like?"

"Angry? Puzzled? Or was he joining in the joke?"

"He looked...annoyed. Not in a rage, but annoyed."

"What happened then?"

"There was a kind of crash and an odd kind of splintering noise. Marcus stepped back. He said something like, 'Oh Christ!' And he went deadly pale. Then he looked up and saw me. I came into the room and walked round the chair so I could see Mary."

He glanced up at Jenny who took his hand and held it hard.

"Her forehead was crushed in. Not much, it seemed, but I could tell she was dead. She still had a cigarette in her hand. I took it out and put it in the ash-tray. Then Marcus started to talk."

"This is very important," said Pascoe urgently. "What did he say?"

"The exact words? I can't remember. He was very very upset. So was I. But he told me he didn't mean it, it was an accident. He kept on saying this. He said over and over again that it was an accident. He begged me to believe him. He became almost hysterical."

"And you, Mr Connon."

"I felt numb at first. Then my head began to ache again

and I felt sick and faint, just like before. But Marcus was in a worse state, I think, and this seemed to help me. I had to help him out of the room. I got him a drink. Then I went to the telephone. I suppose I was going to phone McManus, or the police. I don't really know. It just seemed necessary to phone someone."

"And did you?"

Connon shook his head regretfully.

"No. No, I didn't. He stopped me. He begged me not to, till I'd heard him out. Then he told me his story. He told me about him and Gwen Evans to start with."

"Didn't you know before?"

"Not a thing. He'd kept it very dark. I knew Arthur was very jealous and reckoned that something was going on. Now and then I got the impression he even suspected me."

He laughed shortly.

"I even told Mary. She was very amused."

Pascoe glanced at Dalziel who shook his head almost imperceptibly.

"But he certainly never gave Marcus a thought," went on Connon. "Nor did I. But according to Marcus, Mary had somehow found out. I don't know how, nor did he."

He glanced anxiously at his daughter.

"Don't think badly of your mother, dear. I'm sorry you've got to hear this at all, but it's better now than later."

He looked at Dalziel and added, very clearly, "In court."

"What was Mrs Connon up to, sir?" asked Pascoe. "Some kind of blackmail?"

He kept his gaze firmly away from Jenny.

"Not in the real sense of the word, not in any criminal sense," said Connon urgently. "Believe that. No, according to Marcus, she was just entertaining herself, if that's the word, by ringing Gwen up from time to time. She seemed to have a keen instinct for when they were together. She'd just chatter about this or that, ordinary everyday things, but just slanted so that all the time Gwen knew she knew. When they met, it was the

230 A CLUBBABLE WOMAN

same. Conspiratorial glances behind Arthur's back, that kind of thing. Nothing else though. No threats."

"You believed what Mr Felstead told you."

Another quick glance at Jenny.

"Yes," he said slowly. "I could believe it."

I bet you could, thought Pascoe. I never met your wife and *I* could believe it.

"Let's get back to that Saturday night," said Dalziel.

Connon pulled out a packet of cigarettes and began to light one, then pulled himself up as at an unconscious discourtesy and offered them round.

They all refused. Pascoe was reminded of Stanley Curtis.

"Marcus said that the previous day, Friday, in the morning, Mary had telephoned Gwen to say that she was going to have a drink with Arthur at lunch time. She said it casually, but made it sound full of significance. Gwen was worried sick. She said that Arthur was very strange that night. I don't know whether Mary had seen him or not, or if she had, what she had said."

Again the glance between Pascoe and Dalziel. This time, Pascoe realised, Antony had caught it too.

"But the following night, Saturday, when Marcus called on Gwen just to see her briefly before she went down to the Club, he found her near breaking point. Mary had been on the phone again earlier in the evening. She'd asked if Arthur had mentioned their meeting. Gwen had started to scream at her down the phone, but Mary had just laughed. She'd kept on listening and laughing. She was capable of great cruelty at times."

Times we shall never hear of, thought Pascoe. Is the girl old enough to understand? I hope to God she is for both their sakes.

"So Marcus headed round here?" said Dalziel.

"Yes."

"In a rage? To have a showdown?"

"Yes. I expect so. He told me he came determined to see us

both. He'd been tempted to talk to me for some time, he said. But when he asked where I was, Mary told him I was sleeping it off upstairs. She said I was drunk. She must have been up to see where I was earlier and found me on the bed. She'd undone my collar, I think," he added, as though in irritation.

"Anyway they had a row; or rather, Marcus told me, he yelled and threatened while she just sat and smiled at him. Finally there was a pause and they heard a movement upstairs. I don't know whether it was me or Stanley."

"Stanley?" said Jenny in surprise. "Stanley who?"

"I'll explain later, love," he said. "She got up then and said it was time I came down to hear what my so-called best friend thought of her. She went to the door and opened it, then screamed. Marcus went after her just in time to see someone scuttle across the hall and out of the front door. He'd thrown something down. It was an air-pistol. Marcus picked it up and was going after the intruder, but she stopped him. He said he had a feeling that she thought she knew who it was. If it was Stanley, he was probably right. Well, to cut things short, it all started again. Things got very nasty from the sound of it. Mary suggested they should ring Arthur and ask him what he thought about the affair. Marcus said he was still waving the pistol around. She laughed at him and asked him if he imagined he was a gangster or something. He told me he thought of firing it at her then, but as he lifted it up, he said that the slug came trickling out of the barrel and dropped on the chair beside her. It must have looked a bit absurd. Mary thought it was hilarious. According to Marcus she made a big thing of it, saying things like, 'was he going to kill me, then? With his little toy gun?' That kind of thing. She reached out, he said, and lifted the gun up till it rested against her forehead. That's when I must have come down. Then, Marcus said, still laughing she pressed his finger where it was over the trigger."

He ran his hand over his face nervously.

"I'm glad you know," he said.

"But I don't understand," said Jenny. "What happened? If there was no pellet in it..."

"The pistol was of a type that worked by pressing an inner cylinder into the outer one against a very strong spring as well as the resulting air pressure. Even unloaded, the inner cylinder is jerked out with very great force to an extent of about six inches. Pressed hard against someone's head which in turn was resting hard up against the back of a chair..."

Pascoe didn't finish. Jenny sat down, her face pale. Antony hovered anxiously over her.

"Why didn't you ring the police, Mr Connon?" asked Dalziel. "You still haven't told us."

Connon shrugged hopelessly.

"I don't know. I wish to God I had. He swore it was an accident, but he asked me how it would sound to the police. Would they believe him? I couldn't say they would. I..."

"Go on."

"I half didn't believe him myself. He was my friend, but it was my wife sitting there, dead. I was lost, quite lost. I couldn't see what to do."

"Do you believe him now?"

"Yes. Yes, I think I do. The pellet helped. I thought of it later, but I couldn't find it anywhere. Then I doubted him very much. But it turned up among those objects your people found down the chair. I was overjoyed to find it. It makes a difference, doesn't it?"

"Yes, it does," said Pascoe, more reassuringly than he felt Dalziel would approve.

"Marcus said if I changed my mind later, he'd be ready to tell you everything. But he begged me not to involve him now. He wanted us to let the burglar, Stanley that is, be blamed. But I refused to do that. I said we couldn't do that. I wouldn't risk anyone else being blamed. I suppose once I started arguing on those lines, I'd really agreed to help him. He agreed in the end and in fact it was Marcus who suggested that we should cover up any traces of the intruder."

"He must have realized that if we got on to the burglar there'd be even more chance of us getting on to him," observed Dalziel drily.

Connon ignored him.

"I remembered the bathroom window. We cleaned up the sill and closed the window. Marcus put the gun in his pocket and said he'd get rid of it. I could hardly think straight at all, he had to think of everything."

"The prospect of a murder charge concentrates the mind wonderfully," said Dalziel.

This time Connon answered.

"No, I don't think it was that. I think it was the thought of Arthur Evans more than anything else. Arthur is potentially a violent man. Marcus isn't. He's a terrible tackler, always was. Not frightened for himself, so much as frightened of causing damage. I think he was thinking of Gwen as much as himself."

"He's let it all come out in the open now," said Pascoe.

"I know," said Connon. "I had a letter."

"Where? Where from?" snapped Dalziel eagerly.

"Posted in town, Superintendent. So it's no help, I'm afraid. Oh, you're welcome to see it. He just says they're going. Tells me to tell it all if I have to, not to worry, but says he and Gwen want a time alone, together, without having to worry and lie."

"He needs to worry," said Dalziel. "We'll find him."

Connon gave a sudden smile which lit up his face. "I doubt it, Superintendent. Marcus'll see the papers and read between the lines and in his own time, he'll find you. What happens now? To me I mean. I suppose I've committed any number of offences."

Dalziel loomed menacingly over him.

"You've been bloody stupid, Connie. No, it's no good giving me those nasty looks, Jennifer! He has and he knows it. He's not a stupid man. He just acts stupid sometimes."

"I did it for friendship," said Connon. "Mary was dead.

It seemed to serve no purpose letting my friend be dragged through the courts. But you're right, Dalziel. I knew you were right the next morning. I was even more certain when that letter came to Jenny. I think another week of it would have broken me down, friendship or none. I'm glad you know."

"So am I," said Dalziel. "Don't worry, there'll be no more letters."

"What happens next isn't up to me," Dalziel went on. "You know that. We'll need your statement first. Then a full account of the case will have to be studied by the decision-makers. I hope for your sake they're not soccer men."

He glowered at Pascoe who said, "Whatever happens, Mr Connon, you'll be here for Christmas if that's any consolation."

Connon looked round at Jenny and Antony, who smiled reassuringly at him.

"Yes. Yes," he said. "I think it is."

❀ ❀ ❀

The Fernies watched the police-car drive away with Connon in it.

"If you say 'I told you so,' " said Alice, "I'll hit you so hard you won't be able to sup beer tomorrow, let alone chew turkey."

"No, no," said Fernie. "It's not that. They haven't arrested him. Look at those two, Jenny and that lad. They're looking far too pleased with each other for that."

"Now you're a long-distance psychiatrist too," said Alice. "Hey, get off! What do you think you're on? I've got work to do."

"Mine when, as and how I cared to use it. That's what you told that policeman, wasn't it? You wouldn't like to be got for perjury, would you?"

"Oh God. This'll ruin the stuffing."

"But you're right. You've as much as she ever had. And it is noticeably younger."

❀ ❀ ❀

"He looks so much happier," said Jenny as she drove her father's car after the police-car towards town. "No wonder he was cracking up, with all that on his mind."

Antony observed her curiously from the passenger seat.

"What about you, love? All that about your mother, I mean, didn't it come as a shock?"

"Not really. I don't mean I approve or defend her, but whatever she was like, she was like that when I knew her, so I don't see why I should suddenly change towards her now."

She accelerated to cross a light at amber while Antony stood on an imaginary brake.

"I think that she was just jealous. Women do strange things when they're jealous. You'll find out when we get back to college. I want a ring, I don't care if it's expensive or not, but it's got to be bloody big! No, she was jealous of Gwen, that's all. Wanted to control her somehow. She made a friend of Alice Fernie, you see; condescended to her, could control her that way. But with Gwen it had to be something different. Do I sound very cold?"

Antony looked at her face. Her eyes were brimful of tears.

"No, love," he said. "Not at all. But if you're going to cry, pull in to the kerb before you give us all something to cry about."

Her face broke apart into the Connon grin as the tears overflowed and, glinting in the Christmas lights strung across the streets, rolled down the curve of her cheeks.

❀ ❀ ❀

"She was a bitch. Thank God I didn't know her," said Pascoe thickly.

Connon's statement had taken some time. They had got to Jacko's party very late, but had quickly made up for lost time.

"She wasn't that bad," said Dalziel, more clearly, though

Pascoe knew he'd taken twice as much drink as himself. "Not when I knew her. It depends how you look at them. At least they stayed together."

He had shown a surprising desire to stick in his sergeant's company at the party. Pascoe wondered if his inferior rank made him a more desirable auditor of drunken ramblings.

"Not like the Evanses. She left him a letter. Hey, talking of letters, what did you mean when you said to Connon, there'd be no more?"

"That letter," said Dalziel solemnly. "That letter to Jenny Connon. It was written in green ink."

"Oh yes?" said Pascoe puzzled. "What's that signify?"

"It signifies Arthur Evans wrote it. My copy was in black ink. That signified he didn't."

Pascoe digested this in silence for a while.

"I see," he said finally. "What does all that signify?"

"It signifies," said Dalziel, "that men do bloody stupid things when they're worried about their wives. I spoke to him. He listened to me. He listened to the advice of experience."

"His wife still left him."

"He's still in the Club."

"I suppose that's some compensation," said Pascoe doubtfully. "Better than her being in it, eh, sir?"

They laughed raucously.

"Was she a bitch? She left him. Connon's wife seemed a bigger bitch, but she didn't leave him. Are those the bigger bitches, do you think? Isn't it better to get a letter?"

"My wife," said Dalziel slowly, "my wife sent me a telegram."

Pascoe shifted uneasily, suddenly rather more sober. He wasn't at all sure he wanted to be cast in the role of Dalziel's confidant. Christmas comes but once a year, the jingle tripped incessantly through his mind.

He tried to divert the conversation on to fresh tracks.

"There's a silly game called 'Telegram,' " he said brightly. (Christ! my brightness is more hammy than even his performances!) But neither his brightness nor his attempts at diversion seemed to be noticed. They would be registered, however; that he was certain of. Dalziel's mind might get as soggy as a damp brantub, but sometime, somehow, he would grope around in the clart and come up with these moments clear and sharp as a policeman's whistle.

"Words too harsh to be spoken," said Dalziel. "Words too bloody violent to be heard. Things she couldn't say to me, face to face. Me. Her husband. She wrote them down. On a bit of paper. Gave them to a counter-clerk to count."

(Which of course is what a counter-clerk ought to be doing, thought Pascoe. Or he might have said it. He couldn't tell which one second later.)

"A stranger read them. They were copied. Printed out. Despatched. All those people knowing what I didn't know."

Please God, prayed Pascoe, let him stop. I'm an ambitious man. I don't want to hear him. Besides I'm sure Noolan's wife fancies me. Not so old either. But if I don't move soon I'll have to join a queue.

Somewhere in the house a clock chimed midnight. For a moment everyone was still. Most of the Rugby Club lot, the elders at least, were there. He saw them all it seemed as he glanced round the room. He felt almost fond of them.

He fumbled in his pocket and produced a small cylinder of gay Christmas paper. He hadn't known till now whether he would dare give it.

"Merry Christmas, sir."

"What the hell's this? Apple for teacher?"

That was better.

"Just a little gift. Christmas. And end of case."

Dalziel carefully unwrapped the large expensive cigar and sniffed it appraisingly.

"It's not ended yet," he said. "We've still got to find Felstead."

"What'll happen?"

"God knows. Manslaughter? At least, I should think. But let's catch him first."

238 A CLUBBABLE WOMAN

"Tomorrow, Boxing Day. He's an amateur. And he's got Gwen Evans to attract attention. Five bob they have him in forty-eight hours."

Dalziel shook his head gloomily.

"I won't take your money, lad. Thanks for this, though."

He put the cigar in his mouth and lit it.

"Not a bad party," he said. "Hey, Willie. Where've you been hiding? Take me to Jacko's brandy bottle."

Kids, thought Pascoe. Big kids. Like Jenny Connon, and Antony, and Stanley, and Sheila. Little kids.

He started to cut an efficient path through the crowd towards the ample, mature charms of Mrs Willie Noolan.

Envoi

It was a cold, hard January day, the last Saturday in the month. The weather delighted the hearts of thousands who by car, foot, and train were making their way towards Twickenham.

Connon let himself be swept out of the station by the steady onward flow of the crowd. A loudspeaker warned him that the official programme was on sale only in the ground.

As usual, the police seemed to have invented a new system of pedestrian diversion since his last visit and the route they followed afforded him several tantalizing glimpses of the stands before the final approach.

Even so, there was still half an hour to go before kick-off when he reached the ground. He joined a small queue for an official programme, another for an official cushion. Then he joined a larger queue winding its way into the urinal, and smiled to hear someone say, "Someone's pissing in my pocket." He always smiled at that.

Outside again he paused, buffeted by the purposeful swirl of people all around him. On an impulse he did not head round to the West Bar where he usually met up with old friends, but made his way directly to his seat. It was high in the

East Stand. Round and round he climbed, finally emerging into the bright sunlight and almost frightening spaciousness of the stand itself. A man in a sheepskin jacket and Robin Hood hat looked at his ticket and directed him to his row. He found he was sitting next but one to the aisle.

Far below, an unreal distance it seemed, lay the ground. From up here there was nothing to mar the perfection of the white-edged rectangles of bright green. A military band stood in the middle playing fitfully into the gusty wind. Clusters of notes rose up to the top of the stand and he pieced together a melody from *Oklahoma*. Two boys suddenly ran in from the ringside seats. They carried between them a banner which had painted on it in large red letters "WALES." Boos and cheers rose in almost solid blocks from different parts of the ground. Another group of boys climbed over the fence as the banner was brought beneath the West Stand. The Welsh boys recognized the enemy and ran, but found themselves cut off. There was a brief skirmish and the banner was torn. Around the ground the boos and cheers changed places.

"There's a lot more of this nowadays," said a grey-haired man in front of Connon.

"Too bloody much if you ask me," said his neighbour.

The ground was very full now. Connon looked along his row. Every seat was taken except the one next to the aisle. Down below the band was on the move. It left the playing area and came to a halt on the touch-line. There was a momentary hush from the crowd. Connon leaned forward expectantly. Then out of the tunnel beneath the West Stand came trotting the red-shirted Welshmen. A great scream of welcome went up from the crowd. The red-rosetted man next to Connon waved his arms so violently that Connon felt in some danger. The noise still had not died down when it was overtaken and swallowed by the great trumpeting cry which announced the appearance of the English.

Clapping enthusiastically, Connon thought, the Celts make more noise, perhaps, but there's a touch of hysteria about it. It's partly a threat. *We* roar for love.

They also sing better, he had to acknowledge a few moments later. But then so do canaries.

England kicked off. The wind caught the ball, held it in the air, then dropped it just short of the ten-yard line. The Welsh took the scrum and won the ball. But the English back row were round like lightning and the ball was despatched to touch. It didn't bounce.

Someone took the seat next to Connon.

He didn't glance round, concentrating on the game below.

"Hello Marcus," he said.

The English fly-half had the ball. He sent the defence moving the wrong way with a dummy scissors, but not enough. Kick through! urged Connon mentally. He didn't and was dragged down by a Welsh centre.

"Well Connie," said Marcus. "What are our chances?"

"Fair, if we use the wind properly. That full-back of theirs has got a big bum. He's slow on the turn. How are you?"

"Very well," said Marcus.

The Welsh had the ball from the ruck and were developing an attack down the middle. But the cover was good and too quick to allow a break. Play finally came to a halt ten yards behind the English twenty-five.

"They'll be watching for you, Marcus," said Connon.

"They've found me already," said Marcus with a laugh.

Now Connon looked round. Standing at the entrance to the stairs about ten feet back were Dalziel and Pascoe.

"I think they were disappointed that I came, in a way. They hoped to see more of the match."

"Why did you come, Marcus?"

The English full-back took the ball almost on his own line and found touch near half way.

"I couldn't hide forever, could I? I just wanted a few weeks with Gwen. That's all. In case it goes badly. You never know, do you?"

"You kept well out of the way."

"A cottage in the Lakes. We've been snowed up most of

the time. The local bobby actually ploughed his way through to check if we needed help."

"Did you?"

"It's been the happiest month of my life," replied Marcus quietly.

The Welsh had the ball again. This time their fly-half had room to move and side-stepped the over-impetuous approach of the wing-forward with ease. This took him back towards the packs but he went on happily with an arrogant certainty that his pack would retrieve the ball from any ruck which made Connon's heart sink. They did, but only with a helping hand from the floor. The English full-back indicated he was going to have a kick at goal.

"You've changed, Connie. I don't know how, but somehow," said Marcus as preparations for the kick were undertaken. "You don't believe that I...that what happened to Mary wasn't an accident now, do you?"

"No," said Connon. "But what I did, or what I didn't do, when I found out what happened, later I knew I couldn't have acted like that if somewhere deep I hadn't been glad Mary was dead. I was glad then, Marcus, glad in some dead, secret way. That stopped it from being a real accident. Volition and result, they don't make an accident."

Marcus was aghast.

"Listen, Connie," he urged, "it was nothing to do with you that it happened. You can't blame yourself..."

"Oh, I don't," said Connon. "Not now. Because I found I quickly stopped being glad in any way. Mary wasn't a good woman, I know, and often not a very pleasant person. I'd often wished I could escape her. Get far far away from her, from everyone."

He laughed at himself.

"I got away. To my desert. I got to my desert, and it was just what you'd expect a desert to be. Hot, dusty, empty, killing."

The full-back stabbed at the ball and sliced it badly. An

ironic cheer went up. A Welshman gathered it on his own line and shaped to kick for touch.

"I'm sorry, Connie," said Marcus quietly. "I suppose because I knew, about you and Mary I mean, I suppose I thought it didn't matter as much somehow."

"It always matters. To all of us it matters. It matters to me, it matters to Arthur Evans. I suppose it even mattered to him."

He jerked his head back to where Dalziel was still standing pointing out some feature of the game to Pascoe.

"Now I can mourn properly. Goodbye Marcus. I shall see you again. I'm in a little bit of trouble myself, you know."

"I'm sorry," said Marcus again, standing up. "Goodbye."

He went back up the steps to the policemen.

"Well, I got some use out of my ticket," he said. "Thanks. Why don't you stay, Bruiser, and see the rest of the game? The sergeant here's more than capable of dealing with me, I'm sure."

Dalziel looked tempted for a moment, but shook his head.

"Can't be done," he said. "Would look bad on my report. Anyway we've got a great deal to ask you, Mr Felstead."

"So formal," murmured Marcus. He moved forward, but Dalziel restrained him.

"Wait a mo'," he said.

The Welsh kick had found touch. Now the ball had come back badly on the English side, but the scrum-half got to it. He was pounced on before he could move and the best he could do was to throw out a slow lobbing pass to his fly-half, who had to take it standing still. But miraculously with a simple twist of the hips, he opened a gap between the two Welsh forwards bearing furiously down on him, stepped through it and suddenly accelerated straight ahead.

"Run! Run!" screamed Dalziel.

"Go now!" yelled Pascoe, not quite sure why he felt so excited by this alien game.

"Nothing can stop him," said Marcus with certainty.

He was right. The cover was far too slow in coming across. Head high, ball held lightly before him, beautifully balanced, he rounded the full-back as though he were rooted and touched down gently, undramatically, between the posts.

"Oh, you beauty!" breathed Dalziel. "You beauty!"

He sighed and shook his head as though coming back to reality.

"Right," he said. "Let's go."

"The kick?" suggested Marcus.

"To hell with the kick. He might miss it. Let's go now," said Dalziel.

Marcus took a last glance back at Connon before going through the exit, but he wasn't looking. He was slowly sitting down again after the leap of jubilation which had taken him and thousands of others to their feet.

There were tears in his eyes. He rubbed one away. The Welshman next to him nudged his neighbour and surreptitiously pointed to Connon.

"The buggers have got feelings after all, boy," he said.